Unrestrained

Double D Ranch
Book 3

Jeanne St. James

———

Credits:
Photographer: Wander Aguiar Photography
Cover Artist: Golden Czermak at FuriousFotog
Cover Models: Phillipe, Evan & Kerry
Editor: Encompass Press, LLC.
Beta Readers: Author BJ Alpha, Nicki Holt & Lisa Figueroa

———

www.jeannestjamesauthor.com

Sign up for my newsletter for insider information, author news, and new releases:
https://www.authorjeannestjames.com/

———

**Buy direct from the author here: https://
jeannestjamesauthor.com**

A Note About AI

No Artificial Intelligence (AI) was used to create this novel or its cover (or in any other way). Fiction authors, like me, have been using em dashes and other various punctuation long before AI started being used to write books. All of my books (along with thousands of other authors) were downloaded illegally to train AI systems without permission or compensation (violating copyright laws). This is the reason AI resembles authors' works, not the other way around.

Double D Ranch Series

Chapter One

The annoying blare of his ringtone had Cam groaning and blindly swiping for his phone on the nightstand.

He squinted at the name that popped up on his screen. It wasn't anyone from his job—not his current one, at least—so that was good. Because of that, he could safely assume the ranch resort wasn't burning to the ground. Or being overrun by horny zombies.

He put it to his ear and had to clear his throat to force out, "Hey. It's been a while."

A familiar masculine voice filled his ear. "I'm getting out."

Cam yawned, stretched, then drove his hand down his boxer briefs to tug on his balls. "You make it sound like you're getting out of prison."

"Might as well be," Nolan said.

He hadn't heard from his former co-worker in a few months. Actually, not since the night of Cam's retirement party.

That had been fun, but he normally wasn't a big drinker,

so the next morning had been rough after celebrating most of the night.

He missed talking to Nolan Young, a fellow trooper. They had worked together at the Pennsylvania State Police's barracks in Media. In the last few years before Cam retired, they'd been on the same platoon, had become fast friends and pretty damn close.

He'd been meaning to reach out and felt guilty about not doing so. Especially now that he had finally settled in at Double D Ranch as their head of security.

"It might suck, but at least it's not prison. You know how much they love law enforcement in there."

Silence hit his ears.

"Wait. Have you even done your twenty-five?" Enlisted members of PSP needed to do twenty-five years on the job if they wanted to retire with their full pension and benefits.

Only having to do twenty-five years to get the maximum payout was great when you went into the state police academy at only twenty-one. It was nice to be able to "retire" at forty-six years old.

The biggest challenge was surviving those years on the job.

"No, not yet. But I can't deal with this shit anymore. I thought long and hard about what I'd lose and I'm fine with getting out at twenty."

Damn. That would reduce his monthly pension. But for some, five more years was five too many. "And when is this happening?"

"In two weeks." Nolan paused. "Cam..."

He fought another yawn. "Yeah?"

"I'm only forty-one. I'm too young to retire and do nothing. I'll need to supplement my pension, too."

"I hear you. I'm too old to deal with the bullshit that goes along with police work, but too young to relax in a rocking chair on the porch watching the world go by." Add in the fact that Cam was financially supporting a daughter through college. He couldn't not work.

"I need a slower pace. No freaking fifty-car pile ups due to snow squalls. No domestics. No tweakers. No bullshit."

"I hear you, brother. What do you plan to do, if not board the easy train?"

"Find the kind of gig like you did. Where I can use my experience and skills, but at a much slower pace."

"Security for an old folks' home?" Cam suggested as a joke.

"I said slow, not dead."

"Ouch."

"You know what I mean."

Cam stroked his half chub lazily as he talked. "Some of those residents can get pretty fucking cantankerous. Might have to pepper spray one for assault with a pudding cup."

"Or zip tie their wheelchair wheel to the frame so they can't make a run for it."

Cam chuckled. "They do, you just chase after them using a scooter and do a pit maneuver." A low chuckle filled his ear and caused Cam's nipples to stand at attention.

"Damn, I miss working with you."

"Same, brother." Cam also missed seeing Nolan in the locker room before and after shifts. The man always drew his eye, making him wish Nolan wasn't straight.

Who was he kidding? It didn't matter if he wasn't, Cam had stuffed himself into a closet and locked the door behind him. No way did he want anyone at his barracks, or even in the state-wide law enforcement organization, to know he wasn't strictly batting for the straight team.

He didn't need the hassle. The jokes, the looks, the insulting whispers.

You'd think in this day and age, more folks would be tolerant of how others lived their lives, especially since it wasn't their business. Unfortunately, they weren't.

The only good thing about being bi was that he could bring a woman along to events and get-togethers with his fellow cops and it didn't come off as awkward. Or suspicious.

He could easily pretend to be as straight as the line they made drunks walk during sobriety tests. Only, that was far from the truth. "When's your last day?"

"The fifteenth."

Damn. Now that guilt for not reaching out became even heavier. He should've known Nolan was about to retire. "Then what?"

"Maybe take a breather for a few weeks. Got an offer to work security at the county courthouse. However, the pay is shit, no bennies, and I don't know if I want to deal with some of the crazies that come to court."

"I hear ya. Why don't you come up here for a visit? See what a sweet deal I stumbled into." It would be the perfect time to catch up.

"You're liking it?"

"The benefits outweigh the pay, but hell yeah. I get to live in a rent-free cabin in a beautiful area, the food's awesome and also included, we've got a spa here if I ever have tight muscles and need a massage, I don't have to pay a dime for booze, and I get to spend as much time outdoors as I want. The property butts up against state game land and Moshannon State Forest. I can hunt, run, ATV, whatever."

"Isn't it some kind of sex resort?"

Cam smiled. "Another benefit."

"You're allowed to hook up with the guests?" Nolan sounded skeptical.

"Sure, if they consent. Consent is non-negotiable here. If they want me and I want them? No problem."

"All the sex you want without strings sounds like a damn good benefit."

"As long as I'm off-duty. And yes, no strings. Most guests are only here a few days or a week at the most."

"Sounds like Utopia."

"Pretty close. In fact, they have a whole bunch of kinky playrooms where anything goes named Heaven, if that tells you anything."

Nolan's snort filled Cam's ear. "*Heaven.* I bet."

"Some wild shit goes down in those rooms."

"You get to watch?"

"If I want, sure. We also have security cameras everywhere else and I assure you, those rooms aren't the only place where some interesting shit goes down." They didn't record inside the playrooms unless an emergency button was pushed, but that information wasn't shared outside of management and the security team.

The button was their latest upgrade after Cam suggested it. However, the cameras in the hallway outside of those rooms were always monitored and signage made the guests aware of it.

Nolan's deep chuckle caused Cam's balls to tighten. "And as head of security, you get the privilege of monitoring those."

Cam needed to stop fantasizing about a man he'd never have and concentrate on the guests here who were plentiful.

But so far, since arriving, he'd stuck to women. Despite this resort being judgement-free, it was a hard habit to break. He wasn't quite comfortable yet exposing his true desires, despite the fact that both Dylan and Dayne, the twin brothers who owned the resort, were both bisexual themselves.

"Let me just say, the guests here aren't shy, so shit happens right out in the open. By the pool. By the lake. In a pasture. Nothing's off limits except they don't want people banging on the tables in the dining hall or in the lodge's lobby. And, of course, the bosses' residences are off-limits." Unless invited, of course.

Both Dayne and Dylan Lyons were both in polyamorous relationships and sometimes invited guests to join them.

"Bosses? How many?"

"Three. All siblings. They're great, though. They allow me to do the hiring for the security team and basically let me do what I do best. They don't micromanage."

"Unlike that last lieutenant we had."

"Yeah, Mastriano was a dick. Luckily, I don't have to deal with that shit here. Even better, if I suggest specific equipment for me or my team, I get it. No questions asked. They trust my judgement one hundred percent."

"Like I said, Utopia."

"It's definitely different from PSP. A good type of different." So far, he hadn't had to restrain or get into a scuffle with any guest. Most likely because the guests had to sign agreements before arriving and even more when checking in, so they knew the rules in advance.

The most important rule being consent.

"It sounds like I might have to come up and check it out."

"Anytime, brother."

"I'll let you know. Once I get all my retirement paperwork filed and approved, I might head up for a few days."

"It's been too long and I'd love to see you, Nolan." *See you, touch you, taste you.*

"Same here. I know it's only been a few months, but it seems like years."

Cam agreed. "Just let me know when you want to come up. In the meantime, I'll put you on the pre-approved guest list at the gate. The resort might be a slower pace but you won't be bored. There are plenty of things to do here. Pool, spa, horseback riding, ATVs,"—*sex*—"the list is endless."

"Sounds good, brother. It'll be a nice change of pace and a good opportunity to clear my head."

"It'll be nice to see a familiar face." He had to admit, he'd been a bit lonely, despite being constantly surrounded by guests and fellow employees.

"Is Laurel still attending Penn State Main Campus in State College?"

Talking about his daughter had him yanking his hand free of his underwear. He grimaced. "She sure is. Having her so close is another benefit to living up here. I visit her whenever I can but she's busy with school and her friends." She didn't have much time for dear old dad, she was too busy forging her future.

"She good?"

"She's great. It's hard to believe but one more year and my baby will have her bachelor's degree in Communication."

"You have to be proud of her."

Cam smiled. Both he and his ex-wife agreed, Laurel was the best thing to come out of their failed marriage. "Of course."

"Okay, brother. Got to go. I'll see you soon."

"See you soon, Nolan." He ended the call and set his phone aside.

The wait and anticipation was going to kill him. He had lusted after Nolan since the moment he met the other man, but, of course, he'd always been beyond Cam's reach.

As were all straight men.

Even though Nolan might not be at his fingertips, Cam could pretend he was. All he had to do was wrap those same fingers around his cock again and close his eyes.

Nobody had to know. Especially Nolan.

He rolled enough to reach the lotion kept on the night-stand, did one pump into his palm, then settled in.

Once his fingers circled his length, he gave his cock a good squeeze and began to stroke himself slowly, distributing the lotion evenly. He pulled in a deep breath, closed his eyes, and flipped through his memory bank to find the perfect one.

Oh yeah, that's the one.

Nolan standing in front of his locker at the end of their shift, wearing an Under Amour shirt that fit like a second skin and hugged his six pack abs, broad shoulders, and biceps. When he turned his back to Cam, he dropped his uniform trousers and stepped free. Bending over to pick them up, his tight boxer briefs showcased a perfect peach of an ass.

The one Cam would love to tongue, finger, and fuck.

That memory had him cupping his balls in the palm of his left hand and collaring the root of his hard-on with two fingers like a cock ring. He used his right hand to slowly stroke his whole length. At the top, he swirled his thumb around the tip, then tightened his grip and began to pump it at a fast and furious pace.

With the pressure quickly building, his fist became a blur and his hips danced on the mattress.

Squeezing his eyes shut, he released a grunt he swore came from deep within his soul. He thrusted into his fist one more time and came, the hot ropes of cum creating stripes on his stomach.

Lazily drawing his fingers through the aftermath, he gathered some up and used it to continue slowly stroking as he waited for his heartbeat to slow, as well as his breathing.

He really needed to shower and get ready for the day, but he also wanted to enjoy the bliss that followed a good jerk-off session, even one as short as this one.

He sighed.

Cam appreciated Nolan as a friend. He definitely appreciated him as a man.

And as spank bank material.

For fuck's sake, he was such a damn perv. He should be ashamed for using his friend like that.

But he wasn't. What Nolan didn't know…

Cam chuckled softly. Yeah, he was a complete degenerate.

His next sexual encounter really needed to be with a man. He needed to push past his hangups about anyone knowing.

While he should be ashamed for using an unsuspecting Nolan to get off, he shouldn't be for being bisexual. He was also at a perfect place in his life now where he could be who he was and not hide it.

While hooking up with women was great—and he didn't plan on giving them up—they normally didn't scratch every itch. He simply needed to find the right man since the one he lusted after wasn't available.

Except for in his dreams.

Chapter Two

Cᴀᴍ ɢᴀᴠᴇ his assigned ATV used for patrol a little more power and shot down the stone lane away from his cabin and toward what he called the "back forty."

Like normal, before his morning rounds, he checked in via radio with the guards sitting at the gate, patrolling The Mane Lodge and lake cabins, as well as currently surveilling the cameras.

The Lyons brothers were smart to hire dedicated security staff, not only to protect the resort and guests, but to limit access from outsiders. No one got past the gate unless they had a reservation or were an invited guest. Restricting access to everyone else kept both the guests and staff safe.

And their identities private.

Especially from haters who had a problem with these types of adult playgrounds. Beyond physical threats and verbal abuse, guests could be blackmailed or even have their sexuality outed.

Some guests wanted to keep their sexuality private in

their everyday life but go wild while at the resort. Whatever someone was into, the resort could usually make it happen. If you desired it—and as long as it was legal and consensual—the Lyons family did their best to make sure you got what you wanted.

Their goal was for their guests to leave satisfied in every way possible.

No other resort in the Northeast was similar to the Double D Ranch. Not that he was aware of, anyway.

As he bounced in his seat while tooling down the bumpy lane, Cam recited the resort's motto out loud like a game show host. "Welcome to the Double D Ranch. The adults-only ranch resort where your fantasies become reality. Unpack, unwind, and get uninhibited."

He heard it so many times when guests checked in or staff answered the phone that he could recite it in his sleep. He wouldn't be surprised if he already had.

Cam waved to a couple of the groundskeepers as he passed them, and a small group of guests on horseback, probably headed toward Moshannon State Forest for an early morning trail ride.

After arriving at the farthest edge of the three-hundred acre property, he looped around and headed back.

He made this trek almost daily and never got bored of the view. The backdrop of tall trees and majestic mountains, as well as the expansive pastures and rolling hills, made it a truly peaceful place and a nice change of pace from where he had lived and worked previously.

Peaceful except for the resort's wild themed parties, that was.

His growling stomach reminded him it was time to grab breakfast in the dining hall and also have a face-to-face with the guard assigned there for the day.

While he was their supervisor, he liked to be friendly with his subordinates. Most of the security staff were former law enforcement, like him. Because of that, he trusted them to professionally handle any situations that came up. The Lyons hoped for guests to return, as well as spread the word to their friends, so any incident needed to be handled tactfully.

Cam constantly drilled that into the guards' heads since it was the guests who paid his very nice salary as well as theirs. Without customers, the resort would go under and a bunch of people would find themselves unemployed.

If that happened, it would be devastating for the local economy since most of the resort's employees, vendors, and independent contractors were locals and other job opportunities in the area were limited. The residents of Fisher Falls might grumble about having an all-adult, sex-positive resort in their area, but they realized what an economic boom it provided.

Albeit reluctantly.

Once he filled his gut with strawberry-stuffed French toast, a side of bacon, and two generous cups of black coffee, he went into the lodge's kitchen and filled up his travel mug before heading out on the rest of his rounds.

Since the weather was beautiful, it was going to suck sitting in his office for hours on end to go over reports, schedules, and all the rest of the paperwork he was responsible for.

He shouldn't complain. This job was cake compared to his last one. The only chase he'd been involved in since he started was a fugitive hen that escaped the chicken coop. The motherclucker had needlessly pecked the shit out of him when he was only trying to help.

He had one more area to check before heading over to the farmhouse where all three resort execs—twins Dayne and

Dylan, along with their younger sister Danica—grew up. When they converted the property from a private dairy farm to a public ranch resort, they had upgraded the original family farmhouse and added two wings so each sibling had their own personal space.

However, since then, Dylan and the rest of his polycule, Erin and Ford, built their own house on the property and repurposed his wing as a security office for Cam and his staff. The sole bedroom had been turned into Cam's private office and the rest of the living space now housed desks, computers used for surveillance, and the rest of their security equipment.

For an office, it was pretty damn close to perfect.

Cam stepped out of The Mane Lodge, and on his way back to his ATV, movement caught his eye.

One side of his mouth pulled up. Nothing should surprise him anymore, but every time he thought he'd seen it all, he was proven wrong.

This morning, that surprise came in the form of a woman on the lake's dock doing a little yoga.

Naked, of course.

He guessed early morning was the perfect time to do it, before the threat of getting sunburned in places no one wanted to be sunburned.

Especially with her lily-white assets pointing directly at the sky.

Wait a minute...

He recognized that deep-red hair. That slender, athletic body.

That wasn't a guest, but an employee. Sort of. More like an independent contractor. Or freelancer.

Hope Reed.

When the Lyonses first hired the yoga instructor, Cam figured she'd be into all of that *woo-woo* nonsense and a bit flighty.

From what he'd discovered so far, it turned out she wasn't. Instead, she was more down to Earth. And, of course, took her yoga seriously.

She led early morning yoga sessions only three days a week since she also taught some classes from her home right outside Fisher Falls. Cam had learned all that when he did her background check.

She had also turned down the Lyonses' offer of taking one of the employee cabins and working full-time at the resort. When she was first hired over a month ago, Dylan mentioned that she didn't want to move onsite due to living with her boyfriend.

So while the thirty-year-old woman had caught Cam's eye, the couple of times they briefly spoke, he ignored his interest due to her having a significant other.

However, this morning, his interest—along with his cock—was piqued.

As head of security, he should really go check on her. For her safety, of course. Make sure she didn't pull a muscle doing some of those crazy yoga poses.

He left the ATV parked by the front entrance of the lodge and decided to stretch his legs. As he strode down the grassy incline and toward the dock, he took Hope in as he went.

The loose, long red hair.

The nose ring.

The full sleeve of flowers and butterflies tattooed on her left arm.

He'd admit he'd been wrong judging her appearance at

first; the reason he assumed she was into some sort of New Age spirituality.

Not that there was anything wrong with being free-spirited.

Hope apparently lived her life the way she wanted to live it. He couldn't judge her for that. Just like she shouldn't judge him for having a typical cop's Type-A personality. He was as far from a free-spirit as one could get.

He stuck to schedules and rules, he was never late, he kept himself squared away; habits he was not only born with, but were exacerbated during his career in law enforcement.

There were moments he could be extremely uptight. Since moving onto the ranch, though, he was trying to loosen up, enjoy life more and generally be more easy-going.

However, letting go of his ingrained habits was a slow, arduous process.

He stepped to the edge of the dock, where the stone path ended and the wood planks began. He didn't want to walk onto the dock in case his weight shook it and caused her to lose her balance and fall into the water.

He tipped his head to the side as he studied her. He had no idea what pose she was currently doing, but it certainly showcased how flexible she was.

Whatever the pose was made his cock flex.

It was too damn bad she lived with a boyfriend.

Although, in reality, it was simply easier and cleaner for him to hook up with the occasional guest. Getting intimate with an employee could get sticky if it went badly.

Hope smoothly shifted from one pose into the next. With her palms planted flat on the dock, she walked her hands toward her feet and—

Holy shit.

She was now in an inverted *V* with her bare ass straight up in the air and her not-bare pussy flashing him. He pursed his lips as he checked her out.

Oh yeah, no hippy bush there.

The hair that topped her pussy was neatly trimmed.

With her eyes closed, her head dropped between her arms. After blowing out an extended breath, those blue eyes opened and...

Locked with his.

Fuck!

Busted.

He cleared his throat and redirected his gaze toward the line of beached paddle boats. Certainly not as interesting as a naked Hope. "Sorry."

He heard, "Nothing to be sorry about. If I was worried about catching eyes, I'd do this at home."

When he risked a glance at the dock again, Hope was sitting cross-legged on her yoga mat and facing him.

Now that her breasts weren't hanging upside down, he could appreciate them better. "And why don't you?"

"Because I love to be naked."

When she shrugged, his eyes were drawn to her bouncing breasts. *Yep*, they were very nice. All natural. Just like the color of her hair.

Stop being such a damn perv and ogling another employee. You're head of security, for fuck's sake.

Her next words snapped him out of his depravity. Sort of.

"I love nature. I love yoga. Best of all, I love that I can be myself here."

Cam loved that, too. Especially this morning.

He mentally cringed at his own thoughts. Dirty locker-room talk was taking over his common sense. "Your boyfriend doesn't mind you doing yoga naked in front of"—he glanced around—"I don't know...a couple hundred guests?" While eating breakfast, too.

Her brow furrowed. "Boyfriend?"

"Before you were officially hired, it was mentioned you had a boyfriend."

"Well, I did. Until he had an issue with me working here. He said if I took the job he was leaving."

Damn. "I'm going to take an educated guess that you chose this job over him."

Her lips curled up on the ends. "Didn't I say I loved yoga?"

His lips mirrored the motion of hers. "More than him, apparently."

"He was fun. For a little while, anyway."

Ouch.

"Like a lot of Fisher Falls' residents, Darren was super conservative and uptight." She shrugged again. "I'm far from that. Our ideologies clashed."

"I thought opposites attract?"

"They can. But then it's all downhill from there. Too many personality conflicts. I consider myself an independent free-spirit. I don't like someone giving me an ultimatum or trying to tell me what I can and cannot do. I'm an adult woman who can make my own decisions."

"And you don't need a man telling you what to do or how to think," Cam concluded, because he'd heard this more than once before from women.

"Bingo."

"I assume that means you'd probably never get involved in a Dom/sub relationship." *Oh, good going, genius. Just drop that like a hot potato.*

"Depends on what role I'm asked to take."

His interest in Hope piqued even more after that answer. "And what role would you prefer to take?"

He was bold asking that, but he was truly curious. However, he wouldn't pester her for an answer if it made her uncomfortable.

"That also depends."

"On?"

"On the person I'm with. Sometimes I'm in the mood to give the orders, sometimes I'm in the mood to take them. Of course, I'm speaking strictly sexually and not in everyday life. Like I said, I can make my own decisions."

Cam was the same way. The sexual dynamics could change depending on who he was with and their experience.

He was fine with either implementing the whip or feeling its bite.

If he was with a submissive, he had no problem stepping into the dominant role. And vice versa.

But after twenty-five years of giving orders to others, sometimes it was nice to hand that control over to someone else. And if they were experienced enough to take him into a deep subspace, even better.

Plus, he always looked forward to the aftercare, whether giving or receiving it.

"Have you ever done yoga?"

"No," he answered.

"Well, if you ever want to give it a try, come join my morning class. When the weather is nice, I hold it outside where there's plenty of room for drop-ins."

Yoga? Him? "Is being naked a requirement?"

She laughed softly. "No, not at all. Although, I might have to put another class specifically for that on the schedule."

"Good, because in the position you were in when we made awkward eye contact—"

"It might have been awkward for you, but it wasn't for me."

"Good to know. But my fear is, I might knock myself out in that position, if things get to swinging," he teased.

The corners of her eyes crinkled and she shook her head. "Now, getting slapped in the face with your own equipment while in Downward Facing Dog could be awkward."

"Downward Facing Dog?"

"That's the name of the pose. Anyway, if you don't already know, yoga has a lot of health benefits. You could come to one of my classes and see if you like it. Of course, it's free of charge." She added a wink.

Only if she taught it naked.

He squeezed his eyes shut. He was insufferable. He was riding a fine line of what could be considered sexual harassment.

Something he'd normally be the one investigating.

But it also proved he needed to get laid. And soon. If he had to think long and hard about when the last time he'd hooked up, that meant it had been far too long.

Earlier this morning, he was telling himself that his next sexual encounter needed to be with a man.

Hope was far from that. He'd seen the actual proof. "I'll think about it."

She smiled and rose to her feet. "I hope you do. I guess I should go get ready for my class."

He wasn't ready to end this conversation, especially now he knew she was single. He pointed at her full sleeve. "Those are some tattoos you have." Then he spotted another one he hadn't noticed at first. When she got close, he nabbed her right arm and turned it until he could read the tattoo on her inner wrist. He read the quote out loud, "I am the one thing in life I can control."

Damn. He liked that.

"It's from *Hamilton.* Have you seen it?"

He huffed. "The musical? No." While she didn't try to pull away when he brushed his thumb over the black lettering, he reluctantly released her arm.

"You should. It's great."

"I'll take your word for it."

"If you don't watch awesome performances with catchy tunes, what do you do for fun, Cameron Cook?"

"Not watch musicals. I prefer horror flicks."

"Blood and gore, huh? As a former cop, you'd think you would've seen enough of that while on the job."

"It was one way of desensitizing yourself to it. Otherwise, sometimes those situations could become overwhelming. Especially when it comes to children."

Her brow dropped low. "I can imagine. That had to be rough."

It sure was. And he preferred not to discuss it. He wanted to forget all the real-life horror he'd seen.

He didn't realize how much hate humans could have for each other until after he graduated from the state police academy in Hershey.

She tipped her head toward his left arm. "Your tattoos are something, too."

"Making an appointment was one of the first things I did after handing in my uniform."

"The powers that be didn't want you to have tattoos?"

"Not visible, so I decided to refrain until I retired and go hog wild afterward."

"One sleeve is not hog wild. Unless the rest are hidden under your clothes?"

"If I ever join your naked yoga class, you can find out then."

"Oh, something to look forward to. Both seeing you try yoga for the first time *and* your tattoos. But you might want to strap your massive cock to your thigh if you're worried about knocking yourself out. Or, at minimum, poking out an eye."

Cam laugh-groaned. "Now if you ever see me naked, I'm afraid you'll be disappointed."

A single eyebrow rose. "You're not hung like a horse?"

"Not even close."

"Damn. Well, that's disappointing."

"For me as well." He couldn't stop smiling. That was so unlike him.

"All right. I *really* need to go get dressed and teach my first class."

"Do you normally do yoga more than once a day?"

She pointed to the dock. "This session was for me. The class is for the students. I only show them the pose, then I walk around and check or correct everyone else's."

"Are you usually very hands-on?"

"I always ask my students first if they mind me touching them. Consent and all that. I want my students to feel completely comfortable."

Ah fuck. It just dawned on him that he had touched her without asking first when he grabbed her wrist. He should've known better.

"And do any of them mind you touching them?" He'd be surprised if she said yes when it came to this particular resort.

"I haven't had anyone yet. Anyway, it was nice speaking with you."

As she headed down the dock, he realized no clothes were piled nearby. She had walked to the dock completely naked.

She waved a hand over her bare shoulder and called out, "Have a great rest of the day, Cameron Cook! I look forward to seeing you in a future class."

"Don't bet on it," he whispered, watching her stroll naked up the grassy knoll.

Completely confident about her body.

And what a body it was.

Chapter Three

Wearing a welcoming smile, Hope called out, "Okay, everyone! Please find a mat so we can get started."

Earlier, she had done her own Hatha yoga routine, along with some extra meditative breath work. The same as Monday morning, she'd done it naked since it was the way she felt the freest. Unlike on Monday, she hadn't done it on the dock, but found a peaceful spot not front and center of the lodge during breakfast.

Because of it, she was starting out this class grounded and ready to conquer the day.

Since this was a resort, most of the people joining her class had a mix of experience. Some wanted to simply give yoga a try since it was part of the inclusive package, others did yoga on a regular basis, whether at home or at a studio.

Because of this mix, she always modified the poses to accommodate each skill level as well as the variety of body types. The resort guests appreciated the time and attention they received from her. The classes at the beginning of the week started out small, but by Friday, she always had a full class.

She was thankful for that word of mouth since she really liked this gig. It helped supplement her income, which, if she had to be painfully honest, was pretty pitiful. Running a yoga studio from home barely covered her monthly expenses. Not when her regulars were only Fisher Falls residents.

Not a lot were open to it. Some religious people even called yoga a sin because it was tied to Hinduism.

She mentally rolled her eyes. She certainly wasn't trying to convert anyone. She wasn't even Hindu herself. She simply loved the practice of yoga and only wanted her students to be healthy and happy.

Before the resort opened, she had attended the open house, like most of Fisher Falls, and found herself impressed.

When she ran into Danica, Hope pitched the idea of adding yoga to their activities. The youngest Lyons sibling had been all for it, but with the hustle and bustle of finishing the resort, Hope's proposal had fallen through the cracks.

When she'd crossed paths with Evelyn Lyons, the matriarch of the family and the resort owners' mother, Hope slipped it into their casual conversation.

A day later, she got a call from the CEO, Dylan Lyons, asking her to email him her résumé, a class plan, and fill out the form for a background check. She also had to sign a non-disclosure agreement.

Now here she was, currently standing in front of Double D Ranch guests ready to get their stretch on. Most likely for all the activities they would be doing later, whether it be kinky sex or riding a trail horse.

The nice part about working on the resort was that she had full access to everything the guests did. For the most part. She could eat in the employee area of the dining hall.

She could swim in the pool. If she asked, she could prob-ably go on a trail ride, or milk a cow, or feed the llamas. Or even give the two adopted donkeys some scratches and treats.

The Lyonses were generous with both their guests and the people they employed. Nobody could deny that they certainly helped out the area. They could've simply sold their late father's farm to a corporate developer. The area could've been inundated with condos and an eyesore of a shopping plaza and next thing you knew, the new residents would be bitching about a coyote or black bear wandering through their community.

And the original area residents would be bitching about the new "pansies" who moved in and were attempting to gentrify the area.

Fisher Falls residents didn't take kindly to change. However, most of them begrudgingly accepted the ranch resort. What they considered the lesser of two evils.

Luckily, the Lyonses tried to be the best neighbors they could be. The unorthodox business certainly spurred the economy in the area.

"All right, everyone ready? We're going to start off with a relaxing flow this morning. Everyone stand at the front of your mat. We'll start off with the Palm Tree pose. It's good for your balance and posture, then we'll move on to sun saluta-tions. Are you ready?"

Various responses came from the ten attendees, some enthusiastic, some not so much. She got it. It was early. They probably hadn't had their fill of caffeine yet. And if you tried hard enough, you could just smell breakfast being prepared in the lodge's commercial kitchen.

Normally, by the end of the forty-five minute class and during the final pose, Savasana, growling stomachs—as well as snoring—would be heard over the ambient music she played in the background.

After she demonstrated the proper form, everyone moved into the pose and Hope weaved around the mats and guests, gently guiding anyone who needed it.

As she was about to head back to the front of the class, a large man in a tank top, board shorts, and sneakers with white socks that came up mid-calf, walked through the door of The Mane Event Hall.

While she preferred to hold her classes outside so her students could be "at one" with nature, her weather app, as well as the dark cloudy sky, predicted thunderstorms this morning, indicating it was safer to hold her class inside. She wasn't a big fan of the thought of lightning lighting up her students like Christmas trees. She could safely guess that would be the resort owners' preference, too.

She fought her smile when she recognized that handsome face.

Cameron Cook: head of security and hottie.

Unlike the polo shirt he wore while working, the black tank showed off more of his very delicious body, as well as the sleeve of a black and gray sea monster—possibly a kraken—that took up his left arm.

Cam glanced around with a grimace. "Sorry for being late."

She pressed a finger to her lips in a shushing motion and quickly grabbed him a mat from the nearby cart. She rolled it out at the back of the class. "Better late than never," she said under her breath. "I'm glad you decided to give it a shot."

"I'll let you know if I'm feeling the same once this is over."

Hope suppressed her laugh. Now was not the time to be giggling and flirting. This was supposed to be a Zen moment.

His lips twitched when he whispered, "Should I strip down?"

Nobody else was naked. She hadn't had a chance to run her naked yoga idea past any of the execs. "Completely up to you. If you're unaware, anything goes on this resort," she teased softly, trying not to disturb the rest of the students. "I doubt anyone would be shocked by you doing a Warrior's pose in the buff. However, they might be scared to see your monster. I'm not talking about the one on your arm."

He snorted softly. "I have no idea what a Warrior's pose is but I'll have to take your word for it."

"Even if you take nothing else off"—she pointed to his feet—"you have to remove your shoes and socks."

"Oh, so you're into feet? I have pretty nice ones." He wiggled his eyebrows.

"Are you exaggerating about that the same as your cock?" she whispered.

"You can be the judge."

She wasn't into feet, but his ass when he bent over to remove his sneakers and socks got her stamp of approval.

"Okay, get into the same pose as everyone else." Since he was a complete beginner, she stepped back and waited for him to get set up so she could correct his form.

And, boy, did he need help.

"Do you mind if I touch you?" she asked softly once he got into place and attempted the very simple pose.

The way his deep voice rumbled "Be my guest" caused a flurry of warmth to spiral through her and land at that recently neglected spot between her upper thighs.

She tried not to linger as she adjusted his alignment, but he was tense and she had to keep whispering, "Relax. Loosen your muscles. Don't lock your joints."

The man needed a lot of work, but at least he had shown up. That was more than most people.

However, it turned out that she had to correct his form for every pose. Was he doing that on purpose?

The more she put her hands on him, the more heated his eyes became.

Cam appeared athletic. He probably stuck to doing more "manly" exercises like lifting weights and maybe even running. He was a former cop, after all, and the cops she knew all thought they had to appear "alpha," even when they weren't.

Toward the end of the session, she announced, "Now for the best part. Savasana, or Corpse pose." That got a few quiet chuckles. "Lie in a comfortable, neutral position on your mat. Lengthen your body from your neck through your tailbone, open across your chest, and move your shoulder blades away from your spine. Let gravity help with the rest. Allow your body to feel heavy; let go and sink into the mat. Close your eyes. Notice your thoughts without getting attached to them. Take this time to recalibrate and reset. Your body—and mind —deserve it."

Amazingly enough, that was one pose that Cam didn't need help with, so she shut up and sat cross-legged on her own mat to keep an eye on the class. She grinned when, after a couple of minutes, a few soft snores met her ears. It was inevitable that at least one person always drifted off during the last pose since everyone was so relaxed.

Five minutes later, Hope pressed her hands together as if in prayer and said softly, "May there be love in your heart, peace in your thoughts, and joy in your words as you carry on throughout the rest of your day."

Her students rolled to their sides for a minute or two, then slowly rose to their feet. She was pleased to see how chill everyone appeared. Even the people who might end up bound and whipped with a crop later today.

"I hope to see some, if not all, of you in the future."

When the rest of the class filed out of the event hall, Hope began wiping down the mats, rolling them and stacking them on the cart to put them away. She really needed to sit down with Dayne or Dylan and see if they'd be willing to invest in some desperately needed yoga equipment, like straps, blocks, and bolsters.

The only person who lingered was Cam. Once he pulled on his socks and sneakers, he went around rolling up the mats she hadn't gotten to yet and brought them over to the cart.

She thanked him.

"I never expected it to be such a workout."

Hope smiled knowingly. "Used some muscles you never knew you had, did you?"

"Yes, and I regularly use the resort's gym and pool. Sometimes I even take my bike out or go for a run on the trails, even though running isn't my favorite."

Just what she figured. "You might be sore tomorrow. While yoga is low impact, you're holding poses when your body is used to movement. If you're unaware, the muscle contractions result in microscopic tears to the tissue. Your muscles, tendons, and fascia will grow stronger as your body repairs itself. If you keep coming to my classes, I promise you'll start to feel the benefits. Why do you think some professional athletes do yoga? Even football players."

"To hook up with the teacher?" he suggested with a completely straight face.

Hope shook her head and laughed softly. "Is that why you showed up?"

His sudden smile blinded her. "Of course."

She stared at him.

He shrugged. "I prefer not to lie."

"Like in Corpse pose," she teased.

"That was my favorite part. Also worth mentioning is the guy who farted while we were in Child's pose."

She pressed her lips together. "That happens. It's natural."

"Since I wasn't expecting it, I had to hold my laughter in like a fart. I thought I was going to explode."

A laugh burst from her. "Like the blond gentleman?"

"At least he had some relief."

"So, what did you think? Other than the farting, of course."

Cam shrugged his broad shoulders. "Honestly, I'm not sure yet. I might have to join in on a few more classes to get a better feel for it."

"I hold different levels of classes at my home. So, if these classes get to be too easy, let me know."

"Easy. Sure." He snorted. "How long have you been doing yoga?"

"Since I was a kid. I used to do it with my mother. She's the one who got me interested."

"Does she still do it?"

"She does. But she lives in Arizona now with her second husband, so we don't get to practice much together anymore. Only during visits."

"And your father? Was this a family affair?"

Good lord, the man was handsome with those dark eyes and cut jawline covered in a well-maintained beard. She couldn't stop staring at him. Luckily, since they were having a conversation, it wouldn't come off as creepy. "He never got into the habit. He was more of a drink-a-six-pack-while-watching-a-baseball-game kind of guy."

"Was? Is he no longer around?"

"Oh, he's around, just not in my life."

"Sorry to hear that."

Hope shrugged. "It's better that way. We discussed that whole opposites attract thing the other day. It might be a relationship full of exciting fireworks at first, but eventually, those sparks burn out."

"*Ah*. It sounds like being attracted to the wrong men is in the blood."

"Apparently so. I thought I learned that growing up. Obviously, I thought wrong."

"You just need to find another yoga enthusiast, I guess."

If only it was that easy. "My life isn't only about yoga. And it wasn't yoga that caused the tension between me and Darren."

"Right. You said he didn't like you working here. Why? Did he think you were going to cheat on him?"

"No, he doesn't like this type of resort being in Fisher Falls. He considers everyone who visits or works here as immoral."

"Ouch."

Hope shrugged. "Nothing illegal happens at this resort, as you know." She gave him a pointed look. "The owners are very cognizant of safety and security, as you know. And this place makes people happy—"

"As I know," he finished for her. "Nothing wrong with happy, horny adults doing what adults do. Here, it just doesn't need to be done behind closed doors."

"I wish everyone had that outlook."

"Same."

"Why can't everyone simply live and let live?" Hope sighed.

"Unfortunately, people are always going to judge others. It's human nature." He paused. "Well, time for me to go shower, change, and get to work, despite wanting to be a corpse for the rest of the day. Do you need my help to put things away?"

"No, I appreciate the offer but the rolling cart makes taking everything to the storage closet easy."

He gave her a single nod. "Then, I'm out of here." He headed toward the event hall's double doors but stopped halfway there.

"Did you forget something?" she called out, glancing around for something he might've left behind.

"Yes." He turned and took long, determined strides back to her.

"What?"

He stopped only a couple feet away. "What are you doing later?"

"How much later?"

"Say...six or so?"

She blinked. Was he about to ask her on a date or something? She knew he was single, but...

"I'm not looking for a date, per se."

"You're not?"

He slowly shook his head, then smiled.

That smile spoke volumes.

"*Aaah.* So, no dinner and a movie first?"

"Do you need that?"

Did she? "No. I have dating on hold right now."

"I've had dating on hold since my last relationship ended five years ago."

"Ouch," she echoed him from earlier.

"Hookups are easier and usually less painful."

"Unless someone straps you down to one of those spanking benches and smacks your ass with a spiked paddle."

His head tilted to the side. "That actually sounds better than dinner and a movie."

Her eyebrows shot up. "You're into that?"

"Remove the spikes and I'm not going to say no."

Well, well, well. If that was true, it sounded like the resort was the perfect place for Cam to live and work. "Are you saying you don't want your ass looking like a freshly aerated lawn?"

He barked out a laugh. "That's good."

"Apparently, you don't think so."

"Your joke," he clarified.

"I know what you meant."

She couldn't stop smiling! Holy crap, she hadn't flirted with anyone in a long time. Well, if making jokes about paddling could be considered flirting. "So, six o'clock. Where?"

"My place? Or even yours, now that you don't have a boyfriend."

"Since you got to see me naked, I guess it's only fair that I get to see you the same way. Level the playing field."

"I'm game if you are, but please don't laugh at the size of my cock. It's cold out."

"It's still summer. Even the pool is warm."

"Damn. Okay, then expect the worst so you're pleasantly surprised."

"You're making me think that you have an inverted cock like a belly button. If I push on your stomach, will it pop out?"

He chuckled. "I'll make sure not to eat first. So, my place or yours?"

"Yours, since my neighbors are pretty nosy. At least here, no one will blink an eye if we hook up."

"If?"

She grinned. The man was bold. "When."

"I like that confident attitude."

I like you. "I'll see you at six."

"It's a date." He shook his head. "Nope, not a date. It's a... a..." His mouth twisted.

"Non-date."

"A non-date. See you later, then." He headed toward the exit again.

"I look forward to it."

"Same," he tossed over his shoulder.

With a long sigh, she watched his broad shoulders and very fine ass walk out the door.

Once again, they were proving that opposites *do* attract. Because she was pretty sure that she and Cameron Cook had nothing in common.

Not a damn thing.

But, hey, there was nothing wrong with enjoying the fireworks while they lasted.

Chapter Four

Cam glanced around his cabin to make sure nothing was out of place. No dirty clothes scattered around, all his shoes out of sight, his kitchenette sparkling clean, his bed freshly made with clean sheets...

Instead of having sex in his cabin, maybe he should've booked one of the playrooms up in Heaven. Would she be into that?

It was probably for the best that they started out simple tonight to see if their sexual tastes gelled first.

He lifted his left arm and smelled his pit. Okay, he did remember to roll on deodorant after he showered. Good.

He had also trimmed his nose hairs, pubic hair, and beard for this...

Non-date.

This sexual encounter.

Hopefully it went well. If it didn't, running into Hope around the resort might get a bit awkward.

While he had hoped his next encounter would be with a man since it had been far too long, he couldn't pass up an opportunity to spend some time with Hope. She seemed easy-going, smart, and had a sense of humor. Three traits he appreciated.

She was also beautiful and sexy as fuck.

His cock agreed.

He glanced at the time. 5:55.

For some unknown reason, his pulse began to race. Was he nervous? That wasn't like him. Hope shouldn't be any different from any other person he had been intimate with.

They were only getting together to have sex. He didn't need to impress her with his sparkling personality, his witty charm, or the many accolades he received during his twenty-five year career.

The only thing that mattered tonight was how he performed in bed. Period.

Or wherever they decided to have sex.

He tipped up his face and sniffed the air. His one-bedroom cabin didn't smell musty.

He glanced around one last time.

It was fine. Everything was fine. He was only being a dumbass.

If it didn't work out, then it didn't work out. She didn't seem to be the type who'd hunt him down out of spite. She wasn't some psycho. Her background check had been squeaky clean when he checked it prior to Dayne hiring her.

He glanced at the clock on the microwave again. 5:59.

To him, arriving on time meant you were late. His grand-father taught him at a young age that you always arrived early to make a good impression.

Maybe he should wait out front for her.

No. He was horny, not desperate.

His heart skipped a beat when he heard a light knocking

on the door. Cam pulled in a deep breath and, a few strides later, opened it.

Holy shit. She looked downright edible.

This evening, she wore a white crop top that emphasized her breasts and showed off her firm midriff, as well as forest-green shorts that showcased her lean, tan legs. Her dark-maroon-painted toenails he noticed earlier during class were visible in the sandals she wore. Unlike this morning, her long, deep-red hair now fell loosely around her shoulders.

Apparently, the woman could wear anything, or even nothing at all, and still look great.

"Did you forget I was coming?"

He mentally shook himself. *Jesus, dude, pick your scrambled brains off the floor and stop being an idiot.*

He stepped back and swept his arm toward the cabin's interior. "Sorry. No, I didn't forget. I've actually been looking forward to this."

A smile curled her lips. "Me, too." She stepped over the threshold and glanced around. "This is cute."

"It's small, but I don't have to pay for a mortgage or rent, or even utilities, so I can't complain. And it's only me." Not that he needed to clarify that.

"I've never been inside one yet. As you know, Dylan offered me a cabin, but I didn't need it at the time."

"Do you need one now?" When she turned the cabin down, it was quickly snapped up by someone else. So if she was ready for one, she'd have to wait until one came available again.

"If I sold my home, or even rented it out, I'd have to rent a space to teach yoga."

Right. Because the Lyonses wouldn't let just anyone onto the property, so Hope couldn't hold her regular classes on the resort's grounds. "Couldn't you do it at the community center or the library?"

"The Fisher Falls library branch is too small, but I'd have to see how much the community center would charge me, if they're even open to letting me hold my classes there at all."

He shut the door behind her and watched her wander around his small space, checking everything out. Including the framed pictures of his daughter Laurel at various ages. Those were his most important belongings. He kept them front and center.

He murmured, "I did notice this area sure likes to clutch their pearls over the littlest thing."

"They sure do. You should've heard the scuttlebutt when everyone finally realized what kind of resort this was going to be. You'd think the world was coming to an end. And as innocent as practicing yoga is, some think it summons evil spirits."

He choked out a laugh. "Are you serious?"

Hope turned to face him. "Yes! Some of them act like I'm standing in a pentagram, summoning the devil and sacrificing virgins, instead of instructing people how to deal with tension and stress and how to clear their minds and open their hearts."

"Wait. Are you secretly throwing your students into an active volcano? I don't know how I missed that on your background check. Now I'm going to have to write up a report and give it to Dylan and Dayne."

She laughed. "Oh, please don't! I wouldn't want to have to cast a spell on you!" She waved her fingers at him like she was an evil witch.

She already had. The more he spoke with her, the more he was falling under that spell.

He sure as hell hoped tonight worked out. It would be great if this ended up a solid friends with benefits situation.

This way, if either of them were in the mood to have sex, they could seek each other out.

That would mean he wouldn't need to seek out random female guests unless he was in the mood for something specific. Because he had no idea what Hope was into sexually. It could be she was completely vanilla and only wanted to bang one out and leave. To him, that would be acceptable on occasion, but not on a regular basis.

He was fine with working at this resort because his tastes aligned with a lot of the guests. As well as the owners.

When he saw the job opportunity come up, he jumped on it immediately. A ranch resort based around sex? Hell yes! That was right up his alley.

Shit. He needed to be a proper host, didn't he? "Would you like a drink?"

"Water's fine."

"No wine, beer...shot of whiskey?"

"Oh, well...a glass of wine would be perfect. As long as you're having one, too."

"It's one of the local reds Danica keeps in stock. And yes, I'll join you."

He grabbed a bottle out of the fridge. He appreciated the fact he had a full-size refrigerator/freezer combo in his compact kitchen. It made grabbing a beer or a bowl of ice cream convenient. He didn't want to hike up to the lodge's kitchen for a late night craving.

He pulled the cork and poured. When he turned, he held hers out.

Her lips twitched when she saw what kind of glassware he used.

"Sorry. I don't have any wine glasses. As you can see, my kitchenette is short on space, so some items have multiple purposes." He lifted his own coffee mug. "Cheers?"

Hope chuckled softly and tapped her mug to his. "Cheers. All the wine has to do is go from the bottle to my belly. The vessel doesn't matter."

"Don't let a wine connoisseur hear you say that. You'll be looked upon as a savage," he teased.

"Oh my God, yes." She cupped a hand around the side of her mouth and gossip-whispered, "'Have you heard? Hope Reed was seen summoning evil spirits while sipping on Satan's juice in a *coffee mug*! Can you imagine? Burn her at the stake!'"

"Are the residents of Fisher Falls really that bad?"

She shook her head. "Not all of them, but a few do have some backwards beliefs."

Cam leaned back against the counter, took another sip of the Merlot, and studied her. "If I had to take an educated guess, you're pretty progressive. That makes me believe you're not native to this area. What brought you to Fisher Falls?"

"Not a job, like you. I actually went to Penn State's Main Campus, and after graduation, decided to stay in State College. Three years ago, at a friend's barbecue, I met Darren and he was from this area. We immediately hit it off and, not even two weeks later, moved in together. When we broke up a couple of months ago, he decided he wanted a fresh start somewhere new."

Cam couldn't decide if that had been a dick move or not. He was inclined to say it was. She moved to Fisher Falls to be with her ex and then he left the area, leaving her with the house and expenses.

"And you stayed."

"I considered leaving, but despite some of the backwards thinking, I really like the area. And I *really* like this resort."

"Apparently, so do all the guests. My daughter attends

Penn State as a communications major. What was yours?"
They had at least one thing in common. He looked forward to
discovering others.

"Useless."

He chuckled. "As much as her education is costing me, to
say your degree is useless has to hurt. Was it in interpretive
dance?"

She choked on a laugh while taking another sip of her
wine. "You almost made wine shoot out of my nose."

"Don't you know, that's all part of the interpretive dance
for wine making. You must not have been paying attention in
class."

"As well as stomping on grapes." She made an exaggerated motion of picking grapes, then stomping her feet.

His smile couldn't get any bigger. "Oh, nice. And you
said your degree was useless."

He originally assumed this would only be a fast and
furious hookup, but he was really enjoying their conversation
and didn't want to rush it.

"Does having a daughter mean you were previously
married?"

"It does."

"And?"

"We're friendly still. Our marriage wasn't full of turmoil
or anything. One day I simply realized that..."

That he didn't want to limit himself to only a woman. But
he also didn't want to cheat to fill his needs. He and his ex sat
down together one night and actually had a very reasonable
conversation about it. Luckily, not all divorces turn out to be
ugly.

But then, he was completely honest with Molly and
accepted all the blame. He didn't want her to think it was her
fault. Restlessness had been clawing at his insides.

Sometimes it still did.

"Realized?" she prodded with curiosity in her eyes as she peered at him over the rim of her mug.

"That I needed to be true to myself to be happy. One day I realized I was suppressing some of my urges. I was bottling it up inside and needed to relieve that pressure before I exploded, possibly leaving a path of destruction."

"Urges? Like serial killer urges?"

"No." Of course she was joking, but... "I'm—"

Holy shit. Was he actually going to admit it out loud to someone he hardly knew? Even his family and closest friends didn't know. But...

It was time.

And if he was reading Hope correctly, he doubted she'd judge him for it. "I'm..."

One of Hope's eyebrows cocked and she drew out, "You're?"

He pulled in a deep breath and on the exhale, "Bisexual" escaped.

There. It was now out in the universe.

And the sky didn't fall.

Hope blinked and confusion filled her face. "Okay?"

"Like your yoga, not everyone is open to that lifestyle."

"But this place"—she waved her hand around—"is one of the most accepting places I've ever been."

"Yes. I can freely be who I am here. Without judgement."

"And have you been open about it?" she asked.

"No. Believe it or not, you're only the second person I've told." He was surprised how freeing it felt to finally admit it. Like a heavy load had been lifted from his shoulders.

With her mouth gaping, she set her mug down with a clunk on the tiny two-person table. "Wait a minute. How old are you?"

"Forty-six."

"You've kept your sexuality hidden for forty-six years?"

"Well, the men I've been with had an idea," he half-teased, then shrugged. "Or they assumed I was gay, I guess. The truth is, I've never been in an actual relationship with a man. It's only been casual encounters." Why was he spilling this info tonight?

Instinct told him she'd be fine with him being bisexual. Not all women were.

"In secret."

"Yes."

"Wow. I'm sorry you felt the need to hide it."

"Some of it had to do with my career. I entered the state police academy right after turning twenty-one." He had been so young and only learning about himself at the time.

He had girlfriends in high school, of course, but his eyes had occasionally wandered to his male classmates.

It took him a while to figure out that interest was more than curiosity. He was attracted to men—or, at that age, boys —as much as girls.

At the time, he didn't know what to do with that information. So for a while, he did nothing, hoping that interest would just fade away.

It didn't. It got stronger. Then he met Molly and they hit it off. He hoped she would be enough for him. Sadly, she wasn't.

Again, not her fault. It was his. He wasn't sure how she would take his confession. She'd been surprised since he'd hidden it well enough, and also sad for him. At the time, they decided not to tell Laurel about it, only that they were breaking up due to irreconcilable differences.

The reason wasn't important to their daughter, she'd been more concerned about the fact her parents were splitting up. Now that she was in her early twenties, he'd considered mentioning it, but since he wasn't seeing a man, there really wasn't a point.

He figured it was best to have a reason to bring it up. It might be a bit weird for him to randomly confess that he was into both men and women.

But maybe he was going about it the wrong way.

"I can imagine," she started, "with you being in a male-dominated career, it had to be a bit more difficult to tell your co-workers that you were anything other than a straight, alpha male."

"Especially when we shared the same locker room."

"Usually the people who complain the loudest have something to hide themselves. They're beating themselves up on the inside, so they take it out on others."

"You're probably right," he murmured. "I wish we were at the point where one's sexuality wasn't a big deal."

"A lot of people believe that."

"Not enough."

"I won't disagree. I wish everyone was accepting of others." She quickly downed the contents of her mug and smiled. "Time to play?"

Hell yes. He liked this woman already.

Chapter Five

Hope placed the empty coffee mug in the sink. While their conversation had been great, that wasn't why she had come to his cabin. No, she was there for physical, not mental, stimulation.

She hadn't had sex in at least two months now, ever since she informed Darren she would be teaching yoga classes at Double D Ranch.

"You're really willing to give me up for that little bit of money you'll make from those pervs?"

The perv comment had really pissed her off, so she simply replied, "Yes," and left it at that. She could've told him that she didn't like where he stood on a lot of topics, or how he treated some people, or that their sex life had become mundane, but she didn't need to insult him to make her feel better about her decision.

And that was what it was. A decision for *her* life. Not his.

Whenever they had sex, he also discouraged anything even remotely non-vanilla. Because of that, she'd been suppressing some of her desires in an attempt to keep things between them smooth.

She liked a variety. Darren didn't.

Her ex-boyfriend also held the opinion that teaching yoga classes was a hobby, not a "real" job.

In the end, her relationship with Darren proved two weeks wasn't nearly long enough to know someone before moving in together. Yes, they'd had their good moments, but in the end, their ideologies clashed too much for them to live in complete harmony. She had ignored it for a while, until there came a point she couldn't anymore.

Getting hired by Double D Ranch had been the perfect excuse to end their relationship. She wished Darren well with whatever his future held. Unfortunately, she did not get that in return. He was the kind of man who relentlessly judged others but thought his own shit didn't stink.

Now she was single again and free to do whatever she was in the mood for. And right now, she was in the mood to do the tall, handsome, former trooper that stood only a few feet away.

He was game. She was game. Obviously, it was time to play.

She spun around. "What are you into besides men?"

"Women," he said, tongue in cheek.

"Obviously. Last time I checked, I am one. Other than that?"

"Satisfying sex." He was purposely being obtuse.

"Well, look at that. So am I. What else? You need to narrow it down."

He cocked an eyebrow. "Do I? Or should we just explore?"

"Do you have a safe word?"

"Do you?"

She smiled. "I do."

Cam mirrored that smile. "So do I."

Her smile spread. "I like the sound of that."

"You probably won't hear it."

She also liked a challenge. "Don't bet on it."

"Damn," he whispered. "What's yours?"

"Shanti."

His head twitched. "What's that?"

"It means peace. What's yours?"

"Oklahoma."

She'd admit hers was unique, but his? "Have you been there?"

"No."

Her brow furrowed. "Then why'd you pick it?"

After a slight hesitation, he finally answered. "Johnny Knoxville used it as his safe word in Jackass."

"Jackass? I have no idea what that is."

Cam chuckled. "Maybe it's for the best."

"Got it. As a former cop, I assumed you were either a Dom or leaned toward the more dominant side. Am I wrong?"

"I'm pretty flexible. It all depends on who I'm with. Do you prefer to be submissive?"

"No."

He blinked. "No?"

Hope tipped her head to the side. "Did you expect me to say yes because I'm a woman?"

"No...I...No." He groaned. "Yes. Sorry." He lifted a *let-me-explain* finger. "But not because you're a woman; because you seem to be more of a"—he waved a hand around—"free spirit. A gentle soul, if you will. Please take that as a compliment and not an insult."

"Unlike you, who had no problem cuffing people during

your career?"

"Just because I did it for my job, doesn't mean I enjoy doing it in my down time."

"Good to know."

"But it also doesn't mean I *don't* like to do it in my down time." He shot her a toothy grin. "If you want to be cuffed and stuffed, I'll gladly do that without complaint."

"And if *you* like to be cuffed and stuffed, I will gladly do that as well." As well as plenty of other things.

"Okay, then. How about we move this conversation into the bedroom?" He held out a hand toward the only bedroom in the cabin.

"I figured tonight would be pretty tame. I'm starting to believe it'll be the opposite."

"You do know where we are right now, right?" he asked as he followed her into his bedroom.

"Your cabin?"

"*Welcome to Double D Ranch, the adults-only ranch resort where your fantasies become reality. Unpack, unwind, and get uninhibited,*" he recited.

"Hmm." She tapped her lips with her finger. "I think I've heard that somewhere before..."

He chuckled. "Haven't we all?"

She stopped in the middle of his bedroom and glanced around. It wasn't huge, but it was neat and organized. Nothing had been left out. He was most likely someone who liked everything to have its place.

Police departments were normally paramilitary organizations, so that made sense.

Despite that, she'd love to test his limits, see if she could break him and force him to sing, "*Oklahoma!*"

It had been a while since she'd had that chance with anyone. Certainly not with Darren. She had joked around once about putting clamps on his nipples and he went off about it. That was the last time she mentioned anything even remotely outside of vanilla.

If the Lyonses hadn't turned their family farm into a ranch resort, would she and Darren still be together? She hadn't realized just how dissatisfied and unfulfilled she was in her relationship until after they split.

Maybe her being hired at the resort was a blessing in disguise.

And she certainly couldn't complain about the man whose room she stood in. "So...since you've already seen me in all my pride and glory, how soon do I get to see you?" With what she could see in his shorts and tank earlier, she couldn't wait to see the rest.

"Do you want me to strip?"

She wouldn't say no to a private striptease. "Absolutely." She sat on the edge of the bed, licked her lips and pointed to a spot on the floor directly in front of her. "Stand right there and show me what you got. Hold on." She held up an open palm. "Do I need to grab my purse out of the car and dig out some one dollar bills?"

"You'll only need nickels since my striptease performance might be a bit lacking."

She attempted to sound serious when she asked, "Do you want the nickels thrown at you or slipped into your slot?"

A laugh burst from him, making her smile. He was a good sport and she was enjoying the natural, easy banter between them.

She circled her hand in the air and wiggled her eyebrows. "All right, let's go." She was looking forward to this.

One of his eyebrows cocked. "Impatient?"

"Sure am! I only got a teaser this morning. I'm ready for the complete reveal."

He placed his hand over both of his nipples, pretending like he was shy. "You'll make me self-conscious."

She huffed, "I doubt it."

With a toothy grin, he slowly peeled his T-shirt up and over his head, revealing his very spectacular chest. Holy smokes, it was obvious he hit up the resort's gym on a regular basis. He actually had a well-defined six-pack and not a beer keg.

When he was done sensually sliding his hands down his bare torso, her eyes were automatically drawn to his full sleeve next, the same as they had been that morning. "Did you get the kraken on your arm to match the kraken in your pants?"

"Like I warned earlier, you might be disappointed."

"It's not the size that counts..."

He shot her a look. "Don't kid yourself."

"Just call me Goldilocks. I want the cock that's not too small and not too big, but *just right*."

On a man that was *just right*.

Who also knew how to have sex *just right*.

She was holding on to a lot of hope that Cam was good in bed.

Her anticipation ramped up when he unfastened his jeans and tucked his thumbs into the waistband. Then, holding her gaze, he shucked them, dropping them to the floor before also shoving his boxer briefs down, freeing his erection with a bounce.

Hell yes!

He stepped out of the pants and underwear pooled around his bare feet. "Don't laugh."

She certainly wasn't laughing.

He had a beautiful cock, and that wasn't something she'd

normally say about just any male member. His was a nice shape and size and everything was in proportion.

The pearl of precum clinging to the tip made her mouth water.

"Should I turn in a circle?"

"No." With a shake of her head, she lifted her hand again with the palm out. "Stay there."

She got to her feet and approached him. Slowly circling him, Hope took her time visually inspecting and admiring every inch of his beautiful body she could see.

Hot damn. She just hit the jackpot.

"I'm going to touch you." Normally, she'd ask out of habit from teaching yoga, but tonight wasn't normal.

"I'd be disappointed if you didn't."

She stopped behind him, her hands lightly skimming over his broad back, down to the muscular globes of his ass, before sliding back up and across his wide shoulders.

When she stepped in front of him, she saw him fisting the root of his cock. "I didn't say you could touch yourself, did I?"

His fingers flexed before releasing his hard length and dropping his hands to his sides. "Sorry. Does this mean you'll be giving all the orders tonight?"

"Do you mind?"

It took him a few seconds to respond. "I don't know what you're into." For a seemingly confident man, she was surprised to hear worry coloring his words.

"Nothing too crazy."

"Crazy can be relative."

"You have a safe word," she reminded him. "Although, I don't think you'll need it tonight. I want to get to know you better. Maybe we'll click. Maybe we won't." She hoped they did.

Now she just needed to figure out what she wanted to do to him first. Or if she wanted to order him to simply *do* her.

The main event could wait. His body was like a playground and she wanted to explore it to see what equipment she wanted to play with first.

No matter what, tonight wouldn't be completely vanilla. She wanted to kick it up just a notch. "Do you have a blindfold?"

Again, he hesitated. "Sure. But I'm not really into being blindfolded."

"I don't remember asking if you were. Get it."

Something as simple as being blindfolded would push him out of his comfort zone? *Interesting.* She had to guess that had to do with being former law enforcement. Being tied up, or not having all of your senses, like your sight, could make him feel vulnerable.

"Is it for me or you?"

"You, of course. If I wear it, I won't be able to see what I'm doing."

"And what will you be doing?"

"You'll figure it out. Give it time. And don't forget that safe word if anything I do gets to be too much."

"You're making me apprehensive."

"I promise not to hurt you. Tonight's all about pleasure."

His dark brown eyes held heat. "Would you hurt me if I asked?"

That had her pausing and looking at him in a new light. "As long as we're both getting something out of it, sure. Is that what you want?"

Again, he hesitated. "For now, I'll let you do what you want to do. If it's either not enough or too much, I'll let you know."

"Deal." She held out her hand, palm up. "Now, get the blindfold."

"Yes..." His head twitched and his forehead furrowed. "What honorific do you want me to use?"

She wasn't picky, and that wasn't something she normally required, but she appreciated him asking. "What do you prefer?"

One side of his mouth pulled up. "Mistress."

She preferred that over Ma'am, since that title made her feel much older than her thirty years. "I'm fine with that. How about you?"

"When I'm the top, Master or Sir works. But none is needed, if it makes you uncomfortable."

"Master does, but Sir is perfectly fine."

"Good."

"Good. Now that we have that settled, get that blindfold."

He gave her a single nod. "Yes, Mistress."

Damn. Just that simple title made the heat swirl through her, her pussy clench, and her nipples ache.

Chapter Six

Hope really liked the fact that the former cop wasn't so rigid. She preferred fluidity. A give and take.

She zeroed in on his ass when he went over to the closet and opened it, watching the muscles flex in his broad back as he reached for a box on the top shelf like he was her own personal porn star.

Once he pulled it out and set it on the floor, he squatted down to dig through it.

That was an interesting but eye-popping view.

He was as confident as she was when it came to his nudity. But then, he should have pride in his body. He clearly worked hard to maintain it.

"A toy box?" Her pussy twinged and she mentally rubbed her hands together. "What other goodies do you have in there?"

When he stood and turned, he clutched a black, silk-like blindfold. "May I speak freely, Mistress?"

Good lord, the simple act of him calling her that caused

sparks to ignite inside her. She was looking forward to this more and more by the minute.

"Nothing too extreme since those types of toys can be found up in Heaven. This cabin doesn't have enough storage space."

"I haven't been up to Heaven yet," she murmured.

She meant to check it out but wasn't sure if she'd be allowed. She wasn't a guest and was more of an independent contractor than an actual employee. She had planned on asking Danica if it was okay since she didn't want to do anything that might jeopardize her position at Double D, but hadn't gotten around to it.

"You haven't? I'll have to give you a tour. As head of security, I can get you in anywhere."

Well, that was an even better plan. Now that she had a potential partner to join her in one of those rooms... "I'd love to see it."

His smile was huge when he said, "I'd love to see you in one of those rooms."

"I heard they're themed."

"They are."

"Which is your favorite?"

"Normally I'd say room four, the bondage/restraint room. However, after seeing you do yoga, I'm thinking if you're involved, my favorite might end up being the entertainment room."

"What's in that room?"

"I guess you'll find out during the tour."

"Then I look forward to it."

He winked at her. "You're not the only one."

"Put on the blindfold like a good boy." She kept the tone of her demand more of a soft authority rather than a harsh order.

They went from playful to serious in mere seconds. He pulled the blindfold over his head and adjusted it over his eyes.

She waved a hand in front of his face. "What can you see?"

"Darkness, Mistress."

Unlike her. She could see *everything* on him. "Good. Do you like praise?"

"I don't hate it."

"Does 'good boy' turn you on or off?"

"It's not my favorite, Mistress."

"What do you prefer?"

"I prefer whatever my mistress does."

Well, then. "Then good boy it is." For now. Unless she could come up with something more appropriate. Since she wasn't a hardcore Domme, her BDSM knowledge wasn't extensive. She simply knew what she liked. And as far as she was aware, there weren't any hard and fast rules except for safety and consent.

Sometimes she liked to be the bossy one and at other times, she liked to be bossed around. Only during sex, of course.

"Stay there," she ordered Cam next.

"Since I can't see, I'm not moving until my mistress moves me."

Good point.

She circled him again, raking her nails lightly across his bare, tan skin. Not deep enough to leave marks, but enough to spur goosebumps.

"Beautiful," she whispered as she completely took him in again. Every curve, every hard line, the heaviness of his sack, the perfectly round globes of his ass, the definition of his abs and thighs, the dark hair nestling the base of his cock and lightly decorating his long legs.

He had no tattoos other than the expertly done sleeves that filled both arms. This man had not skimped on finding a good tattoo artist. But then, he waited for decades to get them.

She eyed his erection and knew exactly how she wanted to start this evening of fun debauchery.

He sucked in an audible breath when she whispered, "I'm going to put that in my mouth."

How could she not? It was too beautiful to ignore.

His knees wobbled slightly when she drew her hands down his body, over every ridge and valley, at the same time lowering herself to her knees at his feet. Of course, that wasn't the normal position for someone taking the dominant role, but she didn't care. Again, she didn't hold herself to any hard and fast rules.

She captured the glistening pearl clinging to the tip of his cock on her tongue before raking her nails down his length and back up. Her nipples turned to even harder peaks at the low moan escaping him.

She scraped her nails over him again, this time following along with her tongue.

Cupping his sack, she lightly squeezed as she took his length into her mouth and her taste buds exploded from the salty precum. She'd always loved giving head, and sucking him deep made the slickness between her legs grow, causing her to squeeze her thighs together.

Doing so might have been a mistake, because now she was on the verge of coming hands-free. How was she supposed to be the one in control when she couldn't even control her own reactions?

It was both amusing and frustrating at the same time.

Every time she swallowed as much of his length as possible, his hips jutted forward, and when she pulled back, so did he. Obviously, he wanted to pump in and out of her mouth, but managed to hold himself in check.

Good. Because she wanted to take him to the very edge before pulling him back to do it all over again. She'd wait until he relaxed and his muscles loosened before sucking him harder and faster. Once he tensed and his hips began to jump again, she slowed to almost a stop.

Almost, but not completely. Enough to make him "suffer," but not enough to make him come.

She swore he whimpered when she did it at least four more times. While he didn't voice any complaints, when he finally blew out a loud, frustrated breath, she knew he was at his limit.

With a last sharp tug on his balls and swirl of her tongue around the slick crown, she released him and rose to her feet. His head had fallen forward slightly and small bursts of air came from between his parted lips. His fingers were even curled tightly into his palms.

Oh yes, he'd been fighting it.

"Did you like that?" she asked before leaning in to suck on his small, dusky nipple, flicking the other with the tip of her nail at the same time.

He jerked in response. "Yes, Mistress."

She flicked the nipple she had just sucked next and watched his abs ripple in response. "Do you want me to suck your cock some more?"

"Yes, Mistress, but..."

"But?"

"I might come," he answered.

"You aren't allowed to come unless I give you permission."

"Understood, Mistress."

"Good..." She really didn't like the idea of calling him a "boy." He was far from that. "Stud" might be more fitting. Although, she couldn't confirm if he was or wasn't one yet. Hopefully soon. "What else do you have in that toy box? May I look in it?"

"You may, Mistress."

"Don't move. Not one inch."

"Yes, Mistress."

Hope went over and picked up the box, setting it on the bed so she could dig through it.

Edible lube. Cock rings. Nipple clamps.

Ooo. Yes. She pulled the clamps out and set them aside.

The anal beads made sense since he was bi. She pulled those out, too. "Do you have regular lube?"

"Yes, in my nightstand, along with condoms, Mistress."

"Good," she murmured, continuing to dig.

A small vibrator. Another cock ring that vibrated. A silicone glove that was textured for pleasure and most likely used for jerking off or to stimulate a man's prostate. A silicone sleeve-ring. Also most likely used for self-pleasuring.

Damn, would she love to watch him masturbate. She felt a little trickle between her legs just from that thought alone.

Also in the box were nylon restraints for wrists and ankles, but funny enough, no real handcuffs. Something you'd think a former cop would have in his toolbox.

She also couldn't find any impact toys like whips or paddles. No gags either.

Interesting.

She picked up the black, textured glove and slipped it onto her hand. It was a little big but she could work with it. "You said the lube and condoms are in your nightstand? Do I have permission to get those?"

"Yes, Mistress."

She grabbed the tube of lube and set a couple of condoms aside. Popping open the tube, she generously squirted some on the glove, concentrating on the index and middle fingers. Once it was prepped, she went back over to where he stood and grabbed his arm with her glove-free hand. "This way about five steps, Handsome. Now lean over, place your hands on the mattress, and spread your feet apart."

She didn't miss him quiver as he got into position and she stepped behind him.

She kicked off her sandals and used her own foot to encourage him to spread his legs wider. "Farther apart. Tip your ass up and out."

Now was as good a time as any to get herself naked. She didn't want the silicone-based lube to get on her clothes. She glanced at the lubed glove. Damn it, she should've thought about getting undressed first. "Stay right there. I want to get naked first."

She pulled off the glove and set it carefully to the side before shucking her shorts and panties, then divesting herself of her crop top and bra. She slipped the glove back on and once again moved to stand behind him.

She appreciated the fact he had obeyed and hadn't moved an inch. "Palms stay on the bed, your feet on the floor. Got it?"

"Yes, Mistress."

She smiled. She would soon see how still he kept. She squirted a tiny bit more lube over his tight hole, enough that it glistened, then she gently pushed her gloved index finger against him, encouraging him to loosen up.

As soon as he did, she slipped one finger inside him, working the lube around. His head dropped lower and he groaned.

"Don't move. No matter what I do."

His answering, "Yes, Mistress," sounded more strained this time. Maybe because she was finger fucking him as well as actively searching for his magical spot. As soon as she stroked it, a breath hissed from him.

She continued to stimulate his P-spot until his hole tightened around her and his hips twitched slightly. She pulled back, added her middle finger, and began to fuck him all over again. She didn't want him to come, but she *did* want to take him to that sweet edge.

A noise rose up his throat that reminded her of a growl and he tensed, most likely to keep from thrusting his hips. A quick glance showed that his hands were no longer flat but now clutching the bedding in a death grip.

He released an audible sigh when she pulled her gloved fingers free. She spotted the anal beads she had pulled from his toy box. Removing the glove once again, she grabbed them. It was a string of connected plastic balls, the smallest at around a quarter inch, the largest at the end right before the pull ring had to be about an inch. She lubed it up good.

After going back to him, she asked, "How often have you used the anal beads?"

"Here and there."

That meant he probably used them more often than not. When she pictured him using the glove to masturbate with those beads firmly planted up his ass, more arousal trickled from her.

"I want you to keep them in while we have sex." She doubted he'd complain about that.

"It might make me come faster, Mistress."

"Mind over matter," she told him.

He groaned as she slowly fed the generously lubed beads into his ass. Once they were in place, she stepped back and admired her handiwork. "Beautiful," she murmured. She hooked a finger in the ring and tugged on the beads, then pushed them back and forth a few times.

"Fuck," he groaned again.

"We'll get there. Patience, my handsome stud."

"I want to bury my face in your cunt."

Cunt was such a crude word in everyday life, but when playing, it turned her on. The dirtier the words, the wetter she got.

"We'll get there, too," she told him. She gave his bare ass cheek a sharp slap. "Stand up and take a step back."

When he immediately did as ordered, a thrill rippled through her. She took his place and sat on the edge of the bed. "Now get on your knees."

"Here?"

"There," she confirmed, spreading her own thighs and sliding a finger through her folds. Oh yes, she was soaked. "Now move forward until you're between my legs."

He shuffled forward on his knees until he was wedged between her thighs. As soon as he was, she grabbed his head and shoved his face into her sopping wet pussy. "Now eat me. Do not stop until I tell you. Understood?"

His muffled, "Yes, Mistress," could barely be heard.

His very short beard was rough against her and added to the pleasure, but it was nothing compared to what he did with his tongue and lips.

Holy shit.

Keeping a tight grip on his head to hold him there, she struggled to keep her hips from popping off the bed.

He. Was. *Gooooood.*

So damn good.

He ate her like he'd never eaten anything so tasty.

By alternating sucking her clit and lightly scraping his

teeth over it, she had to bite back a gasp. He flicked it with the tip of his tongue and then *moaned* against her pussy.

That vibration almost made her lose her tightly held control.

He pulled back just enough to ask, "May I use my fingers, Mistress?"

Oh yes, you definitely can.

Chapter Seven

"Yᴇꜱ, Handsome, you can finger fuck me while sucking on my clit." No way in hell was she going to say no to that.

After swiping two fingers through her pussy to gather her arousal, he dove in face-first again, flicking and sucking. At first, he didn't fuck her with his fingers.

No, this man smeared her natural lube on her anus and, using pressure alone, asked for permission to breach that hole. She gave her silent approval by relaxing enough to make it easier on them both.

Luckily, he was good at picking up on silent cues.

But...

Yes. Yes. Yesssss.

He continued to enthusiastically chow down while simultaneously gliding his fingers in and out of her ass; something Darren had had no interest in doing. He thought anything to do with the ass was "gay."

That should've been a red flag. She should've known right then and there who he was at his core. He was set in his ways, and combined with his narrowed thinking, their relationship had been doomed from the start. Only at the beginning had she mistakenly thought he wasn't as bad as he really ended up being.

Lesson learned. Hopefully, it was not one she'd need to repeat.

Despite their issues, she was sad when their relationship failed. She glanced at the dark head presently between her thighs. But maybe it had been for the best.

Once Cam began fucking her ass harder and eating her pussy more frantically, it was obvious he was on a mission to get her to come as fast as possible.

Far be it from her to deny him his reward.

She tossed any thoughts of Darren out of her mind and focused on the man she was with currently. The hot, sexy stud who was certainly not closed-minded. But then, it was probably difficult to be closed-minded when blindfolded with anal beads shoved up his ass.

He sucked her clit so hard that, despite fighting it, her hips shot off the bed. When she slammed her pussy right into his nose, he grunted. Hopefully she didn't break anything. If she did, he kept on going like a true trooper.

But it wasn't long before what started as a small ripple turned into an intense riptide. When it was over, she melted back into the mattress and Cam's head popped up, blindfold askew and wearing a shiny, satisfied smile.

She'd be smiling, too, if she could, but she had to wait out the last few waves of her orgasm.

He slipped his fingers from her ass and sat back on his heels. As soon as she had the energy to move, she sat up and adjusted his blindfold to make sure his eyes were still covered.

Maybe she should just remove it completely. However,

she knew from experience it heightened the anticipation and pleasure. She'd leave it on. For now, anyway.

Getting to her feet, she grabbed his arm and encouraged him to stand. "Climb on the bed, Handsome, and stretch out on your back."

"Yes, Mistress." After getting into place, he waited, his erection long and hard with a tempting string of precum dangling from the end.

"I'm going to grab a towel and washcloth." Not bothering to wait for his response, she walked out of his bedroom and into the only bathroom in the cabin. She found a spare towel and washcloth under the sink, ran the latter under the faucet and, on her way back to the bed, also snagged a waiting condom.

Once she joined him on the bed, she tucked the towel under his very fine ass to protect the bedding, then placed the damp washcloth in his hand so he could clean the lube off his fingers.

As he did so, she got into position by straddling his thighs. "Are you ready for me to fuck you?"

"Yes, Mistress. So ready for you to fuck me."

After ripping open the condom wrapper, his cock flexed within her fingers as she rolled it down his length.

"Hold it for me," she ordered.

He blindly tossed the washcloth aside and held his cock in place. Once she adjusted her position, until the crown was tucked between her folds, she slowly sank down. When he was fully seated, she waited for a second to adjust to his girth, then began to move slowly.

Wait. She was missing something important...

Anal beads. Check.

Blindfold. Check.

Condom. Check.

Lube? Definitely not needed.

The nipple clamps! She couldn't forget about them. Where were they?

She spotted them just out of reach. *Damn it!*

Hope grimaced. She'd have to let it go this time. If there was a next time, she could take advantage of them. Really, she wasn't opposed to them being used on her, either.

"Is there a problem, Mistress?"

"I wanted to use the nipple clamps on you, but...next time." She'd evaluate after this first time to see if there would be a repeat.

He shifted beneath her.

"Have you had them used on you before, Handsome?"

"Yes, Mistress."

She couldn't explain why this sexy hunk of man-meat calling her that honorific sent a thrill through her every time.

She began to move again, sliding up and down his latex-covered cock at a leisurely pace, so she could appreciate everything about the man splayed on his back beneath her. The only problem was, she was currently doing all the work while he laid back and enjoyed the ride. She'd never have any idea about his skill level if he wasn't more involved in the action.

She slowed her pace even more. It could be that he wasn't participating because he was waiting for instruction from her and didn't want to step out of line. If so, it was up to her to switch things up.

"I want to see your beautiful eyes." She ripped off the blindfold and tossed it, figuring it would end up wherever the washcloth did.

His gaze locked with hers and, for a second, she fell into the depths of his expressive, brown eyes.

A bizarre, instant connection fueled the fire inside her to

burn even hotter and her pussy clenched around him tightly. Her rhythm hitched until she recovered from her unexpected reaction.

She'd analyze that more closely later.

Grabbing his hands, she slapped them onto her breasts, giving him an unspoken order to play with them. He immediately sprang into action by kneading them before tugging and twisting her nipples.

She pushed and circled her own clit. With her riding his cock, him roughly playing with her tits, she ground against him, driving him even deeper by both rocking back and forth and circling her hips.

While his eyes were locked on where she played with herself, hers was drawn to his clenched jaw and his Adam's apple stuck at the top of his throat.

The man was fighting for his life.

While she felt pity for him, her goal, first and foremost, was to come again before he did.

Despite not being able to reach the nipple clamps, she couldn't resist pinching them, which she did with gusto.

As she continued to fuck him, they began to mirror each other's action. When she twisted his small, dusky nipples, he did the same to her. When she yanked on them, so did he. When she pinched his hard enough to make him gasp, he growled and did the same to her.

Yes. Yes. Yes!

Leaning forward, she scraped her teeth over the small, hard tips. Of course, due to his position, he was unable to do the same to her. She sucked one, then the other, before dragging her tongue over each puckered nipple.

"Do you like that?" she murmured against his hot skin.

She could actually hear him swallow. "Yes...Mistress."

"Want more, Handsome?"

"I want whatever you do."

He was such a good sport. "I want to come, but I'm enjoying this." No lies were told.

"Same, Mistress."

Sitting up and planting her hands on his chest, she rubbed her thumbs back and forth over his now-red nipples and continued to ride him, increasing her pace and driving him as deep as possible.

As they focused on each other, her heart thumped heavily and butterflies took flight in her belly.

That sensation was so strange and unexpected, catching her off guard. She never had anything similar with Darren that she could remember. Not even when things were new and exciting.

Maybe that had been another sign they weren't meant to be together long-term. Funny how once someone was out of your life, those signs became so much clearer and easier to read. All she had to do was remove her blinders the same way she'd removed Cam's blindfold.

Closing her eyes, she continued to spear herself on his length, dropping her head back and milking his cock by squeezing her inner muscles. That drew out a long moan from deep inside him.

When he squeezed his eyes shut and tensed, she paused.

Oh yeah, he was hanging on by a quickly unraveling thread.

As soon as he relaxed a little, she started all over again by driving him to that very edge before slowing enough, or stopping completely, so that he wouldn't come.

He kept repeating something under his breath, and with his fingers twisting in the bedding so tightly, she was surprised the fabric didn't tear. She wasn't stopping until she came, so whatever he was chanting to himself had better work.

"Mistress..." The plea was strained, but before she could respond, he growled, "My turn," seizing her hips and flipping her onto her back.

Whoa! "I didn't tell you—"

He took her mouth, stopping her flow of words and smothering her surprise.

He circled her wrists with his fingers and stretched her arms over her head, pinning them to the bed.

Okay, then. This was a turn of events she could get onboard with.

He rammed his cock home, ordering, "You need to come...like, now."

He would get no disagreement from her.

She gasped when one sensitive nipple was flicked with his tongue, then the other.

He reared up and gave each one of her breasts a stinging slap before falling over her again to rake his teeth along her neck. She shuddered and moaned when he sank them into her shoulder and used the right amount of pressure for her to ride that thin line between pain and pleasure.

He thrust his cock into her, not skipping a beat. His intentions were clear between his clenched teeth and the determination in his dark eyes.

She closed her own and he began to lead her down that path of satisfaction. But as she was getting swept away, he abruptly flipped her over again and snaked an arm under her hips up to pull her ass even higher while thrusting deeper and slamming into her. Each hard thrust was emphasized by the sound of skin slapping together and his deep, animalistic grunts.

She gasped when he fisted her hair and yanked her

head back, arching her throat. Her hair was used to twist her head so he had access to nip along her back. Not hard enough to break the skin, but enough that goosebumps broke out.

He licked up the indentation of her spine, then shoved her head into the mattress. "Pinch your nipple and play with your clit. When you come, I want an explosion."

That growl caused her pussy to twinge around him.

She was close. So damn close. And she was ready for that explosion, too.

While it had been fun being in charge, she was enjoying this switch of power.

Instead of using two fingers, this time he plugged her ass with his thumb, plunging it in and out of her. *Oh yes. Yes. Yes!*

This. This was what she'd been missing in her former relationship. And, boy, had she been missing it. She was so thankful Cam sought her out the other day when she was practicing naked yoga on the dock so she could get the attention she'd been craving lately.

All of this was right up her alley and she hoped they got to play again in the near future. But it wasn't over.

Yet.

This man was still ramming into her like a piston in a steam engine. Between his thumb and cock filling her and the smooth roll of his hips, her back arched and she began to splinter apart.

"That's it, Handsome. Keep going," she moaned. She shuddered as the waves of orgasm rushed through her, sweeping her away.

Oh yes. Yes. Yes!

How refreshing it was that this man knew how to please a woman. Not only that, but was successful at it, too. In her experience, hot and handsome men like Cam could be arrogant and selfish. More worried about their own pleasure than their partner's.

He definitely broke the stereotype.

Once his smooth movement became choppy, she knew he was about to chase his own release. She smashed her ass into him over and over until he just about stuttered to a stop.

With a tightened grip on her wrists, he jammed himself deep one more time and came with a grunt. After a few seconds, he melted against her with his forehead pressed against her back. His warm breath beat rapidly against her skin while his cock continued to twitch inside her.

"Holy shit," he whispered and flopped onto his back with his chest still heaving.

She settled beside him on the king-sized bed. "I second that."

He slipped the full condom free and tied it off, setting it aside with a long, very satisfied sounding sigh.

She wanted to stretch like a cat, then curl up in contentment, licking her whiskers.

She had not expected tonight to be this good. She had hoped, but...

Thankfully, it blew all expectations out of the water. She also liked the fact he was open to being dominated or doing the domination.

He'd be a great catch. *If* she was looking. And since she was fresh out of a relationship, she was not.

She rolled into him and with a smile, scraped her fingernails along his bearded jaw. "Tell me. How'd you get to be so handsome?"

The corners of his dark eyes crinkled. "Good genetics?"

"Well then, thank your parents for me," she teased.

He huffed, "Can we not bring them into the conversation right now?"

A soft laugh burst from her at his grimace. "Sorry, but I'm impressed that they made such a beautiful man." She wasn't lying

He nudged her with his elbow. "Your parents didn't do a half-bad job themselves."

She sighed with contentment. She got what she came for but she wasn't ready for the evening to be over. "So, now what?"

"For a small cabin, my shower is pretty damn impressive if you'd like to see it."

"Absolutely! I'm prepared to be impressed." If his shower was anywhere as great as the sex, she definitely would be.

Chapter Eight

"Name?"

"Nolan Young."

The guard typed Nolan's name into the computer and not even a minute later, opened the gate. "The boss has been expecting you. Do you know where to go from here?"

"No. Cam only told me to come to his cabin."

The guard jerked a thumb toward the long paved lane that disappeared over a slight rise behind the guard shack. "Head down that road. Once you pass the lodge on your left, keep going. The horse stables will also be on your left and then just past that, the employee cabins will be on your right. He lives in cabin number four."

"Thank you."

"Welcome to Double D Ranch! Enjoy your stay."

Nolan planned on it. He could use this little "vacation" and some time with his friend.

He gave the guard an acknowledging nod and slowly headed off down the lane as instructed, taking his time to look around as he drove. In the distance, sunlight made trees cascading down the steep slopes of the mountain valley glow. To his left, a large lake appeared with a half dozen cabins lining the far side.

Overlooking the serene lake was a looming lodge with a similar appearance to an oversized log cabin. It fit the property perfectly with two-story windows and a mountain stone front. Rustic luxury was the first thing that came to mind.

He drove past guests strolling a paved path, jogging along the lane, or riding bikes.

He was glad he'd decided to bring along his mountain bike. From what he could see so far, this would be the perfect place to go for a long, sweat-inducing ride to clear his head.

Was that a chicken coop to his right? It sure was. When he checked out the resort's website, it did say they locally-sourced ingredients as much as possible. It couldn't get any more local than a good-sized coop full of egg layers.

Movement to his left proved to be a horse trotting around a paddock, tossing its head and kicking up its hooves. Nolan understood that horse's joy. He'd had the same feeling on his last day with the Pennsylvania State Police.

Once the paved lane turned to gravel, he finally spotted the six cabins on the right that housed employees. They weren't huge, but he figured most employees with children would prefer not to live on a ranch that catered to adults turning their sexual fantasies into reality.

Nolan wondered how much of that he'd get to experience during his five nights staying with Cam. The website did state the resort was judgement free, so that meant if he found the right partner, or partners, during his visit, he could be himself and not hide his sexual preferences like he had during his whole career as a trooper.

Only, if he outed himself as bisexual, how would Cam take it? That was his only worry. Would he even want to remain friends with his former co-worker if Cam couldn't accept Nolan the way he was?

Despite Cam's current place of employment being non-judgmental, he worried that his friend would be secretly judging. They had both come from a career where most LGBTQ+ employees kept that information hidden to make life easier.

No one wanted to deal with the harassment or the distasteful "joking" that really weren't jokes. The statement, "I was only kidding," was only a lame excuse for bigotry.

No matter what, it wasn't like his true sexuality needed to be revealed immediately. He could keep that to himself until he ran across the right man to hook up with. Then, if needed, he could mention it to Cam and hope for the best.

However, Cam worked at an LGBTQ+-friendly resort, and by now, Nolan figured that nothing should shock the retired trooper.

Nolan had always been secretly drawn to the man, but the fellow trooper never gave any indication the attraction had been mutual. To avoid unnecessary drama, he kept his interest under wraps and was simply happy to have their solid friendship. He'd rather have Cam as a friend than not have him in his life at all.

After parking in front of cabin number four, he got out and reached for the sky to stretch his stiff muscles. The drive north took longer than he would've liked, but it had been worth it since he was finally going to see Cam again.

Inhaling the fresh air and feeling the warm sunshine on his face, he turned in a circle to take in what he could see from where he stood.

"I hope you don't mind sleeping on the pull-out couch. The bunkhouse is full and so are the employee cabins. Even better, the couch is free, so you won't have to pay out of your ass to stay in a room at the lodge," a deep voice said from behind him.

He turned with a huge smile on his face to find Cam wearing the same as he walked up. He was dressed in a Double D Ranch branded polo shirt that hugged his muscular torso, and khaki pants that emphasized his thick thighs.

Nolan shrugged. "It's only five nights. I'm sure I'll survive sleeping on a pull-out bed." He hoped his back would, too.

When they clasped hands, Nolan was yanked into a bear hug. "Man, I've missed you," Cam grumbled.

Nolan was surprised how long Cam held him close before releasing him. Luckily, not long enough for him to spring a hard-on due to the contact with a man he desired. "Same, brother. It's good to see a familiar face but not in that familiar uniform."

Cam plucked at his own shirt. "It's nice to be able to wear cotton and not that polyester, ball-sweating bullshit."

Nolan chuckled. "Agreed." He turned to check out the cabin. "So this is it, huh? Your new digs?"

"Yeah. It's small but suits my needs. And like I told you on the phone, everything is covered here. The owners are generous with their employees. They want us to be more like family."

"Most employers who say that are full of shit."

"I expected that here, too, but they truly look out for us."

"And in turn, you all look out for them," Nolan assumed.

"Of course. Them and the business. Especially me as head of security."

That made sense.

"Let's get your car unloaded, then if you're hungry, I can take you up to the lodge for a late lunch or early dinner. The food here is the best. Danica doesn't skimp on anything."

Nolan was surprised his stomach didn't growl after hearing that. He'd only snacked on a protein bar during the long trip. "I saw the chicken coop."

"Fresh eggs every morning. Plus, all the meat comes from local farms or the butcher in town. Veggies, too. Everything is top notch here."

"I saw the room rates. They were a bit salty." Way too rich for his blood. Especially since he retired early and wouldn't get his full pension. He would have to live on a budget. That reduced monthly payment was one reason he needed to supplement it with another job.

"The quality of the food is one reason why, but everything is included here. All the activities, the booze, everything. Whatever a guest wants, the owners try their best to accommodate them."

"Can't ask for more than that. I'm assuming most guests leave here happy."

Cam's deep chuckle made Nolan's cock twitch in his jeans. "They leave happy in more ways than one. That's why the resort gets so many returning guests. Hell, from what I've heard, some book their next stay before they even check out."

"Sounds like the Lyons siblings are doing something right."

"They are. And it's a refreshing change from where we both previously worked."

"All that bureaucratic bullshit and red-tape." Nolan murmured, "But that wasn't the only shit we put up with."

"True." Cam slapped him on the back. "But now neither of us have to deal with that anymore. We're free to do as we please with who we please."

That last statement caught Nolan's attention. Was Cam keeping a secret from him as well?

Cam quickly added, "As long as it's legal, of course."

"Of course." Nolan went to the back of his vehicle and began to unstrap his mountain bike.

"Nice," Cam said as he joined him and began to help remove the bike from the rack.

"I figured this would be the perfect place to ride."

"It is," Cam confirmed.

"Do you still have yours?"

"Sure do, but the resort also keeps a few for the guests. As well as ATVs, horses..." One side of Cam's mouth pulled up. "Lots of things to ride."

Nolan cocked an eyebrow. "Guests?"

Cam chuckled. "Of course."

"How many times have you hooked up with a guest since moving here?"

Cam lifted the bike off the rack and set it on the ground, keeping a hold of it since it wasn't equipped with a kickstand. Nolan went around to the passenger side and grabbed his bags from the backseat of his Toyota Sequoia, setting them on the ground at his feet.

He glanced over at Cam, waiting for the answer to his question.

When Cam began rolling the bike toward the cabin, Nolan picked up his bags and followed. "Did you lose count?"

"I don't keep track."

"Like, daily? Weekly?"

Cam shrugged and leaned the bike against the cabin's exterior wall near the front porch. "Whenever someone catches my attention and is also interested in me."

It was difficult to ignore the fact that Cam used the term "someone" instead of "a woman."

Maybe Nolan was reading too much into it.

Or unrealistically hoping Cam was also attracted to men.

Yeah, he had to be delusional.

"On our way to the lodge, we'll drop off your bike in the equipment shed. That's where I keep mine since I don't have any storage. Maybe tomorrow morning we can hit the trails and catch the sunrise."

"How about a tour after we grab something to eat?"

"Absolutely. When I'm not holed up in my office, I'm wandering around checking in with guests and my security guards."

"I like how there's a guard stationed at the entrance."

"Totally necessary for privacy. We don't want just anyone coming onto the property. Not when clothing is optional and the sex is spontaneous. We want everyone to feel comfortable enough to be themselves."

We want everyone to feel comfortable enough to be themselves.

By the end of his five-night stay, maybe Nolan would feel comfortable enough, too.

"Now, let's drop your bags inside and go eat. I'm about to chew my arm off."

Nolan chuckled. "Sounds like a plan since I'm about to chew your arm off, too."

———

Nolan groaned when he heard movement in Cam's bedroom. He glanced at the time on his cell phone. Six.

Holy shit. He hadn't gotten up this early since working the last daylight shift before retiring.

Yesterday's tour had been interesting to say the least. It proved the Lyons family really knew how to make their resort the "complete" experience. Cam had shown him just about every building—and there were a bunch of them—from the stables to the spa and even where the themed playrooms were.

Heaven.

Named appropriately.

Tonight, a mixer was being held in The Mane Event Hall and Cam asked if he wanted to go. There'd be demos for Shibari as well as other kinky play. He also said that any of the guests could participate in a "key party," popular back in the day with swingers.

Nolan had heard of them, of course, but had never been to one. Basically, brave guests could throw their room keycards into a bowl and choose a random one to spend the night with that person. It wasn't quite like the swingers' version since guests who were solo could also participate, whether they joined another single guest or a couple.

While it sounded like fun, Nolan would rather pick the person he'd have sex with. Plus, since he wasn't an actual paying guest, he didn't have a key. Though, Cam said he could grab him a blank one if Nolan wanted to hook up with a stranger.

He sat up on the couch but pulled the blanket over his lap when the bedroom door opened and the man himself came out.

"Morning." Cam's normally deep voice, rougher this morning from non-use, was sexy as hell. He headed directly to the solitary bathroom in the cabin, only wearing snug boxer briefs.

"It certainly is," Nolan responded, unable to tear his eyes away from the very distinct profile of Cam's morning wood.

He blew out a breath when the bathroom door closed behind his friend and his hand automatically dropped to his own erection. He wished he had time to pull one off, but he didn't. If he was this horny after only staying one night with

Cam, he was worried how bad he'd be toward the end of his visit.

He really needed to hook up with someone to distract him from his friend.

He's off limits. Just put him out of your mind and find someone else. Get a blank keycard from the man, like he suggested, and just hook up with a guest to take off that edge.

He didn't care if it was a man, a woman, or another couple.

But the mixer was not until later and he needed to get ready for their bike ride. Hearing the water run in the bathroom, he rose from the couch and tugged on a pair of shorts. The rest of his equipment, including his helmet, was still in his SUV. He could grab all of that on their way out.

When the door opened again, Nolan's gaze automatically landed on Cam's boxer briefs once more. He was disappointed to see the man's erection was already gone. However, Nolan's erection was still raging as he watched Cam move to the kitchenette to grab a water bottle and fill it from the cold water dispenser in the refrigerator door.

His nostrils flared and he turned away. His fingers itched to explore Cam's body but didn't want to touch him without permission.

He also didn't want to get punched.

He set his jaw so he'd keep his thoughts and hands to himself, but *damn*, the man was tempting.

He managed to behave himself during the ride on the trails through the woods and up the mountain. It was exactly what he needed. It blew out the remaining stress from his twenty-year career that had been clinging to him like a sock fresh from the dryer after forgetting to use a fabric sheet.

The only downside was riding behind Cam. It was hard to focus on the surrounding beauty of the area when the man's ass in skintight black bike shorts was *right there* leading the way.

Yes, it might have gotten his mind off of his career, but it certainly didn't help Nolan to stop lusting after Cam.

He worried that even finding someone else to fuck wouldn't help. And if that didn't, nothing would.

Well, except for finding out his friend was a bigot. But in all the years they worked together, he'd never heard Cam say anything derogatory against a specific class of people, like the LGBTQ+ community.

Others? Absolutely. Especially when his fellow troopers thought everyone in the room was straight.

That was one reason he'd wanted to retire early. He'd grown tired of hiding who he was.

Chapter Nine

Cam parked their mountain bikes in a bike rack kept inside the equipment shed. "Shower?"

Yes, please, if your shower is large enough for us both. Nolan wiped a hand over his sweat-beaded forehead and made sure those words did not escape. "I could certainly use one."

"I can use the shower in the security office while you use mine."

"You have a shower in your office?" Nolan asked.

"Yes, from when Dylan lived in it. The twins sure didn't skimp when they added the two residential wings onto the original family farmhouse. The bathroom is pure luxury and I swear the shower can fit a half dozen people."

"That plan works for me." Nolan wasn't sure that Cam would pick up on the double entendre.

But really, even a hose would work to rinse off the dust and sweat. However, if he wanted to find someone to play with later, he really needed a good scrub. He didn't want to turn off any potential partner with musty balls or smelly armpits.

"I'll go back to the cabin with you and grab a change of clothes. Once you're done cleaning up, meet me at my office and we'll head to the lodge for breakfast."

"You need to work today, right?"

"After we eat, I'll catch up on a few things, including checking in on my staff, but I'll take the afternoon off. Or at least be on call, just in case I'm needed. You can explore the property some more while I'm tied up. Feel free to use the pool and attached hot tub. Take a mud bath at the spa or schedule a massage. You can go on a trail ride or take one of the ATVs out. Do whatever your heart desires."

I desire you.

"How about some yoga?" Nolan asked once they rounded the corner of the equipment shed and he spotted about a dozen people in the distance, twisting themselves into all sorts of poses on spread out mats near Nirvana, the resort's spa.

Instead of continuing on back toward his cabin, Cam paused and stared toward the group. Finding Cam's reaction strange, Nolan glanced over at the group again to see if he could spot the issue. "Is something wrong?"

Cam shook his head. "Nothing."

That was when Nolan realized that the head of security wasn't checking out the whole class, but only the instructor; a very attractive, slim redhead.

Hmm. She could have potential in his search for a sex partner. No key exchange needed. "Bet she's flexible."

"She is," Cam murmured.

Nolan's head spun toward him. "You've been with her?" If so, there went his potential hookup.

"Once."

Damn it. "Why only once? Is she psycho or something?" He knew from experience that redheads could be super fiery.

Cam shrugged one shoulder. "No, we just haven't had the opportunity for a repeat."

"But you'd like to," Nolan guessed.

Cam turned his dark brown eyes toward Nolan. "Absolutely. I had a good time. I assume she did, too." His brow furrowed as he seemed to consider his own words.

"Did you want to head over there to remind her that you exist?" Nolan teased. "I can be your wing man."

Cam's eyes flicked back to the instructor, now sitting cross-legged at the front of the group while the rest of the class was sprawled out on their mats on their backs.

Were they sleeping? Weird.

Nolan knew nothing about yoga. He wasn't sure if he wanted to learn anything about it, either.

"I can introduce you, if you'd like. It looks like they're just finishing up."

"By taking a nap?"

Cam chuckled. "It's called...shit, it had some weird name, but basically it's the Corpse pose and ends a session."

"Are you saying yoga is so intense that you die at the end?" Nolan joked.

"Basically. From a distance, most poses look easy, but holding those poses is more difficult than you think. You also need good balance."

"You've tried it?"

"Once."

"So you could hook up with the instructor?" Nolan guessed.

A smile crossed Cam's face. "You know me too well."

Not as well as he wanted to know him, unfortunately.

Cam tipped his head toward the group, now slowly rising

from the ground and rolling up their mats. "C'mon, let's go say hello."

"I guess the sex must have been good for you to head in that direction instead of running away and hiding."

Cam's dark eyes flicked to him as they walked toward Nirvana. "Definitely. I like that she's independent and she's..."

"She's?" Nolan prodded. "She's what?"

"Gorgeous."

It was obvious that wasn't what Cam was originally going to say. Now Nolan was curious about the woman. Did she have some kind of crazy kink? Did Cam?

What was Nolan's longtime friend into? What secrets had he been hiding? Whatever it was, he couldn't hold it against Cam since Nolan was holding on to a secret himself.

When they got to the redhead, she had just finished collecting the rolled-up mats and was setting them on a wheeled cart as her class wandered away. All looking very relaxed, of course.

Her smile was huge and her blue eyes sparkled like topaz gems when she straightened and spotted Cam. "Hey, stranger."

"Hey," Cam returned the greeting. "Sorry, didn't mean to be a stranger." He turned to Nolan. "Hope, this is Nolan Young, I worked with him at PSP. Nolan, this is Hope Reed, she's the resident yoga instructor."

"Wow, it has to be illegal for two men as handsome as you both to be in the same spot. That's not fair to the rest of the men."

Nolan chuckled and tried not to be obvious about checking her out in her tight yoga pants and sports bra as he extended his hand. The woman was certainly in shape. "Hello, Hope. Nice to meet you."

Hope placed her hand in his and shot him a warm, welcoming smile. "Nice to meet you, Nolan. Are you still a trooper?"

Nolan shook his head. "No, I recently retired. That's given me some time to come up here and check out Cam's new gig."

"He's popular around here," Hope said with laughter in her voice. She winked at Cam.

No way. Cam didn't just blush, did he? He must really like this woman.

That sucked for Nolan because, of course, the two people he could see himself having sex with were already interested in each other.

He didn't want to cause any drama between himself and Cam. Especially not over a woman. Luckily, he still had four more nights to find someone else. He might even find someone tonight at the event, whether he participated in the key exchange or not.

"How long are you here, Nolan?" Hope asked him.

"Four more nights."

"Nice. Did Cam give you the nickel tour?"

"He did. This place is certainly impressive."

"Did anything catch your attention?"

Nolan wasn't sure how to answer that weighted question.

"Do you plan on coming to the mixer tonight?" Cam asked her, saving Nolan from answering.

"I wasn't invited," she answered.

"You don't need an official invite. You know you're a part of the Double D family."

One of her dark red eyebrows lifted. "Are you going?"

"Yes. I figured Nolan would enjoy it."

"How about you?" Hope asked Cam.

He tipped his head as he regarded her. "I will if you're there."

Oh yeah, Nolan's friend was definitely interested in the yoga instructor.

"You should come," Cam insisted. "It won't be the same without you."

Now it was Hope's turn to have pink cheeks. "I don't have any plans tonight so maybe I'll stop by. Is it themed?"

"Flashback to the 70s. They're even going to have an optional key party."

Hope squinted at Cam. "Key party?"

"It was popular with swingers back in the day. You throw your keys into a bowl, then you hookup with the person whose key you pulled. They're going to use the keycards from the rooms instead of actual keys," Cam explained.

"I don't have a keycard."

"You don't need one."

Did Cam add a wink onto that? He sure did.

"Oh," Hope breathed and winked back.

While Nolan liked that Hope was both bold and beautiful, the fact Cam and Hope were flirting with each other confirmed that his friend was straight.

Unfortunately.

The key exchange was sounding better and better for him.

"Well, we need to go clean up after our bike ride. Sorry if we've seared your nostrils."

Hope laughed softly. "You haven't. You two smell like the outdoors."

Cam finished with, "Anyway, I hope we see you tonight."

"I second that," Nolan added.

"I'll think about it. If I do, I need to find a groovy outfit to wear."

"We look forward to seeing that," Nolan threw over his shoulder as he and Cam turned to head back to the cabin.

Hell, she'd probably look stunning wearing a black garbage bag.

———

THE DIMLY LIT space vibrated around them with both sexual tension and bass-heavy disco music. Mirrored disco balls spun from the ceiling, reflecting colorful lights all over The Mane Event Hall and its occupants. The floor was packed with people moving and grooving to 70s tunes.

The DJ on stage wore a huge afro wig, oversized rose-colored glasses, and a one-piece multi-colored jumpsuit with a deep V neckline showing off a thick gold chain and hairy chest. The current vinyl he was spinning was *Boogie Wonderland* by Earth Wind and Fire, and anyone who knew the words was singing along.

Nolan shadowed Cam as he worked his way through a crowd full of guests and employees wearing various wigs, as well as huge hoop earrings, platform shoes, and even flared pants.

One man even showed up dressed like Hugh Hefner, with the robe, pipe and all.

The atmosphere was fun, with people dancing, singing, and laughing, most likely a bit tipsy from the spiked punch.

When they paused in front of a stretch of tables full of food typical of that decade, Nolan snagged a pig-in-a-blanket and popped it into his mouth. The spread also consisted of cheese fondue, Jell-o molds, and ambrosia salad.

"Do you think any of these people actually lived through the 70s?" Nolan asked Cam. "I mean, most of the attendees don't seem old enough."

Cam chuckled. "I'm sure some did. You should've seen the 80s party we had a few weeks ago. The guests wore the craziest outfits. The music was great, though."

Cam nodded to one of his security guards when they crossed paths.

"Ah, yes, the 80s," Nolan murmured. "Teased, over-sprayed hair, leg warmers, and jelly shoes."

"I actually saw some of that," Cam said on a laugh. "I worked the event that night but it was still fun and made for great people-watching." He pointed to a large bowl. "There you go. If you want to throw your keycard in there."

He had to write his initials with marker on the blank card Cam got him since he didn't have a room number.

He tossed it in the bowl and crossed his fingers for the best. He really didn't care if it was a man or woman, or even a couple, who chose him. He only hoped there was some sort of spark between them.

Unfortunately, he never asked who was supposed to pull the key. He had no idea how the resort's version worked since his research showed that the original key parties were made up of couples. One half of the couple threw their car key into the bowl and the other chose a key. Nolan didn't have a partner to swap out.

Whatever. He'd go with the flow.

An elbow to the ribs had him turning toward Cam to see Hope making her way over to them. She was dressed in a hot-pink jumpsuit that showed off some cleavage, wore wedge sandals, had a large, fake daisy pinned in her teased hair, and oversized gold hoop earrings hung from her earlobes.

While the outfit was crazy at first glance, she managed to look smoking hot in it.

"Where'd you get that outfit?" Cam asked as she joined them.

With a smile, she showed it off by turning in a circle, and once she stopped, she popped out a hip. "Not from my closet, that's for sure. I asked my neighbor. She was in her 20s during that decade and she hasn't thrown away anything."

"It looks great on you," Nolan told her.

She turned her smile toward him. "Thanks! You should've seen her face when I stopped by her house on my way here. She was thrilled I fit in it."

"You certainly do," Cam murmured, eyeing her up and down.

"Have either of you hit the dance floor yet? I'm loving this music!"

"No, we just got here a few minutes ago."

"Well, then what are we waiting for, guys?" She walked backwards and crooked a finger at them. "Let's go boogie!"

Then she turned and disappeared on the dance floor.

Cam and him shared a look.

"Do you dance?" Nolan asked Cam.

"How hard can it be?" Cam responded with a grin.

It can get pretty hard if I have to watch you moving to the music.

Chapter Ten

While dancing with Cam and Hope, they quickly discovered that neither Cam nor Nolan had good rhythm, especially when it came to disco tunes. Even so, it had been a blast and Nolan didn't regret showing off his choppy, awkward moves. He enjoyed both the music and the company.

After that, he was brave enough to dance with a few random guests before dancing twice more with Hope. She also did a bunch of bumping and grinding with Cam.

Nolan was having so much fun that he lost track of the amount of spiked punch he'd downed in an attempt to quench his thirst from all the activity. But then, it also went down way too smoothly.

As the night wore on, Nolan noticed how handsy Cam and Hope became with each other. A touch here, a grab there, the smiles, the whispers into each other's ear.

He also couldn't miss every time Cam put a possessive hand along the small of Hope's back. It was as if he was claiming her for the evening and wanted the rest of the partygoers to know, even though it was obvious they were attracted to each other and had sexual chemistry.

Good for Cam. Nolan was happy he found someone like Hope, whether it was long or short term. Or simply a friends-with-benefits situation. He only wished it had been him instead.

Stop acting pitiful and don't let jealousy eat at you for something you can't control. Move on and appreciate what you do have...a solid friendship.

Of course, that was easier said than done.

Cam, carrying a full cup of punch, approached Nolan where he stood along the wall and out of the way while people watching.

"They're pulling keys now," Cam announced, offering Nolan the cup.

Nolan shook his head. He was already buzzing and didn't want to get too carried away. Especially when he had no idea how the night would end. "Let me go take my turn then."

Cam stopped him from heading in that direction by grabbing Nolan's forearm. "Are you sure you want to hook up with someone you haven't seen or met first?"

Nolan raised his eyebrows. "You're the one who suggested it. And I'm sure I've already met whoever ends up picking mine. We got up close and personal with a lot of people on that dance floor. Did you throw a key into the bowl, too?"

Cam shook his head. "No, I slipped mine into Hope's pocket."

"That outfit has pockets?"

Cam did a double-take, then burst out laughing. The punch had certainly loosened up his former co-worker tonight. It was nice to see him acting more relaxed and easy-going than when they had worked together.

Out of the two of them, Cam had always kept any emotions locked down tight in the past and was more the typical Type A personality when compared to Nolan, who always leaned more toward Type B.

Nolan and Hope had more similar personalities than she and Cam. Since life was short—and could've been cut much shorter during their former line of work—Nolan didn't want to be so unbendable or uptight all the time. He wanted to enjoy life while he lived it. Another reason he wanted to retire earlier than planned.

The job had been turning him bitter. He had wanted to stop that path before it became too late.

When he walked over to the small crowd still gathered around the key bowl, Cam and Hope followed.

As the last of the group reached in one by one, pulled a key, and found their new partner, they immediately headed off to do...whatever, since the party was winding down.

"Am I supposed to pull a key or do I just wait for someone to pull mine?" Nolan asked, barely loud enough to be heard over the music. Thankfully, it wasn't as deafening as earlier.

"There are only a few keys left and one is yours. See who pulls it," Cam suggested, stepping behind Nolan and squeezing his shoulders.

Nolan's stomach churned as he waited for someone to do just that. He'd never been on a blind date nor hooked up with some random stranger before. And while he didn't mind putting himself out there, he hoped it wasn't a complete disaster.

Nolan held his breath as the next person stepped up and pulled a key. The male guest held it up and it was clearly marked with Nolan's initials.

"Well, that isn't good," Cam grumbled, stiffening behind

Nolan and releasing his shoulders. "He'll have to pull another key."

"It's fine," Nolan assured him. "That was a risk I took when participating."

Cam stepped around Nolan with his brow furrowed and confusion filling his face. "Nolan..."

Nolan kept his expression blank. "What?"

"You don't have to do this."

"It's a resort based around sexual fantasies. Why wouldn't I take advantage of it?"

"Because..." Cam shook his head. "It's another man."

"I can see that."

"You're not gay."

"You're right, I'm not," Nolan confirmed.

"Are you sure you're okay with this?" Hope asked.

"Who's key is this?" the guest asked, still holding up the key.

"Mine." Nolan stepped forward, raising his hand slightly.

"You...just be safe," Cam said behind him as Nolan joined the other man.

"Nolan said he isn't gay but he's okay going off with a man?"

Cam was as confused as Hope. He scraped his fingers through his hair. "He just confirmed he wasn't. If he is, he never told me."

"Did you ever tell him that you're bi?"

Cam pulled in a breath. "Of course not."

"Do you think he is?"

Cam stared in the direction Nolan disappeared. With a *man*. What the hell! "I mean, I figured bringing him to the mixer tonight would give him a taste of what goes on here at Double D, but I certainly wasn't expecting that."

Her eyes also flicked toward where Nolan disappeared. "Looks like he's getting a good taste for sure." She blinked up at him. "You're attracted to him."

Should he share that with the woman he wanted to fuck tonight? From what he had seen with Hope so far, she didn't seem the type to get bent out of shape if he told the truth.

Plus, it was probably best to be up front with her. Keeping secrets tended to create problems. Obviously.

"I always have been, but I never told him. I didn't want things to get weird between us. Especially since we worked together."

"Well, you don't work together anymore. You should tell him, Cam," Hope chided softly. "He's your good friend, and if I'm not mistaken, he's into men."

"How do you know he's not just going with that guy for shock value and really doesn't have any plans to have sex with him?"

"Ask him."

"You mean chase him down?"

"Or wait until morning when he returns to your cabin. He's either going to be smiling or laughing. Smiling because he was fucked good or laughing because he pranked you good."

Hope could be right. He could be pulling a prank on Cam since Nolan never gave any indication he was attracted to men. Because if he would've known...

Shit.

Too late either way. He was gone already.

But damn, if Nolan was going to have sex with any man, Cam wanted it to be him. Only, how did he broach that touchy subject? Because even if Nolan might be bi, it didn't mean he was sexually attracted to Cam. He didn't want to make things awkward between them as friends.

"As you know, in the BDSM world, communication is key. Actually, communication is key in all worlds, not just in the BDSM community."

Hope was right on that point.

"Do you want to dance some more?" she asked, then tucked her bottom lip between her teeth to hide her smile. Though, the corner of her eyes wrinkling gave it away.

"Do you?"

"I think I've boogied myself out for tonight, but there's another form of dancing I wouldn't mind doing with you."

He cocked an eyebrow. "Horizontal dancing?"

She finally let her smile free. "I'm not sure how horizontal our dancing will be, but...I'm definitely in."

"Good. Check your pocket."

She slipped a hand into her hidden pocket and pulled out the keycard with his initials written on it. She held it up and laughed. "Oh, I see. You wanted to make certain I'm a sure thing."

He chuckled softly and pulled her against him using a firm grip on her hips. "Well, there's a bowl over there if you'd rather choose for yourself."

"Now why would I want to exchange my very handsome prize for a complete unknown?" Her blue eyes twinkled.

"For excitement?"

"Are you planning on boring me?"

He tipped his head toward the exit. "Let's go find out."

Chapter Eleven

Of course, it was just Nolan's luck.

The man who pulled his key turned out not to be bi or even gay. While they were both disappointed with the situation, they had a good laugh about the odds of him picking another man. Especially since the ranch guests' genders seem to be evenly divided.

They ended up grabbing a drink at the lodge, anyway, and had some interesting conversation. After the guest left—with neither of them having any hard feelings or hard cocks, unfortunately—Nolan decided to hang out at the lodge a bit longer, trying to give Hope and Cam enough private time in the small cabin.

But by one a.m., he was yawning so badly—especially after getting up early to hit the bike trails—that he finally headed back to the cabin.

He tried not to make much noise as he undressed and used the restroom before heading to the pull-out couch. While it had been quiet when he entered, an unfamiliar vehicle was parked in front of the cabin. Obviously, Hope hadn't left yet.

If Nolan was lucky, they had tired themselves out and fallen asleep. Because he was pretty damn sure he didn't want to hear Cam having sex with someone other than him. To be fair, they probably assumed he'd be gone for the night with the man who picked his key.

Nolan had expected that, too.

To add insult to injury, just as he was drifting off, the unmistakable sound of two bodies doing what two bodies do drifted to him from the bedroom.

Again with his shitty luck. He sighed.

Unfortunately, his cock also recognized the moans, grunts, skin slapping, and headboard knocking against the wall. With a groan, Nolan drove a hand down his boxer briefs and wrapped it around his now very interested and very erect cock.

Despite being tempted to join the couple, he didn't want to freak them out. And it would be kind of weird to invite yourself to your friend's bed. Consent and all that, being the primary concern. The other being, he was afraid to tell his friend how much he wanted him, mostly out of fear of rejection.

But at least tonight wouldn't be a total bust.

He closed his eyes to watch the movie playing in his mind that corresponded with the sounds he heard. Nolan visualized Hope and Cam getting each other off as he began to tug on his own cock.

He yanked the elastic waistband of his boxer briefs down enough to tuck it under his balls before cupping his sack in his palm and squeezing gently as he continued to jerk on the base of his cock. He'd occasionally slide the pad of his thumb over the tip, gathering the pearly beads of precum and spreading it over the head.

He quickly got lost in the rhythmic and guttural sounds coming from the bedroom as well as in his fantasies.

Hell yeah.

His hips lifted off the couch with each quick stroke until finally, he grabbed the pillow and jammed it over his face with one hand as he kept tugging on his cock with the other at the speed of light.

He was right there...

Right there!

He could practically feel himself driving deep into Hope's hot, slick pussy as Cam jammed himself just as deep into Nolan's ass.

Fuck yes. To be in the middle of that scenario would be perfect.

He was bummed it would never happen. He would never screw over his friend by fucking the woman Cam had an interest in.

How was his life so pitiful that he was reduced to masturbating while listening to others have sex when he was staying at a damn resort that focused on those same activities? Not to mention, full of guests with the same mindset?

His ass shot off the couch one more time and seconds later, strings of warm cum landed on his stomach when he came like a fountain.

When he dropped back to the couch with a grunt, he threw the pillow aside and continued to milk every last drop from his cock while his heartbeat thumped in his ears and he attempted to slow his breathing.

He glanced down at his stomach, grimaced, then took a quick glance toward the bedroom door before sliding his eyes over to the only bathroom in the cabin.

Shit. Shit. Shit.

Since they had no idea he had returned, either could walk out to use the bathroom and catch him like this at any moment.

After yanking up his underwear—careful not to smear the cum—he rushed into the bathroom before they discovered him along with the aftermath of him jerking off. That would be fun to explain.

He'd rather not, actually. It was just one more secret he'd be keeping to himself.

After cleaning up, he hit the couch once again. Luckily, he passed out quickly enough that he avoided any questions about why he'd come back to the cabin before morning.

Though, he was sure Cam would be asking plenty of questions come tomorrow morning during their bike ride.

———

Nolan released a contented sigh while sprawled on the lounge chair by the sparkling pool. The early afternoon sun was warm on his skin and the air smelled clean and fresh with only a hint of sunscreen. He sipped on a cold local brew one of the servers had dropped off from the nearby pool bar.

This was the life.

However, he couldn't spend the next decade or so getting a tan, sitting in the hot tub, and people watching, even as entertaining and eye-opening as it had been.

Well, he would if he could. Only, it wasn't realistic or practical. He was only up here in paradise for three more nights, then he had to get back to his condo in West Chester and continue the frustrating search for another job.

Now that one life chapter had closed, he was ready to

start a new one. One where he didn't have to hide who he was. He only hoped that chapter paid well.

What he wanted could very well be a pipe dream. Just like lusting after his very hot friend and former co-worker.

When he had cracked open his eyelids that morning, Cam's bedroom door had still been closed. But not five minutes later, Cam came striding out, dressed and ready to tackle the trails on two wheels.

Nolan had to guess that the sex must have been great since the man sure looked relaxed. As well as worn out.

It was at that point that he realized Hope somehow managed to sneak out without waking him.

As expected, Cam had been very interested in how Nolan's night went. He explained that he and the other gentleman had a good laugh about the situation over some drinks.

The expression on Cam's face when he mentioned that caught Nolan's attention. He couldn't tell if his friend was relieved or disappointed.

And that didn't make much sense. Nor did the fact that Cam was pretty quiet during the whole ride through the woods.

Did Cam think Nolan was lying? That he was actually gay and he didn't approve?

Nolan really didn't want this misconception affecting their friendship. Maybe he should simply come clean and deal with any fallout.

When his cell phone chirped by his hip, he squinted as he read the text from Cam: *Stop by my office when you're ready to go for lunch. I have news.*

News?

Did Cam somehow figure out that Nolan jerked off while

listening to him and Hope fucking each other? If so, that would be embarrassing.

He glanced at the time and was surprised it was almost two already. Time to go change out of his bathing suit and find out what "news" Cam wanted to share.

Nolan only hoped it was good news.

———

"I HAD a meeting with the owners and we discussed you."

He did? Did he do something wrong? "Me? Why?" Nolan's heart skipped a beat.

"Because I can't be the only one in charge of the security team. I can't—and don't want to—work twenty-four-seven. I need someone to help me." Cam lifted a finger. "Someone with experience and training. I also need someone I work well with and can trust."

Nolan stared at Cam as those words sank into his brain. "What are you saying?"

With his fingers spread out, Cam pressed his hands onto his desk and looked pleased with himself. "I'm offering you the assistant head of security position. Are you interested?"

Assistant head of—

Hell yes, he was interested!

"There's only one problem."

Of course.

"The bunkhouse is currently full and the employee cabins are all claimed. But until a spot opens up, you can stay with me."

Nolan blinked. "On the couch?"

Cam shrugged. "It's the best we can do right now."

"Won't that put a kink in yours and Hope's relationship?"

"I wouldn't call it a relationship. We fucked twice."

From what he could guess, they fucked at least twice last night alone, but he wasn't pointing that out.

"This is their offer." Cam slid a piece of paper across his desk. "I talked you up and insisted they make it worth your while. I also mentioned you'd be a huge asset to the team."

Nolan sank into one of the chairs facing Cam's desk before pulling the paper closer and scanning it.

Holy shit. Not only would he eventually have a free place to live plus all the perks of the resort, but he'd get to work with his close friend again? Not to mention, having a sexual playground at his fingertips...

How could he say no?

Cam's lip pulled downward. "Is that offer not fair enough? It's damn near exactly what I was offered."

Nolan closed his gaping mouth and met Cam's eyes. "No, it's...it's more than fair. But, Cam, I didn't come up here to get a job."

One of his eyebrows cocked. "So, you don't want it?"

Nolan quickly scanned the document again. If he took the job, his reduced pension wouldn't be stretched thin. He wouldn't be stressed about money at all.

Better yet, this place was truly paradise for someone like him. Between being surrounded by nature and plenty of sex, great food, the financial benefits—and Cam, of course—he'd be a fool to say no.

Luckily, his mother hadn't raised a fool. "I want it. It's perfect and exactly what I was looking for. I hope you didn't feel pressured to do this."

"Not at all. You mentioned you were looking for another job. You seem to like it here. And I would love to have you here. So that had me thinking, if I need someone backing me up—and I do—I can't find anyone better than you."

"That's quite a compliment." It also stroked his ego a bit.

"One well deserved."

"How soon would you want me to start?"

"As soon as you're ready."

"I would need to sell my condo and put my stuff in storage."

"You don't need to be living there to sell it. It might be easier if it's empty."

That was true. If he moved out before listing it, he wouldn't need to vacate his home every time prospective buyers wanted to see it. He also wouldn't need to worry about keeping it clean and tidy.

"Are you okay with bunking with me for a while? At least until a spot frees up in the bunkhouse? Then I'll make sure you're at the top of the list to get one of the cabins as soon as one's available."

Was he okay with waking up every morning and having Cam so close but not close enough? Will listening to his friend have sex with others, and not him, eventually drive him mad? Make him bitter?

Every silver lining was attached to a dark cloud. You had to take the good with the bad.

"I appreciate that." The sooner he could move into a cabin, the better. He'd just have to suck it up and suffer through his insatiable lust over Cam—and now Hope—until that happened.

He could do it. He'd done it before when they worked together. The only difference now would be them living in close quarters. And the possibility of hearing them fuck if Cam and Hope's relationship progressed.

Maybe Nolan should drop a hint for them to do the bump and grind at Hope's place instead. "Do you have any idea how soon a cabin will open up? I don't want to infringe on your privacy."

Comprehension filled Cam's expression. A second later, he grimaced and scrubbed fingers over his forehead. "I'm sorry if you heard us last night. We figured you'd be gone all night."

"So did I." Nolan waved a hand around. "It's fine. You didn't know and I didn't want to interrupt to announce that I had returned."

"I'm not sure if we'll hook up again, but if we do, Hope has her own place."

Luckily, his subtle message was received. Only... "Why wouldn't you? She seems great. Did you two have an issue last night?"

"No, not at all. The sex was as great as she is. However, I'm not looking for a commitment and neither is she, since she just got out of a relationship. As such, I don't want to assume the sex will continue. We don't owe each other anything. If it happens, great. If not..." Cam shrugged.

"You won't be disappointed if it doesn't?"

"Of course, but..." Suddenly Cam masked his expression, sat back, and stared at him. "Nolan, I have to ask you something."

"Shoot."

"You indicated you didn't have sex with that guy last night, and I could see you were attracted to Hope when you first spotted her, but..."

Here it comes.

Cam pulled in a breath. "I'm not sure how to approach this."

"We've been friends for a long time, brother. I would hope you'd be comfortable asking me anything." *As long as I'd be comfortable answering it.*

"I'm worried that I'll be wrong and you'll be offended."

Nolan had a good idea where this was heading. He should put Cam out of his misery. "Cam, before you ask me your question, I've got a confession to make." And it might be the answer his friend was looking for.

"About?"

"About what I think you're struggling to ask." Nolan pressed a hand to his chest. "About who I am."

Cam's head twitched. "I know who you are. I worked with you for years."

"Do you ever really know somebody unless you know their deepest, darkest secrets?"

"I guess not. What's your deepest, darkest secret?"

It was better to know how he'd react now rather than after Nolan moved in with him and things became unbearably uncomfortable.

Not to mention disappointing.

Or maybe after his confession, Cam would want to pull the employment offer. While that would suck, Nolan needed to know the truth before completely uprooting his life.

"The truth is..." *Now's the time to pull off the damn Band-Aid. Get it over with.* "I'm bi." Nolan squeezed his eyes shut for a moment and waited for Cam's reaction, good or bad.

When he didn't hear anything, he opened them and saw that Cam had deflated in his chair, as if all the air had fled his lungs. Nolan had no idea what to make of that.

He quickly followed up with, "If you no longer want to offer me the position, I'll understand."

Cam blinked and shook his head in confusion. "Why would I want to revoke the offer?"

"Because I hid the fact I'm bisexual." *And I've lusted*

after you for a long time. Plus, had plenty of fantasies about you.

Cam's brow dipped low. "Why would that matter? That doesn't affect how you do your job."

"But I was afraid how it would affect our relationship."

"Because you're bi?"

"Because of how attracted I am to you."

Chapter Twelve

When Cam surged from his desk chair, it shot backward and slammed the wall behind him. He rushed around his desk, grabbed a surprised Nolan's shoulders, and pulled him out of his chair.

They stood toe-to-toe, only inches apart.

Cam had not been expecting that revelation. He never had an inkling that Nolan wasn't straight. That Nolan was just like him.

They both had been hiding that secret for years. Actually, for more than a freaking decade.

If he couldn't figure out Nolan's sexuality without it being stated out loud, that meant Nolan hadn't figured out Cam's.

Holy shit, he'd been as clueless as Nolan. To be fair, he needed to do a little confessing himself.

Cam locked his gaze with a wide-eyed Nolan. "I also have a confession to make."

Nolan's lips parted slightly and a soft breath puffed out. "What?"

"I'm bi, too."

"What?" came out on almost a shout.

Cam nodded. "It's true. But... I've only known you to date women."

"I've also dated men. I just didn't discuss it. But, damn, I always thought you were straight, too. You were married and —" Nolan closed his eyes and shook his head. When he opened them again, he said, "We're idiots. Of course you were married. Of course I dated women..." He slapped a hand onto his forehead and groaned. "We're *both* bisexual. I kept a lid on it because I was worried about being harassed at work."

"Same." Cam sighed.

"I have another confession to make..."

What could be bigger than what he just revealed?

"I've wanted you since the day I've met you."

Holy shit. He thought he was surprised from the first confession, but this just blew that out of the water.

"I wish you would've said something sooner because I've wanted you for years, too."

Nolan's mouth gaped. "I wish *you* would've said something."

They'd both been fools. Their reasoning had been the same: their careers. But two friends should be able to be open with each other. "Jesus. We've wasted so much time."

"I'm not sure it could've been avoided. Even if we didn't keep the secret from each other, we would've had to keep it from everyone else."

"Not everyone," Cam murmured.

Unfortunately, that realization was too little, too late. However, they could make up for that mistake now. And Cam planned on doing just that.

He cupped Nolan's face with one hand while grabbing

his hip with the other to pull him even closer. Close enough that their warm breaths kissed each other's lips and their hips pressed together. "Do you still want me?"

"You have no idea," Nolan whispered. "Do you still want me?"

The uncertainty in his hazel eyes stabbed Cam right in the chest. "Absolutely."

"Then I don't want to waste another min—"

Cam captured the rest of Nolan's words when he smashed his mouth against his friend's. *Loyal* friend and hopefully soon to be lover.

The fire in his gut started as a flicker, then grew to a roar as their tongues clashed and tangled. As their groans meshed.

His cock, now as hard as steel, began to pulse. It was like an arrow seeking its target.

That target happened to be the man he was locking lips with.

Nolan's fingers dug into Cam's waist as they held each other close and ground their erections together.

While the kissing was great, Cam wanted nothing more than to be inside Nolan. But he needed to keep his head. He was at work. In his office. And he had a team that reported to him and could enter the outer office area at any time.

Not only that, but Cam reported directly to the resort owners. He didn't want to risk this job. It was perfect for him and would only be getting better once Nolan joined the team.

Nolan pulled his head back just slightly. "I want this—boy, do I want this—but I don't want this to ruin our friendship."

"We won't let it," Cam murmured against Nolan's neck before sucking on it.

"That might be out of our control."

"We control our destiny." Okay, that belief might be

somewhat lame, but it was true at its core. At least it didn't cause Nolan to burst out laughing.

They might not be able to fuck in Cam's office. He didn't keep lube or condoms in his desk, anyway. Plus, he had no idea yet if Nolan preferred to pitch or catch.

Despite that, Cam really needed to get his hands on him. To finally touch Nolan as he had dreamed about for so long. To make sure this was real—the *man* before him was real— and not one of his fantasies. "Tell me this is real and finally happening."

With his head tipped to the side, Nolan moaned as Cam sucked on his warm flesh even harder before giving it a sharp nip.

"It...it might be. Do it again and I'll get back to you," Nolan encouraged.

Cam smiled and captured his flesh between his teeth, gently tugging on it before swiping his tongue over the same spot. He ran his nose up Nolan's pounding pulse and took his mouth again, but this time he also grabbed the man's ass and squeezed.

That ass would be his soon enough.

He hoped so, anyway. Because Cam was not a bottom and never had been. If Nolan wasn't either...that could be a problem. But they could talk about that detail later, couldn't they? Why ruin the moment now?

Not when he'd wanted this for *years*. And it sounded like Nolan had wanted the same.

We can't fuck in my office.

We can't. Can we? No.

But maybe...

Maybe...

He released Nolan and went over to lock his office door.

On his way back to his long-time friend, heat smoldered in Nolan's hazel eyes.

"What are you doing?"

"Giving us some privacy."

"Cam..."

Cam pressed a finger to Nolan's lips and shook his head. "We're limited on what we can do in my office, but I've been waiting forever to get my hands on you. Give me this at least."

Nolan's eyelids became heavy and his voice husky. "What do you want to do?"

"Besides this?" Cam locked his lips with Nolan's again in another very thorough kiss. He dragged his tongue through the other man's mouth, exploring every inch.

Cam swore every drop of blood in his body was now pooled in his aching cock. When he finally ended the kiss, he didn't wait for Nolan's response. Instead, he spun his former—and future—co-worker around until he faced the desk.

Cam reached around and fumbled with the button on Nolan's jeans.

Nolan stopped him with a hand over his. "Are you sure about this? Are you sure we're not making a mistake?"

The only thing he was completely sure about was that he wanted to fuck Nolan.

Cam pressed his raging erection to Nolan's denim-covered ass. "How would we ever know it was a mistake unless we make it?"

Nolan blew out a breath. "I don't want to screw up our friendship. Or this job opportunity."

Cam reluctantly released him and stepped back, raising his hands chest-level in surrender. He didn't bother to hide the disappointment in his voice. "I get your concern."

Still facing the desk, Nolan dropped his head and groaned.

"But I also want this so badly. I want you, Cam," he whispered, giving Cam some hope. Nolan turned around, opened his jeans, and shoved them and his underwear down just enough to release his cock. "This is how much I want you."

Cam's eyes followed every stroke of Nolan's fist. When he lifted his gaze and met Nolan's, the need filling the other man's eyes was apparent. He was sure his reflected the same. "Turn around."

"Condom and lube?"

"Not needed."

"But—"

"Not for what I'm going to do," Cam assured him, before saying more firmly, "Turn around."

Nolan only paused for a second.

Cam wished the man was naked, that they had the time and were in the right place to do more than what he was about to do next, but they didn't, so this would have to do until later. When he wasn't working. When the threat of one of his team, or one of his bosses, interrupting didn't exist.

Cam pressed his erection against Nolan's ass, wrapped an arm around his waist, holding him close, and shoved his face into Nolan's neck once more. He inhaled the man's very recognizable scent. He used to get whiffs of it when they were changing in the locker room at the police barracks.

He replaced Nolan's hand on his hard length with his own. "Let me," he whispered against his warm, smooth skin. "I want to touch you, make you come."

"I want that, too," Nolan whispered back, reaching behind Cam to cup the back of his head as he thrust his hips forward.

Cam slid his hand up and down Nolan's length in a steady rhythm, occasionally sweeping away a pearl of precum. Nolan's cock was hot and like velvet-covered steel. His hips moved in time with the pumping of Cam's fist.

"Cam," Nolan groaned. "I've wanted this for so long that I'm not going to last."

Good. The sooner he came, the better. Otherwise, Cam might end up yanking Nolan's jeans down and bending him over the desk. Lube and condom be damned.

Of course, that would never happen. No matter how desperate Cam became, he would never do anything to hurt his friend and, soon, lover. He only had to dig deep for his willpower. A little suffering now could pay off in the future.

"I'm going to..."

Dropping his arm from around Nolan's waist, Cam cupped his hand under the crown of his cock and kept stroking...squeezing...tugging...

Nolan tensed and his cock pulsed within Cam's fingers.

Cam leaned forward and pressed their cheeks together to get a better view. "Come for me."

An audible rush of air accompanied Nolan's hips twitching, before he thrust forward one last time. The thick, warm cum filled Cam's palm and he continued to milk Nolan's cock until he'd squeezed out every last drop.

With a contented sigh, Nolan collapsed against Cam, leaning into him for support. Cam reluctantly released the man's cock and held him close for a few seconds, waiting for Nolan to catch his breath and his own pulse to stop racing.

Now, if only his own cock would behave and stop screaming at him for relief.

Once Nolan gathered himself and pulled up his jeans, Cam turned him around and they shared another slow, ball-tightening kiss.

When they finished, "I want to eat your ass," slipped out of Cam's mouth.

Fuck. He hadn't meant to say that. Not yet, anyway.

Nolan's head jerked back and his eyebrows shot up his forehead. "You're into that?"

"Not with everyone, no. But you? I can't wait to dive in." *Before I fuck you into next month.*

Shit, they still needed to have a discussion about whether Nolan minded being a bottom.

"Jesus, Cam," Nolan whispered. "You're going to make me beg for you to call off the rest of the day so we can go back to your cabin and you could do just that."

At least he wasn't against having his ass eaten. "Don't tempt me."

"What about you?" Nolan tipped his head toward Cam's painful erection.

Cam shook his head. "I'm fine."

"You don't look fine."

He chuckled softly. "I don't mind a good edging. I can wait." Cam lifted his hand and looked at the cum pooled in his palm. "I need to clean up."

"Me, too. But we're not done yet."

We weren't?

Nolan plucked several tissues from the box on Cam's desk and grabbed his messy hand. He wiped away the cum, then tossed the tissues into the small trash can next to his desk.

"I could've washed my hands in the bathroom."

"No. Not yet."

Nolan's wicked smile made Cam pause. "What do you—"

His question was answered when Nolan slowly sank to his knees.

Hell yes. Certainly unexpected but definitely appreciated.

Keeping his eyes locked with Cam's, Nolan managed to unfasten his khakis and yank them down far enough so Cam's erection sprang free.

"Nolan, you don't need to do this." *But if you insist, I'm not going to fight you off.*

"I know. But I want to. Do you think I haven't fantasized about doing this to you?"

"You have?"

"More times than I can remember."

"Well then, we have something in common." His words morphed into a moan as Nolan wrapped his lips around Cam's cock and stroked the underside with his tongue from tip to root and back.

Holy hell.

He loved getting head. What he loved even more was that it was Nolan doing it.

Cam turned his head and listened carefully to make sure no one had come into the outer office.

They'd been lucky so far, but he didn't want to press that luck. Normally, he'd hate the idea of rushing through a blowjob, but it was smart not to let it go on too long.

Luckily, he was already on the precipice of exploding from jerking Nolan off.

It was when Nolan gently kneaded Cam's balls while sucking the crown of his cock that he knew his release would come quicker than expected.

Yes, he knew this needed to be expeditious, but he hated that it would be *that* fast. They really needed to make up for it later. When they were alone in Cam's cabin.

Or maybe up in one of the playrooms in Heaven. He might have to book a room to test each other's limits.

But not tonight. Tonight, he didn't want an audience. He wanted to get to know Nolan in a more intimate way.

Cam tensed as his friend took him all the way to the back of his mouth, practically swallowing him whole. His fingers flexed as he resisted grabbing Nolan's head to thrust hard and deep.

Fuck, he was about to blow.

When Nolan wrapped his hand around the base and continued to suck the head, Cam called it a wrap.

He. Was. *Done.*

"I'm going to come," he warned, barely in time.

But Nolan didn't pull back, he kept sucking and stroking. Cam squeezed his eyes shut, tilted his hips, and shot his load down Nolan's throat.

It had turned out to be a good day.

He hoped the evening would be even better.

Chapter Thirteen

"WHAT ABOUT HOPE? Will she be mad?" Nolan asked. *Or at least upset?*

After eating dinner at the lodge, they had stopped over at Heaven and stood in front of a few playrooms that had open blinds until they were both hard as a rock and ready to get down to business with each other.

Some of the resort's guests certainly were into roleplaying, whether pretending to be a doctor or even a stripper.

Nolan wasn't sure if he'd try it himself, but he found himself surprised when a foursome in Room Three, the Puppy Playroom, turned him on. While he'd heard about puppy play before, he'd never seen that kind of kink in person.

Three of the four occupants in the room wore leather canine masks with ears, muzzles, and even anal plugs with dog tails attached. The sole woman in the room appeared to be the canine pack's "trainer." She disciplined "bad" dogs with a rolled up newspaper or a sharp yank on a pronged collar. One "bad dog" was even caged in an oversized dog crate.

It certainly was a different dynamic, but exciting nonetheless.

However, as turned on as Nolan became, Cam still insisted they continue on to his cabin instead of taking care of each other in Heaven's hallway, where there were security cameras. Nolan figured it had to be due to Cam being the head of security.

Nolan could understand how uncomfortable that might get if your subordinates watched you getting off, especially with another man, when he wasn't yet out to his staff or the owners.

As they headed back to Cam's place, the anticipation was killing Nolan.

"Mad about what?" Cam's question brought him back to the conversation.

Oh, that's right. He had brought up Hope. "Us hooking up."

"Having sex twice doesn't make a relationship. Or a commitment."

While that was true... "You don't think she'll have an issue?"

"No," Cam confirmed.

"Good." A smile spread across his face. "Because I can't wait to have sex with you, but I also don't want to screw over Hope." Nolan glanced over at Cam, who matched him stride for stride. "But you do want to fuck her again, right?"

"I wouldn't say no. I also wouldn't say no to a chance at your ass, either."

Nolan's feet stuttered for a second until he recovered and continued on. "Why do you assume I'm a bottom?" Did he come off as one?

"I wasn't assuming. I was hoping." Cam glanced over at him. "Are you?"

They stopped in front of the cabin's door, and while waiting for it to be unlocked, Nolan nodded and smiled. "I am."

Cam tucked his keys into his pocket and turned to face Nolan. "Good. I was worried that might be a problem."

"Do you ever bottom?" Nolan asked out of curiosity.

"I prefer not to," Cam answered. "Do you ever top?"

"I will if asked." He wasn't against it, but it wasn't his preference when it came to men.

Cam opened the door and tipped his head, indicating Nolan should go inside ahead of him.

"Do you know how hard it was—hell, how hard *I* was—listening to you fucking Hope last night?"

"Were you jealous?"

Nolan shook his head. "No. The truth is, I wanted to join you. Both of you."

"I wish you would've." Cam's low chuckle sent sparks flying through Nolan. Of course, they all landed in his cock. "But I'm not sure how Hope would've reacted to you inviting yourself into the mix."

"That was one reason I didn't. Add in the fact I didn't know you were bi. If I had burst in ready for action and you weren't, that might've been really awkward."

Cam laughed as he ensured the cabin's door was locked, then went straight to the fridge to grab two bottles of water.

Nolan accepted one and cracked the lid to down a third of it. His mouth was as dry as the Mojave Desert. It had to be nerves.

Today was completely changing the dynamics of their long friendship.

Cam leaned back against the counter and studied him. "You're trembling."

Damn. Busted. "I'm always worried about the first time with someone new." *Particularly when that someone is you.*

"I'm not new to you." Cam tipped the water bottle to his lips and Nolan got sucked into watching his throat work as he swallowed.

"We were friends, not lovers. That's a huge change, Cam. A friend's expectations are different than a lover's."

"I'll give you that. Would you rather wait and go slow? If that's what you need..."

Nolan shook his head. "I've known you a long time. I trust you. This isn't your first time and it certainly isn't mine. I think we'll be okay." *Or at least, I hope so.*

Cam set his water bottle on the counter, took two long strides over to Nolan, and pulled him close. When their eyes met, he whispered, "You expressed your concern about this ruining our friendship and I want you to be absolutely sure about this. I want you to be comfortable."

Nolan nodded. "I'm sure. I've wanted this forever. I just didn't think it would ever happen."

"Same." Cam released him and tipped his head toward his bedroom. "Let's go. I can't wait to fuck you."

Nolan lost his breath for a second. As soon as he recovered it, he followed Cam inside and eyed the king-sized bed. It was definitely big enough for two, but would it be big enough for three?

He wouldn't mind Hope eventually joining them. If she'd be into that, of course. Because he wasn't sure if this ended up long-term between him and Cam that he'd be okay with Cam being with Hope without him.

Again, Nolan didn't want to alienate Hope. He liked her.

Clearly, they had the same taste. He didn't mind sharing but he didn't want to feel like a third wheel.

However, they needed to get through tonight successfully first. Later, they might be able to figure out a way to include Hope.

Besides simply outright asking her.

"I hope you don't mind, but that time we spent up in Heaven has made me want to get right down to business."

"You said you like eating ass," Nolan reminded him.

One of Cam's eyebrows cocked. "I do and I'd be glad to oblige. Not sure how long I'll last doing it, though. I'm so ready to be inside you."

"I'm ready for that, too. If you want to skip it for now, we can." Though, Nolan had been looking forward to it since Cam mentioned it. He'd had it done to him only once before and, once he got over being self-conscious, the experience had been *amazing*.

Unfortunately, he never found anyone else who was into it. Until now. "Just like you said you could wait for relief earlier in your office. I can wait for this, too."

"But you didn't make me wait," Cam reminded him.

"Since this is our first time together, Cam, I'm okay with waiting for that. Like you, I'm anxious for you to be inside me."

"Okay, well...I'll give you an I.O.U." Cam grinned.

It should be illegal for the man to be so damn handsome. As well as hot and sexy. Not to mention, fuckable.

Had Nolan won the lottery? Because he felt like one lucky man right now.

When Cam sat on the bed to remove his shoes and socks, Nolan joined him to do the same. But once they both were back on their feet, Cam stopped him from removing the rest of his clothes. "Let me."

Nolan held his breath as Cam peeled off his shirt with excruciating slowness. His fingers skimmed here and there over Nolan's heated skin. He peppered kisses on each spot being revealed.

A stroke of a tongue, a brush of fingers, a scrape of teeth...

Nolan jerked when Cam flicked one nipple, then the other, before leaning in to take turns sucking them both.

Nolan's sigh ended on a groan.

They were actually doing this. His fantasy was finally coming true. The years of suppressing his desire for Cam had finally come to an end.

A sudden thought caused Nolan's brain to spin: If this turned out to be a disappointing experience, it would crush him. If after having shitty sex, could they really go back to who they were prior?

The anxiety of possibly losing Cam as a friend began to ramp up and take over. Maybe they should rethink this before it was too late.

He swallowed to loosen up his tight throat, but failed.

Cam unfastened Nolan's jeans. "Are you okay? You seem tense."

"I'm—"

His jeans were yanked down in a flash. Cam spun him around, then squatted down and sank his teeth into Nolan's ass, making those muscles bunch and tighten.

"Fine," Nolan managed to finish. He needed to get out of his head and stay present in the room. Continuing to worry would ruin the moment. Hell, ruin the whole night.

"Are you sure?" Cam tapped Nolan's ankle so he would lift his foot free of his gathered jeans and boxer briefs.

No. "Yes." Nolan lifted his other foot.

Cam swept away the pile of discarded clothes and surged to his feet. "Good." Still completely clothed, Cam went over to the nightstand and pulled out a strip of condoms and a tube of lube, throwing them onto the bed.

"Are we going to need all of those?" If so, Nolan might be a bit sore tomorrow.

"I guess we'll see. Better to have them readily available, than not."

Nolan perched himself at the bottom of the bed. "It's unacceptable that you're still dressed. Get naked. I want to see every inch of you."

"Every inch?"

"Every single, delicious inch."

Cam tossed each piece of clothing onto a nearby chair as he stripped down in record time. Nolan wished he'd gone slower, but the result was still the same...

Worthwhile.

But instead of immediately approaching the bed, Cam stroked his cock while standing a couple feet away from where Nolan sat.

Oh yes, he was about to be the luckiest man on the Earth. Or at least on Double D Ranch. His mouth watered when Cam squeezed the head and a pearly drop appeared at the tip. "Don't tempt me to suck you off again."

"If you do, it'll derail the rest of the evening."

"I'll save that for another time, then."

"Since I gave you an I.O.U., I'll take one from you for that. I'll never say no to you wrapping your mouth around me."

"So, I didn't suck," Nolan teased.

Cam grinned. "You did suck and it was great." After two more fist pumps, he stalked toward the bed. When he reached it, Cam shoved Nolan's shoulder, knocking him onto his back. "Get on your hands and knees."

Nolan's breath shuddered. "I thought we were waiting for that."

"We are. I only want a quick taste and to give you a little preview. Move farther onto the bed, and I want you head down, ass up."

He didn't need to tell Nolan that twice. He quickly turned over and moved up the bed on his hands and knees until he was in the center, where he planted his forehead.

The mattress shifted as Cam followed, only stopping once he was between Nolan's spread legs. Cam's warm lips dragged over his flesh before he separated his ass cheeks.

"I feel so exposed," Nolan grumbled.

"Because you are. And let me just say, it's a beautiful sight."

The tip of Cam's tongue tickled his hole, warm and wet for just the briefest of moments, before pulling away and reaching for the nearby lube.

Oh yes, Nolan would definitely take Cam up on his offer to have him do this in the future.

The snap of the cap on the tube, then the squirting sound of lube made him tremble even worse from anticipation.

He was never like this with anyone else, but he couldn't shake this nervousness from being with Cam for the first time.

First, he heard the tear of the condom packet, then felt the slight shake of the mattress as Cam rolled it on.

Seconds later, lube dripped onto his ass and slipped down his crack before Cam gathered the excess and circled his entrance, distributing it.

But it was when those thick fingers slipped inside him and began to plunge in and out, that he groaned again. And once more when Cam stroked his prostate. By doing so, his friend was entering dangerous territory.

"That alone makes me want to come," Nolan warned.

"Resist."

"I'm trying."

"Try harder."

"Cam," Nolan whimpered. "Take mercy on me, unless you want me to come right away."

Cam slipped his fingers free and nipped at his ass cheek. He tapped Nolan's hip. "Flip over."

"I don't know if I can stare you in the eyes when you fuck me for the first time."

Cam stilled. "I thought you wanted this."

"I do. I'm afraid I'll be distracted."

His eyebrows pinned together. "Why?"

"Because I might be staring into your eyes the whole time, wondering if this is real."

The concern on Cam's face was replaced with understanding. "Stay on your hands and knees, then. I'm fine with that. This time."

The blunt latex and lubed, covered crown pressed against his hole. Nolan relaxed as much as he could.

This was the moment they couldn't return from. The moment where things would shift between them. From friends and former co-workers to friends and lovers.

Chapter Fourteen

Cam was surprised when Nolan didn't want to face him, but he understood. He also wanted Nolan to be completely comfortable.

Pulling in a deep breath, he pressed the tip of his cock against Nolan's puckered entrance and paused.

This was it. It was finally happening. While he was excited, Nolan's worry about things changing between them was valid.

Because they would.

It was one thing to be friends, quite another to be lovers. Realistically, it could end up being a friends-with-benefits situation. Only, that wasn't what Cam wanted. Not with Nolan taking the job and moving up to Double D.

He didn't think he could tolerate watching the man have sex with others. Though, strangely enough, he wouldn't mind sharing him with Hope—if she was into it—because he would also insist on being a part of that dynamic.

None of that might come to fruition anyway, so he

couldn't worry about it right now. They could figure all of that out later.

Cam pressed forward, breaking the tight seal, taking Nolan inch by slow inch until he couldn't go any farther. Until he was balls deep in the man he'd lusted after for years.

With his eyes closed, he paused again and pulled in a breath, appreciating the tight squeeze around him. His cock was urging him to slam Nolan hard and fast while his muddled brain was warning him to keep it slow and steady. At least at the start.

"Fuck me."

The whispered plea had him opening his eyes and taking in the man on his hands and knees, all lean muscle and hard lines, a dark dusting of facial hair accentuating his strong jawline. Cam dug his fingers deeper into Nolan's hips and began to move, making sure to drag his cock over Nolan's P-spot.

With Nolan's groans and encouraging words, along with squeezing and releasing him with every thrust, Cam slipped dangerously close to the edge much too quickly.

He should warn Nolan, tell him to stop.

But he didn't want to.

If things went well, they could do this again.

Hell, with Nolan moving onto the ranch, they could do it often. They could try all kinds of things. It would make working in this paradise even better.

This first time wouldn't be any kind of marathon; it would be a sprint. They could take their time to explore and figure out each other's preferences later.

Tonight was about breaking that seal. The one they put in place when they met each other years ago. The one that concealed their desire for each other.

If they had only known...

Cam couldn't dwell on that. They couldn't go back and fix it. They could only move forward.

No matter what, before Cam came, he wanted to make sure Nolan did, too. When Cam reached around to get him there, he discovered a string of precum swinging from the tip of Nolan's cock with each thrust. Gathering it in his palm, Cam used it as lube as he began to stroke Nolan's cock.

He also tipped his hips to make sure he continued to stimulate Nolan's prostate.

"Fuck, Cam...I'm going to come."

"That's the point. I want you to." Cam gritted his teeth. As soon as Nolan got his release, Cam would quickly follow.

Too quickly.

"Okay, well..." Nolan's hips jutted forward and his cock pulsed in Cam's hands.

Damn, he never had a chance to catch Nolan's cum. He'd worry about that later, too, because...

"Fuck," he moaned, jammed himself deep one more time, and spilled inside of Nolan.

He closed his eyes and dropped his forehead to Nolan's back while he waited for his balls to finish emptying.

When his cock finally stopped twitching, he straightened and glanced down at his friend-turned-lover, still positioned face down, ass up.

Right then and there, Cam decided no more avoidance. They needed to face each other next time.

He collared the condom and carefully slipped from Nolan. "I'm going to get rid of the condom and clean up."

Nolan flopped onto his back, barely missing the wet spot. "We should've put a towel down. Sorry I made a mess."

Cam climbed off the bed. "I helped make that mess. It's easy enough to change the sheets."

"It's much easier to throw a towel in the hamper."

"True. Next time."

Nolan sighed and stretched. "I like the sound of that." He tucked an arm under his head. "As soon as you're done, I'll clean up and we can change the sheets."

Cam lifted his eyebrows and jerked his head toward the bedroom door.. "How about we clean up together?"

"I'm definitely not saying no to that."

———

"Do you still want the job?" Cam asked cautiously.

Fresh sheets covered the bed and they were both squeaky clean from the almost hour of playing in the shower.

"Absolutely," Nolan answered from beside him.

While they had been changing out the bedding, Cam had a worrying thought that Nolan might not want to mix business and pleasure. That was exactly what it would be. Especially since Cam would be his immediate supervisor.

"Do you still want to stay with me until a spot in the bunkhouse or cabin opens up?"

"Will I have to sleep on the couch?"

Cam chuckled. "What do you think?"

After their escapades, there was no reason for Nolan to stay on the pull-out couch, his bed was plenty big enough for them both.

"Do you think this bed will fit three? That is, if you convince Hope to join us."

"Well, since she has her own place, she won't be moving in. We'd only need to make the bed work during certain activities. Plus, this property has plenty of other places we can play."

"I wonder if she's ever had a threesome before," Nolan murmured.

"A threesome with two men," Cam reminded him.

"Hopefully she's not the jealous type."

"She actually encouraged me to tell you I'm bi. I would think if she was jealous or, for whatever reason, wanted to keep me for herself, she wouldn't have done that."

"Let's hope."

"Anyway, some of the great perks of this job..." He rolled into Nolan and patted his cheek playfully. "If you don't feel like shaving, you don't have to shave. If you want to get all tatted up, no one will stop you. The uniforms are comfortable. We have no reason to wear Kevlar. Think of it as working security in an adult amusement park. Other humans are the rides."

"Not the horses? Or that Sybian I saw up in one of Heaven's playrooms?" Nolan joked.

"I was making a point."

Nolan chuckled. "Just busting on you. I miss that."

"I miss it, too. I try not to joke around with any of the security guards under me, so our relationship stays professional. Even though you kid, I would love to see you getting fucked by that Sybian."

Of course, the blinds would need to stay closed.

"When can you start?" For Cam, the sooner, the better.

"Well, I was thinking about ending this trip early and heading home to start getting my stuff packed up and into storage so I can sell my place."

"So...a week?" That still felt like too far away, especially if he left early.

Nolan's eyebrows shot up. "A week? Probably more like a month."

"I'd hate to waste another month."

"That'll give you time to work on Hope."

"You won't mind us hooking up when you're gone?"

Cam asked cautiously. Their sexual relationship was in its infancy stage, he didn't want to derail it before it got on solid ground.

"No, actually. The thought of you two together doesn't bother me at all. As long as she's the only one, Cam."

"I'll work on her. See if she'd be open to that."

"I hope she is."

"Me, too."

"And if she's not?"

"We'll deal with that once I talk to her. Warning, she leans toward being dominant."

"No way. The free-spirited yoga teacher is a Domme?"

"Surprising, right? But I wouldn't give her that official title just yet. She likes to dominate, but I also think she'd be perfectly fine if someone else took the lead. Don't expect to see her in some leather get-up, whip in hand." Though, that was more of an assumption than a fact. He and Hope were still getting to know each other.

"What's more surprising is that you'd let her dominate you." Nolan rolled so that they were both on their sides, facing each other. He brushed the back of his knuckles down Cam's whiskered cheek.

"Only during sex. I don't mind letting her take the reins. If she wants to dominate you, too, is that a problem?"

"Not at all. I actually expected you to be that way."

"I'm okay with either role."

"How about if she wants to paddle my ass until its red, then afterward, you fuck me?"

"Damn, you're going to make me hard again. But, sure, if that's what you want, I'd be glad to oblige. We can run that scenario by her." He chuckled. "Personally, I would love to see her sitting on your face while you're getting fucked by the Sybian."

Nolan blew out a breath. "Now you're going to make *me* hard again."

"When do you plan on heading home?"

Nolan's head twitched. Probably from the sudden subject change. "I was thinking about leaving in the morning."

Cam shoved Nolan to his back and climbed over him. He dropped his head until his mouth hovered over Nolan's. "Then let's make the most of tonight, shall we?"

"I'm game."

It was only the beginning for them. Cam couldn't wait to see what the future held.

Chapter Fifteen

"Where's your friend, Handsome?" Class had wrapped up and the majority of the guests had left. "Or didn't he want to get up early to join us for yoga?"

Cameron finished rolling up his mat, tucked it under his arm, and stood. "He went home."

Hope hadn't expected that answer. "Oh. I thought he was here for five nights?"

"That was the original plan." He set his mat on the nearby rolling cart and began to collect the rest of the yoga mats the other students had left behind.

"Why did he leave early? Did he hate it here?" She couldn't see how anyone would dislike the Double D Ranch, unless they were a prude. Or shy. She doubted Nolan was either of those.

"No, just the opposite."

"Then, why would he leave early?" Did they have a disagreement?

"I offered him the assistant head of security position and

he accepted. He decided to head back early to begin packing and get his place ready to sell."

"Oh, wow! Good for him. And you, too, of course, since I'm assuming that'll help with your work load?"

"Yes. This way I'm not the only security supervisor on call all the time. I'll be able to split those duties with Nolan."

Hope carried the last two mats to the cart, then turned to take in Cam's good looks. His chiseled, bearded face, his thick, sculpted thighs...

She mentally sighed. The man certainly turned her on. All through class, she could barely take her eyes off him as he moved through the poses. "You did better today. You're already more balanced and becoming more flexible."

Cam glanced around, most likely checking to make sure the rest of the students had left. "At least the teacher didn't have to scold me like a bad boy today."

Her lips twitched. "*Ah.* Would you rather I did?"

Cam chuckled. "No. Not during class."

Hope lifted an eyebrow. "But after?" They hadn't had sex since the night of the key party. She wouldn't mind doing it again. And soon. "What are you doing later?"

"No plans. What about you?"

No point in beating around the bush. "I was thinking about doing you."

Cam's sexy smirk made her clit throb.

"Great minds and all of that, but..." His lips quickly flattened out. "Hope, I have something to tell you first."

Uh oh. "That sounds ominous."

"It's not. I told Nolan I'm bi."

"Oh, good! Do you feel better about no longer keeping it a secret?" That had to be a heavy load lifted from his shoulders.

"Yes, but now I wish I would've told him sooner."

"Why's that?"

"Because he's bi, too."

Hope stared at him as she digested that info. "And you didn't know."

"No. I had no idea. But that's not all."

"Why do I suddenly feel like I'm in an infomercial? *But wait*"—Hope lifted a finger—"*that's not all!*" She expected him to chuckle at that. When he didn't, her gut twisted.

"We fucked."

Hold on. Did he feel guilty? He shouldn't. "Cam, we don't owe each other anything. You didn't need to tell me that. But I'll understand if you don't want to risk your relationship with him over me." That had to be why he was bringing it up, right?

Cam shook his head. "That's not it. He's into you, too."

In hindsight, she was less surprised than she thought she'd be. Like with her and Cam, an obvious spark had existed between her and Nolan, but since Cam and Nolan were friends, she had tamped down her interest to avoid issues between them.

Her eyebrows pinched together. "So, what does that mean for us?"

"He brought you up because he didn't want to hurt you by having sex with me. I told him you and I only got together twice."

And twice did not a relationship make.

"Does this mean he wants to hook up with me without you?" She really didn't even know the guy outside of the fact they were attracted to each other. Not that she knew Cam well the first night she went to his cabin, either.

"No, he wants the three of us to hook up together."

She hadn't been expecting that revelation. She closed her gaping mouth. "Oh. Is that something you also want?"

"I'm interested if you are."

Hope pursed her lips at this new twist. "A threesome, huh?"

"Have you ever had one?"

"No," she answered. "Have you?"

"No."

"Has he?"

Cam grimaced. "Shit. I didn't ask. But if I had to guess? Probably not."

"Then, this would be new territory for all of us."

"Only if you're into it. Are you?"

It was cute the way he asked that. Almost like a wide-eyed kid in a candy store asking for one of those giant lollipops. "I never gave it any thought before. I'm not saying I'm against it, but..." She shook her head when the reality hit her. "Who in their right mind would pass on having sex with both of you?"

"Someone uncomfortable with the idea?" Cam countered with a chuckle.

She smiled. "True. I'm definitely not against it, but I'm assuming threesomes can either be really great or go really wrong." Two personalities could be difficult enough, but adding a third?

"While that might be true, look at the Lyons twins. Both are in rock solid triads. As long as everyone is on the same page, it should work."

That was over-simplifying it. "I'm sure they have problems like every other relationship."

"As long as the threesome keeps communication open..."

"Though, this wouldn't be a relationship like theirs," she reminded both herself and Cam.

"True. It would be for fun."

"And loads of orgasms."

That heart-stopping grin was back. "Of course."

"If it doesn't work out, there'd be no hard feelings, right?" A threesome could end up being a total disaster and she worried if it was, things would end with Cam too soon.

"Of course. If one of us ends up being uncomfortable or feeling left out and doesn't want to continue, then..." Cam shrugged. "Hopefully that doesn't happen."

"Does this mean you don't want to meet up later? Do you want to wait until Nolan returns?" She didn't want to wait, but she would.

"No. He made it clear he wouldn't mind us getting together without him in the meantime. It might be a month before he returns."

Hope trailed Cam as he rolled the cart full of yoga equipment to the storage closet.

He pushed it inside, closed the door and turned to face her. "So, if it wasn't clear: Yes, I'd love to meet up later. In the meantime, do you want to join me for breakfast? We can discuss this in more detail and maybe make plans for tonight?"

She wasn't turning down that offer. "How can I say no to great food and even better company?"

Cam jutted out his hand and she clasped it. "Then, let's go eat."

———

IN THE LAST MONTH, every time Cam reserved a playroom for them up in Heaven, he requested the blinds be closed. Earlier, he had booked Room Four, the bondage/restraint room, for tonight. The week prior, they had played in the medical-themed room where they switched things up. They reversed the dominant roles when Cam ended up being the doctor and her the patient.

It had been fun and stimulating, as well as orgasmic.

Cam was a great sex partner. No doubt, tonight would be the same. Especially since Hope was back in charge.

She wanted to use some toys on him that might give her an idea of how far she could push him before he said his safe word. The first thing she did after ordering Cam to undress was buckle a wide leather collar around his thick, corded neck and inform him, "You're my pet tonight."

Simply announcing that sent shivers of excitement through her.

She wanted to make him wear a cock cage, but he was hard the moment they walked into the playroom, locked the door, and pulled the blinds. She would have to save that treat for another time.

Like the first night they hooked up, Hope blindfolded him. But unlike the first time, she remembered to add the nipple clamps. Of course, once his nipples were being pinched without mercy, she tugged a few times on the chain connecting the two rubber-tipped metal clamps.

Just to make sure they were secure, and to remind him who was in charge.

While this playroom wasn't specifically set up for impact play, it still had plenty of toys available to leave a mark or two. And, lucky her, Cam said she could do whatever she wanted to him.

She liked the sound of that so much she almost rubbed her hands together with glee.

She warred with herself whether to use a ball gag since she wanted him to easily be able to use his safe word, but seeing his strong, chiseled jaw locked open was too good to pass up, so she devised a way for him to notify her if anything got to be too much. He was to use a thumbs up for "go," give a thumbs down for "slow down or ease up," and hold up all five fingers for "stop."

Those signals would be definitely needed, since she requested he book this room solely for the stockade. It was made of polished wood and bolted to the floor to prevent from tipping and injuring the people involved.

With Cam's head and arms locked in it, he had no choice but to bend over, giving her the perfect access to his muscular ass. One she planned on decorating a little by using a wooden paddle with holes in it for greater impact.

But before she did that, she clipped a leash to the chain on the nipple clamps, making it easier for her to tug on them while she swatted his ass.

"Don't forget your hand signals," she reminded him, even though when she came up with them, he insisted he wouldn't need them at all.

Stubborn man.

But so far, in the few weeks since Nolan left, no matter what she did to Cam, he hadn't once uttered his safe word. He either had a high pain tolerance or got off on it.

Hope smoothed her hand over the wooden paddle before smacking it against her palm a few times. "Are you ready?" Her question made him quiver, which, in turn, made her smile.

When she slapped her palm harder so it made a sharp sound, he jerked forward. She waited until he relaxed again and eyed her very impressive target...

When the sharp crack of wood against flesh filled the room, Hope still heard his grunt around the ball gag. Since he didn't give the signal for her to ease up or stop, she struck him again.

And again. Not giving him time for second thoughts or to relax between blows.

After a half dozen hard whacks, she paused and looked at her handiwork. "That looks so pretty."

She licked her lips before deciding her tongue could be used to soothe the redness left behind. But with as hard as she was striking him, she had no doubt those areas would swell, maybe even bruise. He might not even be able to sit comfortably for a day. If not longer.

It gave her pleasure to think that every time he went to sit, he'd think of her.

Whenever she pulled her arm back for the next strike, his ass would clench in anticipation. When he did, she'd hold off and wait until he relaxed again, smoothing her hands over each heated cheek while murmuring sweet, encouraging words.

Once it got to the point where his pink skin was turning a deep red, she figured he'd had enough. Of course, he was still being bull-headed and refused to give her the sign to ease up or stop.

Since she had no desire to injure him, she made that executive decision for him. Plus, it was time to move on, anyway. She had more in store for Cam.

Setting the paddle aside, she went over to her bag to grab the large, realistic dildo she'd brought along. "I've got a surprise for you."

Since he was gagged and blindfolded, the only response she got was a grunt.

Grabbing the bottle of lube the resort supplied in each room, she separated his ass cheeks and dripped some over her target. He twitched with each drip.

Oops. She forgot to ask him if he liked giving or getting anal, or if he was good with either. But, he *did* say she could do anything and seemed fine with the anal beads, so she'd assume he was okay with ass play.

His hips shot forward when she used the head of the realistic latex cock to spread the lube around his entrance. She generously coated the dildo and pressed it against his hole again. She took her time working it in, again, not knowing if he was used to having a cock inside him or not. She kept one eye on what she was doing and the other on his hand, watching for his hand signals.

When the dildo was halfway in, she paused, giving him time to adjust and for her to check in. She softly stroked his heated butt cheek. "Are you okay, Handsome?"

Despite giving a thumbs up, it had a slight shake to it.

"Okay, then. I'll keep going," she warned. She pushed the fake cock in another inch and paused, then repeated it until the dildo was fully seated. The man had to be feeling quite full. "Are you good?"

When he gave another thumbs up, she took him at his word and began to fuck him with it. She had no way of knowing whether it was stimulating his prostate without a reaction or him telling her.

She ignored that for now and continued on, plunging the fake cock in and out of his ass. Muffled groans worked their way around the ball gag, but since he didn't give the signal to stop, she had to assume he was enjoying it.

Only, the dildo wasn't doing what she intended it to, which was have him begging for mercy. So after a few more thrusts, she slowly pulled it back out and set it aside. She did not miss the fact every muscle in his body immediately loosened.

Could this be the first time he'd ever been fucked? Was she the first one to do it? She'd ask him once he could talk again.

In the meantime, she grabbed a latex glove from a nearby cabinet full of toys. She pulled it on her right hand and lubed two fingers up well.

Since the dildo didn't work as she'd hoped, what she was about to do next might. And not because it would be painful, but because it would be too pleasurable.

When she went back to stand behind Cam, he tensed due to not knowing what was coming next. She was definitely keeping him on his toes.

When she worked two fingers inside him—much easier after being stretched by the dildo—he clamped down around her for only the time it took to find his walnut-sized "start" button.

It was time to "turn him on."

She stroked him there until his hips began to hump the air uncontrollably. That reaction made one side of her mouth pull up. He was saying something but she couldn't make it out. However, unless he gave her the signal to stop, she'd continue until he ran out of juice or couldn't take the stimulation anymore.

She squatted down to see his erection hanging heavily between his legs and prostatic fluid dripping off the head of his cock and onto the floor.

"Do you like me milking you like that, Handsome?"

Chapter Sixteen

"Do you like me milking you like that, Handsome?"

Did she really expect him to answer? His mouth was being forced open and filled with a rubber ball.

Of course, *if* he could answer, it would be a resounding yes, but he could only take so much of it. Just like that big dildo. Her using it on him confirmed why he didn't bottom.

He wasn't fond of the fullness or the uncomfortable stretch.

However, he had told her to go wild. He'd have to rethink that for next time. Even so, she was milking his prostate like a pro. And while he couldn't see the result of it because of the blindfold, he sure could feel it.

The more she stroked his P-spot, the more fluid escaped him. While he hadn't come yet, he was teetering dangerously. It wouldn't take much more for him to succumb. Only, once he did, he'd lose his erection. Though, that might be her goal and she wouldn't care that he couldn't fuck her.

At least not until he had time to recover.

They only had the room for an hour and he had lost track

of time. Given his current position, he certainly couldn't check it.

When she reached between his legs and slapped his balls lightly, he jerked forward in surprise and was unable to breathe for a second or two.

What the fuck? At least being restrained in the stockade kept him from collapsing to his knees. Maybe even curling up and crying like a baby.

No matter what, he refused to tell her to stop.

She must be getting back at him from all the "torture" he inflicted on her last week in the medical room. That night he had turned the tables on her. Now she was flipping those tables over.

When she moved to his side but still continued to finger fuck him, he knew she had something up her sleeve and he would soon be done.

"It can't get any more perfect than that," she whispered, using downward strokes to pull on his cock as if she was milking a cow. "Time to move on."

Thank fuck.

However, "moving on" to her meant slipping her fingers free of his ass, then getting on her knees and wedging herself between his feet and the base of the stockade.

What was she doing?

She tapped his leg. "Give me more room to work, Handsome."

He wasn't sure he liked her using the term "work." Especially after she had slapped his damn balls. Did it mean she was going to work him over? She already...

Wait.

Okay.

He gave two thumbs up, even though he had no idea if she could see them. But he was fully onboard with her wrapping her mouth around his aching cock. But why did she need his legs wider?

Oh yes. For that...

If he had more than two thumbs he'd be raising them all.

While sucking his cock, she had reached through his thighs and plugged her two fingers right back into his socket so she could continue to push his power button.

Holy shit. Between her going to town with her hot, wet mouth and the stimulation of his prostate, he wasn't going to last long.

Hell, he wasn't going to last, period.

One Mississippi, two Mississippi...

Hold up. Why did he care how long he lasted? He had no reason to hold out.

Instead, he cleared his mind and let her do her thing. Consequences be damned.

While gently kneading his still stinging balls, she swallowed his length all the way to the back of her throat, sucking while stroking the underside with her tongue.

Between her magical fingers and blowjob skills, she was soon going to get a mouthful. With the gag, he had no way to warn her, so he would simply let nature take its course. She was fully aware of what she was doing to him and what the end result would be.

He thrust into her mouth one more time and tensed as his cum exploded from him. Hope didn't even attempt to pull free. Instead, she sucked him harder and deeper, drawing every drop from him until he was completely drained.

She needed to stop overstimulating his prostate because it was quickly going from ecstasy to torture. *Real* torture. Not the pleasurable, playful kind.

His cock slipped from her mouth at the same time she removed her fingers and moved away.

With the blindfold, he might not be able to see her, but he could still picture in his mind what she looked like by the memory of how she appeared the last time she sucked him off.

She had looked sexy as hell with her messy hair, flushed face, glossy lips, and heated eyes. Not to mention the satisfaction on her face.

Though, guaranteed he was more satisfied right now than she was.

He'd had some really bad head in the past, but Hope did not fall into that category. Not even close.

A rustling sound, then the water running in the tiny attached bathroom meant that Hope was most likely cleaning up. A few minutes later, he felt her heat as she stopped in front of him. His first thought was, *"Oh boy, what's next?"* He sighed in relief when she finally removed the ball gag.

"I'm going to release you, Handsome, but leave the blindfold in place for now. I'm debating what I want to do with it."

Could he still even form words? Did his mouth still function? He worked his stiff jaw around. It was easier to nod, instead.

Once she freed him from the stockade, it took him a few moments to be able to stand straight. After being bent over like that, his back was killing him. It was a good excuse to book an appointment at Nirvana.

As for now, he was still coming down from his own slice of nirvana.

With his energy drained and feeling like a limp dish rag, all he wanted to do was take a nap, but doubted that was what Hope had in mind.

When he heard the leash being unclipped from his nipple clamps, he expected those to go next.

But no.

Hope tugged on the shorter chain connecting them and in a husky voice said, "This way, Handsome."

He followed like an obedient dog as she led him over to the small bed in the corner. The one with restraint hoops at all four corners of the metal bed frame.

Was she planning on tying him up there, too? Their time in the room had to be running out.

"Get on the bed and on your back, Handsome."

"How much time do we have left? I don't want to piss off my bosses by hogging the room and—"

She cut him off with, "This isn't going to take long at all. You're wasting time, Handsome. Chop. Chop."

Chop? Chop? Cam swallowed his chuckle since he certainly didn't want to be *punished* for laughing at her choice of words.

Once she released the chain, she placed his hands on the bed so he could find the edge and climb on. With the way his poor back was aching, it would be a relief to lie flat.

He got comfortable on the mattress that was covered in waterproof material for good reason. Since he was now completely soft, he had no idea what her plan was.

He yelped and jerked his foot back when her fingernail scraped a line along the bottom from heel to toe. A soft snort burst from her due to his overreaction.

Holy crap. Who knew he'd be so sensitive there? "Are you going to tie me up?"

"No need."

"Then, what do you plan on doing with me?"

She also got on the narrow bed, only big enough for one person to fit comfortably. Unless you stacked them.

Since it was too soon to get an erection, she couldn't be planning on riding his cock...

Before he could ask her anything else, she straddled his head.

Of course. He licked his lips in anticipation.

He couldn't wait to taste her essence and had no doubt she was soaked from his time in the stockade.

"I thought about keeping you blindfolded, but I really want to see those beautiful brown eyes of yours as you eat, Handsome."

The blindfold was quickly whisked away.

He winced when the sudden change of light hit his eyes, then blinked a few times as his pupils adjusted. But once his vision cleared, he saw Hope was now totally naked like him, unlike in the beginning before she had blindfolded him.

Her rosy nipples were puckered tight and it was impossible to miss the sheen on her inner thighs.

Just as he thought. Playing with him made her hot and bothered. Because of that, everything she had done to him so far had been one hundred percent worth it.

Well, maybe not the ball slapping. She could've omitted that.

Hope rose on her knees and shuffled forward until she was hovering over his mouth. He raised his head and used the tip of his tongue to tickle the damp curls hiding her clit.

That was only a taste and he wanted more. The scent of her arousal was making his mouth water. He was more than ready to chow down on the rest of the meal.

"Tap my leg if you get to the point you can't breathe."

"Maybe I won't be able to since my hands will be busy. Who said I won't shove two fingers up *your* ass?"

She smiled down at him. "Then use your other hand to tap my leg."

"That's going to be playing with your clit while I tongue fuck you."

Her smile quickly disappeared and heat filled both her eyes and her cheeks. "I think we need to stop talking and start doing. You were right. We're running out of time."

"*Now* you're in a rush?"

"Hush," she scolded gently and dropped down until his face was buried in her cunt.

That was a good way to shut him up. His preferred way, actually.

He lapped up the sweet, tangy goodness and sucked hard on her clit, causing her to whimper.

He'd hooked up with a few guests in the months that he'd worked on the ranch, but none had been as responsive as Hope. She never held back on her reactions.

"Fuck me. With your tongue. With your thumb. Make me come, Handsome. Make me squirt all over your beard."

He'd be glad to help with that by tonguing her pussy while thumbing her clit.

Seconds later, little whimpers filled his ears and she began to rock back and forth, grinding her pussy harder on his face.

"Yes, like that." With a long groan, she continued to circle her hips.

He didn't even attempt to be gentle as he sucked each fold into his mouth and scraped his teeth along the sensitive flesh. Then he went back to stabbing his tongue as deep as he could into her slick slit.

While he couldn't see it, he knew exactly when she reached back and grabbed the chain to the nipple clamps. How? Because she ripped on that damn chain, making his back bow.

She did it one more time before sinking almost all of her weight on him, effectively smothering him.

He was worried for a moment there that he might actually have to tap out.

Luckily, seconds later, she screamed, "I'm coming!" and he caught the rush of arousal on his tongue. She moved before he started gasping for breath and smiled down at him. "Look at that messy beard. I did that," she announced proudly.

He refrained from wiping his face before returning that smile. "I helped."

"You certainly did, Handsome."

Now they needed to do a quick clean up and vacate the room before one of his own security officers began banging on the door to evict them.

Chapter Seventeen

Nolan blindly stared inside the open refrigerator, the cool air kissing his skin as it escaped the interior.

He jumped when thick, muscular arms circled his waist and a pair of soft lips, accompanied by a scratchy beard, brushed over his bare shoulder.

Cam's husky question filled his ear. "What are you looking for?"

"World peace?"

"You won't find it in my fridge."

Nolan turned within his arms. "I don't think we'll find it outside of your fridge, either."

They shared a quick kiss.

Why did standing in Cam's kitchenette make him feel so content? Make him feel at home when he'd only moved in less than forty-eight hours ago?

When Cam finally pulled away, Nolan mourned his touch for a second before grabbing a bottle of water from the fridge door and shutting it. "I can't believe I'm here for good." He cracked the lid on the bottle and swallowed a mouthful.

They had just come back from their morning bike ride and had "saved water" by showering together. Though, they did get a little dirty in the shower.

His condo was now on the market and all the items he wouldn't need at this point had been moved into a storage unit close by in Fisher Falls. Since living with Cam was only temporary, he'd need all his belongings and furniture later when he found his own place.

When he'd arrived late two nights prior, after a long, exhausting drive, he had parked the box truck he'd rented by the resort's equipment shed. Once Cam was done with work the next day, they, as well as some of Cam's security guards, had unloaded it in a much shorter amount of time than it had taken him to load it.

But because they'd been busy since Nolan returned, they hadn't had time to get together with Hope.

After he had talked to her, Cam had called to share that she was willing to give a threesome a try and Nolan couldn't wait. In fact, it had made him pack even faster.

Despite never having had a threesome, being bi, Nolan saw it as being potentially the best of both worlds. As long as everything went well. If not, hopefully there'd be no hard feelings.

Especially between him and Cam.

If hooking up with him made Nolan worry about their friendship, adding a third person ramped up that anxiety even more.

All three of them were supposed to get together that night for the first time. In the five weeks he'd been gone, Cam had kept him updated on what he and Hope had been doing together, sometimes even describing it in explicit detail. Enough to make Nolan as hard as a rock. Enough to make Nolan masturbate as soon as he got off the phone with Cam.

During a couple of those conversations, they had both jerked off at the same time while still on the phone.

It had been super hot. And unbelievably satisfying.

But now he was here with Cam in the flesh. Sharing his bed. Sharing his shower. And starting on Monday, they'd be working together. Like old times but better. No uncomfortable uniforms. No reason to carry lethal weapons. No more answering to asshole leadership.

Nolan's immediate supervisor would be Cam himself. And yesterday, he met with the Lyons siblings: the twins, Dayne and Dylan, along with their younger sister, Danica.

All three had been very welcoming and easy-going. Except for when they busted on each other like typical siblings. For a moment, it made him regret that he had been an only child.

"I have to return the box truck and car dolly today." That was going to be another long drive all the way to State College. Luckily, nowhere near as long as the drive from Media.

"Do you want me to come with you?"

Nolan shook his head. "No, I can take care of it since you need to work."

"I don't think the bosses will mind if I take a few hours off. Plus, it's a good excuse to visit Laurel at school. And I'm sure she'd be happy to see her 'Uncle Nolan.'"

"Does Laurel know you're bi?"

"No, I saw no reason to tell her. I told Molly back when we split."

"But now?"

"I'm not ready to tell her yet."

"You don't think she'd understand?"

"Maybe. Maybe not. But things are new with us. And she loves you."

What did that mean? Was Cam worried his daughter would be devastated if things didn't work out between them?

Nolan would be. But that was a risk with any new relationship, whether serious or casual.

Or was he more worried that Laurel wouldn't be accepting when it came to her father being bisexual? Or even in a relationship with another man?

Could he blame Cam when it came to being cautious? Nolan kept his bisexuality under wraps, too. Even from his family.

Cam was right. This was brand spanking new.

They needed to give this a chance before announcing it to their families.

As well as the world.

———

"I'm the director tonight, boys."

Nolan had no idea whether to be excited or scared at Hope's announcement not even thirty seconds after walking into Cam's cabin.

When she eyed Nolan up and down, his asshole puckered a little.

Hope hooked a thumb toward Cam. "I call him Handsome. Now I need a pet name for you. *Hmm.*" She pursed her lips. "Hunk? How about Hot Stuff?"

Okay, good. She wasn't about to suspend him from the ceiling and paddle his ass until he couldn't sit down. Cam had complained about a bruised and sore ass a couple of weeks prior.

Though, Nolan had wished he'd been here to watch that action.

"I'm fine with either," Nolan answered.

"Mistress."

Shit.

Cam had said she wasn't an official "Domme," only that she liked to dominate. But demanding Nolan call her that honorific proved otherwise. "I'm fine with either, Mistress."

She stepped up to Nolan, grabbed his crotch through his jeans and squeezed gently. "I'm leaning toward Hot Stuff." After releasing him, she turned toward Cam next. "Handsome, grab us a large towel for the bed and a couple of small hand towels for quick cleanup. I don't want anyone lying in the wet spot tonight and I guarantee there will be one."

"Yes, Mistress."

When Cam quickly left the bedroom to do her bidding, Nolan noticed his friend—and now lover—had an erection. He was about to be in the same boat.

"We're about to fuck and we haven't even kissed yet," Hope murmured. "I think we should remedy that, Hot Stuff, don't you?" She cupped her hands on either side of his face, stepping even closer. "I've been wanting to taste your lips."

He could say the same, whether they were the lips on her face or the ones between her legs. He loved eating pussy as much as he loved giving head. He was an equal opportunity oral—

Damn. He didn't even know what to call it. Oral opportunist?

Not that it mattered. His thoughts scattered when she pressed her lips against his. Hers were soft, but powerful as she swept her tongue through his mouth to claim it.

She kept control at first, but as soon as she backed off, their tongues tangled. The semi he'd been sporting was now a full blown erection.

He cupped her breast over the yoga-themed ribbed tank top she was wearing to find she was not wearing a bra. Most likely because she came straight to the cabin from her house. He supposed that, with as fit as she was from all the yoga she did, she certainly didn't need one. Especially at Double D Ranch, a judgement-free space.

Footsteps behind them had them separating. Nolan turned his eyes toward Cam, who was acting like his two lovers kissing each other wasn't out of the ordinary.

Cam removed the bedspread and top sheet from the bed and tucked them out of the way in the corner of his room. He then spread a large towel in the center of his king-sized bed before stacking a couple of hand towels within arm's reach.

"Thank you, Handsome."

"No reason to thank me since I benefit—" All Hope had to do was raise an eyebrow and Cam quickly said, "You're welcome, Mistress."

Nolan rolled his lips under for a second before asking her, "How do you want us?"

Hope tapped a finger against her lips as she took both of them in. "Well, I want you naked, first of all..."

"A given," Cam said. "Do you want any toys?"

Hope pursed her lips as she glanced toward Cam's closet. That piqued Nolan's curiosity. Did she already know what was in there?

"Yes, do you have a remote-controlled vibrating plug?"

Nolan wondered who that was for. So far, she was keeping her plans close to the vest.

"I do, Mistress."

"Get it."

Cam went to the closet and slid out a box that had been stored on the floor. After opening it, he dug around for a second, then held up a butt plug and small wireless remote.

"Perfect," Hope purred, going over and plucking it from his fingers. She held the plug out to Nolan, but as he reached for it, she tipped her head toward Cam. "This isn't for you. It's for him."

"You have a plan," Cam surmised as he pulled a strip of condoms out of the nightstand's drawer and a bottle of Swiss Navy, the water-based lube they used whenever he and Cam had sex.

"I do now."

"Let's get naked before we go any further," Cam suggested to Nolan. "Would you like us to undress you, Mistress?"

"No, I can do it. But thank you for asking."

Since Nolan already knew what Cam looked like naked, he kept his focus on Hope as he undressed. This was the first time he was getting to see her totally naked. She looked great in clothes. She also looked great in her yoga gear. But naked?

Holy shit. So much better than he ever imagined. No wonder Cam was drawn to her. Especially since he said the first interaction with her after being hired on at Double D was while she was doing naked yoga on the lake's dock.

Her pussy wasn't bare, but the reddish-brown hair was trimmed into a neat pattern. Her arms and legs were tan, smooth and sculpted. Truly a sculpted piece of art.

Her stomach was flat and her breasts neither too large or too small for her five-foot-six athletic frame.

Yoga must be some powerful shit. Unless she also did some weight training, he was surprised it did a body *that* good.

Her blue eyes flashed when she noticed Nolan eyeing her up. "Very nice, Mistress."

She ran a hand down her torso. "I'm glad you approve. Now...grab that bottle, Hot Stuff," Hope ordered, "and generously lube up that plug."

He grabbed the lube and began to ready the silicone butt plug that had a unique swirl to it.

He also snuck a few glances at Cam as he did so. Since he was a top, he probably wasn't used to having things shoved up his ass. Especially plugs of this size.

One exception might be the dildo Hope had used on him. He almost skipped telling Nolan that part when describing the night they had played in the restraint room up in Heaven.

Nolan glanced at the remote. With three speeds and seven different vibration patterns, he actually looked forward to it being used on him in the future.

"Handsome, please get into your preferred position," Hope instructed Cam.

Cam and Nolan's eyes locked. Smothering a grin, Nolan promised, "I'll be gentle, *Handsome*."

"Great," Cam muttered before going over and planting his hands on the bed and sticking out his bare ass.

Nolan stepped behind him, separated Cam's cheeks, and began to slowly work the lubed plug in and out. He drove it deeper each time, until it was fully seated.

Clearly, Cam hadn't bought that butt plug for himself, otherwise, his back wouldn't be currently arched like a camel and his hands wouldn't be curled into fists.

Nolan brushed a kiss over Cam's hunched back and patted his ass. His new roommate and lover slowly straightened and clenched his cheeks together.

"Are you okay? Nolan asked.

Cam grimaced. "It just needs some getting used to, is all."

Nolan turned to Hope. "What would you like us to do next, Mistress?"

She climbed onto the bed and settled in the middle, leaning back on her elbows. "I want your face between my thighs and your ass in the air. You're going to eat me while Cam eats you."

Okay then. While he liked the sound of that, Nolan wondered what Cam thought of the idea. Not that he had a choice. Hope had taken control the second she walked through the door and it didn't seem as if she would be letting that control go anytime soon.

Hope cocked her knees and spread her legs. Making a *V* with her fingers, she separated her folds, showing off his next meal.

"What a pretty pink pussy, Mistress," Nolan murmured, licking his lips. He was looking forward to diving in and experiencing what Cam had for the last couple of months.

It hit him then that this was actually happening. He was about to experience his first threesome. And not with some random strangers, either, but with two people he was highly attracted to.

"Let's go, boys. Stop dawdling. The night might be young, but I've got a lot of ideas to put into play."

That sounded promising. And a little intimidating, if he had to admit it.

While shuffling forward on his knees to get into position, he focused on her spread open pussy. It was shiny already from arousal and he couldn't wait to dive in.

"Handsome, you know what to do. So do you, Hot Stuff."

Nolan would be the one in the middle, both eating and getting eaten. He couldn't think of a better welcome to this new chapter in his life.

Hope held her hand out, palm up. "Hot Stuff, hand me that remote."

He quickly located it and gave it to her. Nolan had a feeling that Cam was in for a wild ride.

Hope grabbed his head and pulled it down, shoving his face right between her legs. "Now eat like this is your last meal."

Chapter Eighteen

HOPE'S PUSSY pulsed at the thought of Nolan's mouth on her. Despite the fact that she had no idea what to expect since this was their first time together.

She'd had some great head in the past as well as some head that was absolute shit.

Cough Darren. *Cough*

Luckily, Cam was great at it. He didn't flick his tongue a few times in the direction of her pussy and call it a day. No, he tackled it like a pro. As if he was participating in a competitive eating contest.

She was pleased to find that Nolan wasn't timid at all, either, when he began tonguing her pussy with gusto and grinding his thumb against her clit.

Oh yes, he was definitely taking this task to heart.

When his groan vibrated against her, sending waves of pleasure through her body, Hope raised her head enough to see Cam's face buried in Nolan's ass.

She had never eaten anyone's ass and wasn't sure she ever

could, but if Cam was into doing it and Nolan was into getting it done, more power to them. She'd never judge.

As Nolan's long fingers worked in and out of her, his thumb circled her clit even faster, driving her hips into motion and causing that place deep inside her to begin to tense.

She rolled both of her tightly puckered nipples between her thumbs and forefingers. It hammered home the fact she really wanted their mouths there. Cam on one side, Nolan on the other. Unfortunately—more like *fortunately*—their mouths were a bit busy at the moment.

She could wait. But she would definitely add it to their to-do list. For round two. Or three. Or maybe even four.

When another groan vibrated against her pussy, her breath escaped her in a shudder. Hope had no idea if his moans were due to what he was doing to her or what Cam was doing to him.

It could very well be both and she had a feeling Nolan was simply matching Cam's energy.

The stubble on Nolan's face scoring the delicate skin between her inner thighs caused another wave of heat to rush through her and her walls clamped down around his fingers.

The sensation of his tongue swirling on her clit and the vibrations of his moans radiated through her core, hauling her to the peak of the mountain she'd been climbing, but she didn't fall over the top just yet.

No, she hovered right there, enjoying the trip.

Until Nolan scraped his teeth over her clit, shooting a jolt of electricity into the pit of her stomach and causing her to breath to hitch and her body to jerk. That was the moment she began the downward slide.

With her toes curling, she dug her fingers into his hair and her hips shot up as a climax ripped through her. Wave after wave, she tumbled, throwing her head back and not bothering to bite back her loud cry.

As she came down from the high of that earth-shattering orgasm, she realised that her body had clamped down around Nolan's face and most likely sealed off his airways.

Holy shit. That had been intense.

Once her orgasm subsided and she came back to Earth, she lifted her head to see Nolan doing the same. Only, unlike her slack mouth, he wore a shit-eating grin.

He had every right to be cocky. In fact, he deserved a medal.

Cam now sat on his haunches, also looking quite satisfied himself. "What's next, Mistress?"

Certainly not kissing him since she knew where that mouth had been. "Now we fuck." She dropped her gaze to Nolan. "Did you enjoy what he did to you?"

That sexy grin remained in place. "I did, Mistress."

"Do you want him to fuck you?"

"Yes, I do, Mistress."

"Do you prefer to bottom? Or should I make him take your cock the same way I used the dildo on him?"

Oh, shit! Because of how expertly Nolan ate her pussy, she forgot all about the butt plug! Damn it. Cam got away easy.

But not for long.

"I prefer to bottom but will do whatever our Mistress wants."

It was such a rush to have two men willing to do whatever pleased her. Especially when what she desired was something they normally wouldn't do.

When she turned her eyes toward Cam, they briefly dropped to his raging erection. That had to be uncomfortable and, no doubt, he was hoping for his own release soon. "And how about you? If I switch it up and make Nolan fuck you, would you be okay with it?"

Cam's jaw shifted slightly. "Are you giving me a choice, Mistress?"

She raised both eyebrows at him. "I'm asking you a question. I expect an answer in return, not another question."

Cam's mouth dropped open slightly and his eyes turned even darker.

She lifted her hand with the forgotten remote. "You got off easy. Don't expect it to stay that way."

Cam dipped his head. "Yes, Mistress."

She'd never been power hungry. In fact, she had always been a "live and let live" kind of person, but holding control over two former state troopers was heady. Especially since all she needed to do to get them to bend to her every sexual whim was use her words.

Oh yes, she could get used to this. She shouldn't be surprised that holding that authority within her fingertips turned her on. It always had, but never to this extent.

The fact she'd been suppressing her dominant side during her former relationship should've been another red flag. In the future, she needed to stop ignoring those signs. Even in casual relationships like the one with Cam. And now potentially with Nolan as well.

Thankfully, at this point, she hadn't witnessed anything concerning with either of them. At least not yet. Cam had been flexible and open—even if apprehensive—to everything she'd suggested so far. She had a feeling Nolan would be the same.

Of course, she hadn't given them any unreasonable demands as of yet. If she did, the truth was, she wouldn't have a problem with either of them saying no. "I'll ask again: Would you be against Nolan fucking you?"

Cam's chest expanded. That alone was Hope's answer. He would not be comfortable with that scenario but would do it if told.

"Mistress, I'd prefer Nolan not fuck me. I'll understand if you need to punish me for that."

Sex was supposed to be fun, pleasurable and satisfying in the end, and that's what she looked forward to most at the end of the day. For all three of them. So she wouldn't force Cam to do something he wouldn't enjoy. "No reason for that. I prefer honesty over a lie."

Cam's eyes were filled with relief when they met hers. When he gave her a chin lift, she answered with a single nod.

Respect was as important as communication.

There were times where all of them should be pushed past their comfort zone, like what she did with Cam and the dildo, but tonight was not one of those times.

"Hot Stuff, have you ever had a threesome before?"

"No."

Shit. That meant this was the first time for all of them. They'd have to wing it. Would adding a third person complicate things beyond the fact it meant extra limbs and holes?

Common sense told her to not concentrate on one man more than the other. She needed to focus on both equally. Unless she found a specific reason to humiliate or "punish" one. Of course, all in good fun.

She could also see the benefit of forcing one to watch while she had sex with the other. But even then, in the end, the one temporarily left out would get their own satisfying conclusion.

Even better, she might want to try sitting back herself and see how horny she became simply watching the two men pleasure each other. She mentally added that to her to-do list. Yes, it could be quite the thrill to be able to watch

Cam and Nolan together without any distractions pulling at her.

Again, not this time.

The simplest way to keep things equal for their first time would be for Cam to fuck Nolan as Nolan fucked Hope. She quickly worked out the logistics in her head.

Since she'd only had anal once before, her being in the middle was out. At least for now. She was definitely for it but knew it would take some time and preparation for double penetration. She quickly added that to her ever-expanding list, too.

It would probably be best to keep Nolan in the middle, with him fucking her and Cam fucking him.

Keep it simple. They could experiment with different positions later, once they worked out the kinks.

The only thing that needed to be decided in that moment was if she was to be the front of this three-person train, did she want to be on her stomach or on her back when Nolan fucked her?

Her back was the clear winner. She wanted to watch the men interact. Her pussy twinged with anticipation and excitement.

Please let this go well.

She worried about being too bossy, or not bossy enough. The beginning of a relationship—even a casual one—could be difficult enough when trying to learn what one partner liked, loved, or hated, but with two?

Even if it turned out to be complicated, she believed it would be worth the effort. On the remote chance it wasn't, it would still be an experience she'd never forget. One she never expected to check off her sexual bucket list.

But here she was.

The clearing of a throat brought her focus back to the bed.

Oops.

She hadn't meant to make them wait and edge them this way. If anything, she was surprised they didn't get started without her.

But both men stared at her with more patience than she ever would've had. She gave them a smile of apology and pulled herself to the top of the bed. "Condoms?"

Cam held up two before passing one to Nolan, who immediately went to work rolling it down his thick, veiny cock. Cam did the same before grabbing the nearby lube to drizzle some on his own erection.

Before he was done, he paused and looked up with his brow furrowed. "Mistress, you didn't confirm if—"

"Nolan will be in the middle."

With another relieved nod, he continued generously lubing his cock in preparation of what was about to come next.

Which, if everything went smoothly, would be all three of them.

Hope extended a hand to Nolan. "I'm more than ready for you, Hot Stuff. If your hip action is anything like your tongue action..."

Nolan grinned and stroked his cock. "I aim to please, Mistress."

Hope spread her legs farther apart, making room for him as Nolan moved into place, still stroking. She doubted his cock needed any encouragement to stay hard.

Or did it because she was a woman?

Shit. Don't let the doubts take over.

When Nolan planted his hands on the mattress, he leaned

down and brushed his lips over hers, light, gentle, his breath mingling with hers as the thrill of what they were about to do began to pool in her core. He dipped his head, pulling one of her aching nipples into his mouth as he slid the head of his cock through her slick folds, from her clit all the way down to the place she knew might get a rude awakening if the sexual relationship between the three of them progressed.

But after he did it about a half dozen times, she realized Nolan was only teasing her.

"Hot Stuff..." she warned.

"You're ready for me to fuck you, Mistress."

Of course she was! "As if you can't tell."

One side of his mouth pulled up. He was so damn handsome that it made her toes curl. They both were.

"I'm ready to make you squirt all over me like you did when I ate you out," Nolan told her.

"I hope that's not a promise you can't keep," she said as he pushed the head of his cock against her opening. No more teasing.

"If I fail you, Mistress, then I accept any punishment you'll dole out."

She wasn't into any punishment that wouldn't be fun for both parties. She wasn't a true Domme. She was simply having a blast playing one in this case. Of course, Cam already knew that. Maybe he hadn't shared that with Nolan?

It didn't matter. If he was determined to get her to squirt as well as come, she'd be a fool to deny it.

Digging her fingernails into his ass, she pulled him forward. Instead of sliding into her in one sudden stroke, he moved slowly, giving her his cock little by little.

Now *that* was what she would call punishment.

She wrapped her legs around him and lifted her hips to encourage him to go faster. She *could* order him to hurry up and get to business, but she'd rather just let it play out naturally.

"Oh *yessss*," she hissed when he was filling her completely and deliciously stretching her.

"Stay there still until I get settled," Cam murmured to Nolan as he shuffled forward on his knees.

With Nolan's hard-on deep inside her, it was difficult not to automatically thrust against him and encourage him to do the same.

With his head turned, Nolan watched Cam over his shoulder as he did the same thing Nolan had done to her. After dripping more Swiss Navy between Nolan's cheeks, he dragged his cock up and down, spreading the lube.

When Cam caught his bottom lip between his teeth and focused on his target, Hope knew the party was officially starting.

All systems go.

Nolan met her eyes as Cam pushed forward. She searched carefully for any signs that he was in discomfort.

He was not.

In fact, his expression turned soft and his mouth went slack, making it obvious how much he wanted Cam. Or at least wanted Cam inside him.

Hope could understand that. Cam was an experienced and attentive lover.

"You move," Cam told Nolan in a strained voice. "You can pick the pace."

When Nolan slowly dragged himself from her pussy, she realized he was also pushing himself back onto Cam's cock, his deep sigh of pleasure only ratcheting up her own.

He started out moving slowly, most likely seeing how this all would work and probably trying not to dislodge Cam's cock, but the intensity in his eyes quickly sharpened and he quickly found a pace that worked for all of them.

He could've been choppy and awkward, but he was far from that.

Just as the beginnings of her next orgasm began to build, she hit a button on the remote to the butt plug.

A sound she never heard before came from Cam, just before his hips pistoned forward, causing Nolan to cry out in what she hoped was pleasure and slam into her to the hilt, the fullness nearly overwhelming her.

If that was how Cam reacted when she had it turned low, she couldn't wait to see what happened when she cranked it up a notch. Or two.

Because that was her plan. She needed to wait, though, since she didn't want him to come too quickly. That toy would cause him to lose his mind if it was seated properly and hitting the right spot.

However, she *could* use it to edge him.

Now *there* was an idea! Especially since he declared he would never use his safe word. She was now determined to be the reason he did.

Not because of too much pain, but because of too much pleasure.

Chapter Nineteen

NOLAN STRUGGLED to control his breathing. He wanted to snort and paw and ram Hope like a horny bull. However, he reminded himself that he couldn't screw this up. He was the one in the "hot seat," after all.

While it was one thing to fuck Hope, it was quite another experience to have Cam fucking him at the same time. It was an effort to concentrate on both what he was doing to Hope and what Cam was doing to him.

The vibrations of the plug cam wore working their way into him through the man's cock certainly weren't helping anything.

He needed to keep his head and keep a hold of his control. He wasn't sure how Cam was managing it himself. Maybe from staying still, for the most part, and letting Nolan spear himself on his cock.

At least concentrating on moving like he had ball-bearings in his hips helped keep Nolan from coming in thirty seconds flat.

Because damn...

To be balls deep in a hot, slick pussy at the same time he had a man balls deep in him...

If he'd known how crazy good this felt, he would've participated in a threesome sooner.

What was he thinking? No, he wouldn't have. He was doing it at the right time with the right people. Two people he was attracted to and with whom he had a connection. They weren't some random sex partners hooking up to simply get off.

Cam was much more than that to him. Hope could be that, too, if she wanted the same.

When Hope turned up the intensity on the butt plug once more, Nolan gritted his teeth and tried to ignore it. He failed when Cam blew out a sharp breath that whispered along his spine and tensed. He pulled back to the point that only the tip remained inside Nolan and his fingers squeezed Nolan's hips almost to the point of pain. The tension in his plea, "Mistress..." was obvious.

Clearly, the man was struggling.

"Is it too much?" Her question sounded husky. Oh yes, she was getting off on edging poor Cam. She held a lot of power in her palm with that little remote.

"Yes—"

"Too bad. What was your safe word, again? The one you think you'll never have to use?"

Nolan must have missed something. Was she trying to force him to say it?

"Oklahoma."

His head spun to glance at Cam behind him. *Oklahoma?* Cam could explain that choice later. When they were less busy.

She grabbed Nolan's chin and turned his face until their

gazes locked. No surprise, she wore a sly grin, confirming that she was purposely edging him.

"Do you have a safe word, Hot Stuff?"

Uh oh. "No."

"Now you do. It's Sequoia." At least she picked a word familiar to him. He owned the one parked out in front of the cabin, after all.

"Sequoia." Nolan repeated, testing how easily it slipped from his tongue.

"Will that work?"

Did he have a choice? "Yes, Mistress."

"I doubt you'll need it tonight, but it can't hurt to be prepared."

Hurt was an interesting choice of word. It would make his asshole pucker if Cam wasn't already stretching it open.

CAM WAS ABOUT to lose his shit much sooner than expected if she kept playing with the setting on that damn vibrating toy shoved up his ass.

Normally, he'd be into it, but nothing about tonight was *normal.* This was unchartered territory for the three of them.

His teeth were clenched so tightly, he was surprised he hadn't shattered them. A muscle in his jaw ticked fiercely as he continued to fight an orgasm.

It was too soon to come.

It was too soon to come.

Nolan ramming his ass into Cam's cock before shifting forward to ram his cock into Hope was already making him unravel. Adding that damn toy, though...

Did she want this threesome to go sideways?

Two—or three—could play at that game.

He wrapped one arm around Nolan's hips to indicate he

should sit up more, and as soon as he did, Cam reached around the man with his other arm to find Hope's clit. He just needed to make her forget she had that little torture device in her palm before she turned it up to the max setting.

Because if she did, he might end up flopping around on the floor like a fish out of water. Or scream "Oklahoma."

Since he already said it once, he was determined not to say it again. He couldn't wait to torture her until she cried out her own safe word. *Shanti*, wasn't it?

But not this time. It would have to be when both he and Nolan could concentrate solely on her. Maybe in one of the playrooms up in Heaven.

Hell yes. He and Nolan might have to come up with a plan. Let her think she'd be in control, then turn the tables on her.

Tie her up and turn her ass red. Fuck her mouth, her pussy, *and* her ass...

Going down that rabbit hole was not helping his dilemma. In that moment, his goal was to get Hope to come soon, so Nolan and he could do the same.

Because Cam needed to come five minutes ago. *That* was the real torture. Not having a vibrating butt plug jammed up his ass.

Suddenly, Nolan began to pick up the pace, slamming back onto Cam and then forward into Hope. She threw her head back and cried, "Oh my God. That's it. Right there. Both of you keep doing what you're doing."

He didn't need that order. He had already planned on doing so since he was on a mission. And now it seemed so was Nolan. He was probably clinging precariously to his sanity, too. One of them had to go first and he needed it to be Hope.

Rocking forward from the impact of Nolan's thrusts, she

grabbed one of her breasts and squeezed. Of course she kept that damn remote securely in her other hand. Maybe if she didn't have that, he wouldn't be in such a panic.

Who was he trying to kid? He was fucking the man he'd lusted after for years. And that man was fucking the first woman in the last few years who Cam wanted more than once in his bed.

Cam dragged his fingers from her sensitive clit to where Nolan was pounding her, to the point where they connected. A place he had also claimed thoroughly.

When Nolan grit out a, "Fuck," Cam pressed his face against his warm, damp neck and went back to thumbing Hope's clit with a vengeance.

But instead of pushing back against Cam in another thrust, Nolan's hips twitched and his asshole began to tighten.

Shit.

"Hold on," Cam whispered against Nolan's ear. "She's almost there."

"I—"

"Hold on. As soon as she comes, we can, too."

"I'm not sure—"

"You can," Cam said more forcefully. But then, what he was telling Nolan he was telling himself, too.

Hold on just a few more minutes.

But, damn, Nolan's ass was so damn tight and he made it worse every time he clamped around Cam.

He wanted to cry with relief when Hope's back arched, her eyes squeezed shut and her mouth opened on a silent scream.

"She's coming," Nolan announced unnecessarily. His head was hanging down and he was white-knuckling her hips while she slammed her pussy against him a few more times before collapsing back to the mattress.

"Come for me," Cam whispered.

When Nolan thrust one last time, Cam went with him. Keeping him close, driving deep.

Nolan's canal pulsated around Cam's throbbing cock, setting of fireworks in his vision and sending his head spinning.

And—

What the fuck?

Hope turned that damn thing on high and he just about hit the ceiling, his vision momentarily fading to black with the intensity.

She lifted her head, opened her eyes, and did a half-assed attempt to smother a smile. "Oops."

He snagged the remote from her hand, switched it off, then tossed it out of her reach. "Ever hear the saying, paybacks are a bitch?"

"I look forward to it," Hope said with a wink.

"We'll see," Cam warned.

Hope, with her chest still heaving and beads of sweat clinging to her forehead, asked, "Why did I wait so long to have a threesome?"

"Maybe because we weren't in your life?"

Hope laugh-snorted. "That could be one reason."

Cam tapped Nolan's hip. "Okay, let's disengage before we leave a real mess. Ready?" He collared the full condom, and as soon as Nolan nodded, Cam slowly pulled free. He slipped the condom off while watching Nolan do the same with Hope.

Once they both took their turn in the bathroom cleaning up, Cam and Nolan settled on the bed on either side of Hope.

Cam was pleased to see that she looked completely relaxed and satisfied. A soft smile curved her lips and her eyelids were heavy. It wouldn't take long for her to be out, and based on the slow, lazy circles Nolan's fingers were tracing on her hip, he wasn't far behind her. Cam understood the feeling.

They needed to save up their energy so they could do this all over again. Except next time they would switch up the configuration. "That worked out better than expected. I really thought our first time together would be a disaster, with arms and legs all over the place. And a severe lack of coordination."

"Same," Nolan whispered, his eyelids also drooping. "Next time, Hope should be in the middle."

"That would mean..." Cam let that drift off.

"Double penetration," she finished. "I'm up for working towards that goal, but not tonight."

Nolan's yawn turned into a grin. "There's always your mouth in the meantime. We can take turns."

Hope chuckled softly. "Already scheming, I see."

"We'll take your cue. Whatever you want, Hope." Cam twisted his head toward her to see her blinking up at the ceiling. "Do you plan on staying?"

"The night?" she turned her head enough to meet his eyes.

"Of course," Cam answered.

"You don't think the bed will be too crowded for actual sleeping?"

It might be a little tight but they could make do. It was better than sending Hope home. "I don't think I have the brain cells left for another round. I don't think any of us will have a problem sleeping."

"Good point." She released a loud, exaggerated sigh.

"Fine. Twist my arm. I'll stay. Luckily, I threw an overnight bag in my car just in case. And it certainly will shorten the commute for my class tomorrow morning." She lifted her head and looked back and forth between them. "You boys are joining me for that, aren't you?"

"We usually hit the trails in the morning."

"Riding a mountain bike through the woods is great cardio, but it isn't going to help with your flexibility. And that needs to improve if we're going to continue doing this."

Nolan snorted. "Are you saying we were stiff?"

She reached out and patted their cheeks at the same time. "You two were certainly stiff. But seriously, I only teach yoga here three days a week. You can ride on those other mornings."

"Do we have to?" Nolan teased, his voice petulant through his grin.

Hope laughed. "Do I need to make it an order?"

"We'll be there," Cam assured her. "But in the meantime, how about we get some shut eye since your class is at the crack of dawn."

"The class is at seven."

"Same thing. I consider anything before my first cup of coffee the crack of dawn."

"Maybe it's time to stop drinking coffee," she sassed.

"I'm rethinking the invite for you to spend the night," Cam grumbled.

Chapter Twenty

Strong, tanned arms with sexy-as-fuck veins appearing like roads on a map caged Cam against the dresser. Nolan's mouth pressed to his ear. "I just wanted you to know that you are the reason I never had a long-term relationship. I could never settle. I figured I'd be single for the rest of my life because no one lived up to you. No one made me desire them as much as I desired you."

Those whispered words made his heart swell.

All those years they wasted pining for each other...

If only they had sat down and had an honest conversation.

But he understood.

Cam turned within his lover's arms so he could face him. "We've been doing pretty damn well making up for lost time."

Nolan grinned. "My ass agrees."

"It's a very nice ass."

"I figured, since you're always staring at it."

One side of Cam's mouth hooked upward. "I do more than stare at it."

"You know, I thought I caught you staring at it in the locker room a few times, but back then, I chalked it up to wishful thinking."

"Well, you didn't imagine it. I couldn't help myself. I kept hoping it would be mine one day. And now it is."

They were in the midst of getting dressed for dinner with Hope at The Mane Lodge. Afterward, they planned to spend a couple of hours playing up in Heaven.

Over the last few weeks, they had worked on preparing Hope for double penetration. She was determined to take both Nolan and Cam at the same time.

Far be it from Cam or Nolan to discourage it, despite both of them assuring her it wasn't necessary. They were perfectly fine with everything she had done so far.

The sex had been great. The intimacy great. The company great.

They had fallen into an easy companionship.

Sometimes Cam took the lead, but mostly it was Hope. Nolan didn't care either way. He was happy doing the fucking or getting fucked.

He had quickly settled into his position as assistant head of security. Of course, compared to being a state trooper, the work was so much more stress free. His presence had definitely freed up some time for Cam.

They took turns being on-call. Though, rarely was there an incident worthy enough for one of the guards to contact either of them during those late hours.

A guest would have to become belligerent, be trashed out of their mind or harassing employees or other guests. Cam or Nolan were the only two, outside of the execs, who had the power to make the final decision on whether a guest was eighty-sixed from the property. And if they were, they did not get a refund.

In all the months that Cam had worked at Double D, only one guest had made a total ass of himself. The man was quickly escorted off the property and blacklisted from ever returning.

The guy had become overly jealous and possessive over another guest he had hooked up with the night before. He didn't want her hooking up with anyone else.

That behavior was not tolerated at the Double D Ranch.

For the most part, the resort's guests were happy. The food was great, the property and views stunning, the activities endless and, of course, not too many people were disgruntled after having loads of dirty, kinky fun.

Quite the opposite, actually.

Which was why Cam didn't worry when Hope practiced her naked yoga somewhere on the property. He had zero concerns about her being assaulted, or even insulted. She had the complete freedom to be her confident self.

A few weeks ago, he caught two of his guards watching her do her routine on one of the live cameras. They hadn't been focused on her nudity, they were more impressed with how she could fold herself in half with ease. Or do a perfect headstand. Or contort herself into what she explained was the Scorpion pose.

And those were only a few of the advanced poses she could do.

Nudity and sex out in the open was so normal at the Double D, his team no longer blinked an eye when seeing it.

Cam agreed with his team members. Her flexibility was impressive. He was still struggling not to fall over when trying to balance on one foot in the deceptively simple Tree pose.

"When will Hope be here?"

Nolan's question pulled him from his wandering thoughts. "Soon."

"Then I should let you finish getting dressed."

"We have time."

Nolan cocked an eyebrow. "For?"

"This." Cam grabbed both sides of his face and crashed their lips together. He couldn't get enough of making out with Nolan. His lips were soft, but firm, and he was a hell of a kisser.

As their tongues tangled and their breathing meshed, Nolan grabbed Cam's hips and yanked him closer to grind their cocks together.

Cam was tempted to have a quickie. Just yank down Nolan's jeans and bend him over. Knowing Hope, if she showed up in the middle of it, she would simply lean against the door jamb and watch until they were finished, then probably make them repeat the scenario again whenever they got up to Heaven.

As hungry as Cam was—not just for Nolan's mouth, but for actual food—he was impatient for dinner to be over so they could go play.

When he checked Heaven's schedule and found the sensory playroom was free, he was able to book Room Five for two whole hours.

This would be the first time Cam got a chance to use it.

Designed for the users to explore all their senses, the room had a fridge full of food that could be used during sex play, like whipped cream and strawberries. The freezer section had items like ice cubes and popsicles. Other food items were also stocked that stimulated the senses like bananas, Pop Rocks, and flavored syrups.

Whoever had added Pop Rocks to the list was a genius.

He might have to toss some in his mouth and suck Nolan's cock or Hope's nipples while they crackled and popped.

If she was willing, they'd strap Hope down to the massage table and drive her out of her mind by using feathers, hot wax, an electro whip, and maybe even a vampire glove.

To start.

While Hope might not be ready for double penetration yet, her mouth could be used for something more than licking chocolate syrup off either man.

If it was up to him, he'd skip dinner completely, but a growling stomach wasn't sexy. Food was fuel and they'd need to keep their energy up for their two-hour sexcapades.

Cam tipped his head back enough to end the kiss. "You keep kissing me like that and dinner will be delayed."

"I'm sure Hope won't—"

A knock on the door had their heads twisting toward the front of the cabin and their eyes meeting in confusion.

"Did you lock the door?"

Cam shook his head. "No."

They normally left the door unlocked and Hope walked in whenever she arrived. They were past the point of formality, especially since she now stayed over the nights before her early morning yoga classes on the ranch. They occasionally went over to her place on other nights.

They had fallen into an easy rhythm. Sharing meals, beds, and orgasms.

They spent a lot of time together, learning each other's hopes, dreams and secrets as well as exploring new territory when it came to sex.

Of course, they had a lot of it.

Luckily, Hope had no issue when it came to the men having sex without her. In fact, she actually encouraged it, whether she was there watching or not.

"Maybe it's one of the guys needing something," Nolan suggested.

Cam's eyes flicked to the portable radio he kept in the cabin, or on him when he wasn't at home, so he could be easily reached by anyone on his team.

Another rap at the door had them separating and Cam taking long strides through the small cabin with Nolan trailing more slowly.

When Cam opened the door, his head jerked back. Standing on his tiny porch was someone he had not expected.

Laurel.

His heart leapt into his throat as he stared at his daughter.

Both he and Nolan were bare-chested and barefooted. While Laurel knew Nolan was coming to work for her father, she did not know they were sharing a cabin.

Or a bed.

Shit.

Cam swallowed his pounding heart back down as he stepped back and gave her space to step over the threshold.

"Hi, honey. It's good to see you." He did his best to sound convincing.

"Dad," she greeted and paused next to him to rise up on her toes to kiss his cheek. When she was flat on her feet again, she directed a smile toward Nolan. "Nolan, it's good to see you. It's been a while."

"It has. Look at you, all grown up."

Laurel flipped a hand in his direction. "Look at *you*. Nice chest." She lifted an eyebrow.

Grimacing, Nolan turned to Cam and mumbled, "Let me go grab a shirt." He rushed back into the bedroom and, of course, shut the door for privacy.

Damn it.

Laurel's head tipped to the side as her gaze sliced from

the closed bedroom door to Cam. "You seem to be missing yours also."

Cam scratched his ear. "We were getting ready for dinner."

Laurel's gaze landed on the couch. "I thought Nolan was only staying with you temporarily."

"He is. It's only been a...month." Or so.

"I thought it was only for a few nights, not weeks. But... you're sharing your bedroom? I thought your couch was a sleeper sofa."

Cam's nostrils flared as he pulled in a breath, then puffed out his cheeks to delay his answer.

Laurel's dark brown eyes drilled into him and suspicion laced her next words. "What's going on here, Dad?"

It was past time to let his daughter know the truth. He'd hidden it long enough. She was either going to accept him being bisexual or she wouldn't. And if she wouldn't, he needed to know this now rather than later when Nolan and he were in it even deeper.

However, he and his ex raised a well-rounded, intelligent woman. As far as he knew, she had no issues with the LGBTQ+ community. However, her dad having a relation-ship with another man might hit a little too close to home.

He hoped he was worrying for nothing. "Nolan is more than my number two guy, Laurel. He's my number one."

She shook her head. "I know he's your assistant head of security, but does that mean he's taking over your spot?"

"No." *He's taking over my heart.* "We're...more than friends."

"Yes, you're co-workers."

"More than that."

Every second ticked off in his head as he waited for her to figure it out.

"Dad!" Her eyes went wide and she did not temper her exasperation. "You're lovers?"

Ding. Ding. Ding. "Yes."

She snapped her gaping mouth closed. "Holy shit! I knew you two were close, but I had no idea you felt *that way* about Nolan."

"Neither did Nolan."

She pressed her fingers to her lips. "Wow, so both of you are gay." It wasn't a question but a surprised statement.

"No, not gay. We both like women, too."

"So, that's how you kept it a secret. And Mom? Does she —*did* she know?"

"Yes. It was something we discussed in depth when we separated. But nobody else knew." He was now glad he'd had that in-depth conversation with his ex. Laurel might not like the idea that Cam hid his sexuality from her, but she would hate it even more if he had hidden it from her mother.

"Why did you feel the need to hide it?"

That answer was easy, and one she'd understand. "I did what I had to do while I worked at PSP."

Her eyes filled with sorrow. "Dad..."

He hated when his baby girl was sad. He'd wiped too many of her tears away while she was growing up. He didn't want to be the reason for more. Only, she wasn't upset about him being bi, but because he had to hide it. He was proud of how she turned out to be so accepting of others.

"It's fine, honey."

Her shoulders pulled back and her chin raised. "Well, now you're free to do what you want to do."

There was the confident warrior he helped raise. "Yes and nobody here will look at me any differently."

"Well then...I'm happy that you can finally live your truth, Dad."

She sounded a lot more confident in that than what he felt. "We'll see."

"Did Nolan hide it, too?"

"He did."

"So both of you wanted to be more than friends but never admitted it?"

Unfortunately. "Yes."

Laurel rushed over, wrapped her arms around his waist and squeezed him tight. "Oh, Dad." She rested her cheek on his chest. A good reminder that he was still shirtless.

He enveloped her more tightly, because what father didn't love his girl's hugs?

Now that his daughter was here, tonight's plans would have to change. Or at least be delayed. He tucked two fingers under her chin and tipped her face up. "Why didn't you tell me you were coming?"

"I wanted to surprise you. I figured you were lonely since we haven't had much of an opportunity to spend time together. I had no idea—"

"Laurel, I live on a resort constantly full of people. I hardly have a chance to be lonely."

"I mean be with someone who loves you..." When she pulled out of his arms, her brown eyes were wide. She slapped his bare chest and stage-whispered, "Wait. Do you love each other? Is this like, serious?"

He wasn't sure how to answer that, especially with Nolan right on the other side of the door. He shot a glance toward the bedroom. He kept his voice low when he explained, "It's leaning toward serious, but we haven't said the *L* word."

Yet. Cam knew what was in his heart, but he wasn't sure about Nolan.

Anyway, they were in no rush since they were still getting to know each other as more than friends. A lot more.

Plus, a relationship hit differently when you spent just about twenty-four-seven with someone.

Besides his ex-wife, Cam had never lived with anyone before. And the cabin was small enough they could easily get on each other's nerves. While that hadn't happened yet, it didn't mean it wouldn't eventually. If their relationship continued to grow, they might have to find a bigger place.

However, if it came to that, he doubted it would be on the ranch.

"But you feel that strongly about him," Laurel concluded.

"I have for a long time, but being"—*sexually involved*—"together just made it stronger."

"So, *Uncle* Nolan might become *Daddy* Nolan?"

Chapter Twenty-One

Cam grimaced at the term *Daddy*. In certain situations, one adult calling another adult Daddy hit differently. "You're rushing things, honey. This is all new for us. Just because we're...uh...seeing each other doesn't mean a wedding is in the near future." Or ever.

"New? You've known each other for years."

"Yes, but in a different capacity." He needed to change the subject before Nolan came out of the bedroom. It certainly didn't take this long to tug on a shirt, so he had to be giving them some privacy. "We're heading to dinner, Laurel. You'll join us, right?"

She shot him a huge smile. "Of course! I was hoping you hadn't eaten yet since the food was excellent the last time I was here. I actually planned on spending the night, but I don't want to intrude."

When she wiggled her eyebrows, Cam silently groaned in his head while forcing his expression to remain neutral. "You can absolutely stay the night. You're the reason I have a pull-out bed in the first place."

Her staying the night meant their regularly scheduled programming would definitely be preempted since his daughter would always be priority.

The front door opened and a female voice preceded the person it belonged to. "Hey, whose Honda is in my spot? I had to park—" Hope's feet stuttered to a stop as she took in the scene. "I hope I'm not interrupting something important? You said six, right?"

"I did." He glanced at his daughter to see her brow furrowed.

Surprise, honey! Not only am I doing a man, I'm also doing a woman at the same time!

He swallowed all of that back down.

Hope's eyes flicked between the two of them as she hovered near the door. "Should I go?"

"No. Please stay!" Laurel practically shouted with quite a bit of enthusiasm.

Shit.

"Let me introduce you two. Hope Reed, this is my daughter, Laurel. Laurel, this is the resort's yoga instructor, Hope."

Laurel spun on him. "Wait. You're now into yoga? Any other surprises you need to tell me?"

"I'm definitely benefitting from yoga," he said carefully.

Nolan chose that moment to exit the bedroom.

"And so is Nolan," Hope added so helpfully.

"You're doing yoga, too?"

"Only when guilted into it," Nolan answered. "How's school, Laurel?"

"Boring compared to this."

Cam turned to Nolan. "Do you want to take Laurel over to the lodge? We'll catch up in a few minutes. I need to finish getting dressed."

Laurel linked her arm with Nolan's. "I'm starving and I

can't wait to hear more about you and Dad." She glanced at Hope. "And you too, Hope."

Hope, Nolan, and Cam shared glances. Nolan gave the slightest nod, enough so Cam knew he understood the assignment. Which was basically: careful how you answer.

As Nolan guided Cam's daughter out the door, she asked, "So, how are you liking it here, Nolan?"

At least she didn't call him *Daddy* Nolan to his face.

Once the door closed, Hope said, "I guess her visit wasn't planned?"

"No." He tipped his head toward the bedroom. "I need to grab a shirt."

Hope raked her gaze over his chest. "Shame. But the rules are the rules."

The restaurant was one of the few areas on the resort where nudity or public sex was forbidden.

Hope followed on his heels. "I'm assuming our plans are cancelled for the evening."

He'd need to cancel the playroom's reservation once he got to the lodge. "Yes. Sorry. She arrived right before you did so I didn't have time to cancel your trip here."

"It's okay, Handsome. It's not like I'm sex starved or anything." She laughed. "Anyway, Nolan can come home with me after dinner if you want to spend some time alone with your daughter."

"Knowing what you two will be doing will be distracting, but yes, that might be for the best. Laurel has known Nolan for a long time but not in this capacity." Though, Nolan going home with Hope would most likely open up a whole new discussion.

His daughter had a good head on her shoulders and not much got by her. Just like her old man.

"She seems to be taking it well."

He pulled a polo shirt out of his dresser drawer and slipped it over his head. "We raised her to be open-minded and to treat everyone equally."

But would she be open-minded enough to accept that her father was not only in a relationship with Nolan but with Hope, too?

Should he even bring it up at all at this point? Their little triad hadn't made any commitment to each other. They were simply going with the flow right now. He saw no reason to rush into anything serious.

"How about this? Why don't we have dinner and hang out for a bit at the lodge. Afterward—if Nolan's okay with it, of course—we'll head to my place." She gave him a naughty grin. "Or he and I can use that playroom you booked."

Cam finished tucking in his shirt and fastening his belt. "Oh no. You two are not using that room without me. I was looking forward to trying it for the first time."

"Then reschedule. I'm looking forward to it, too." Hope lightly scraped her short nails down his beard. "I'll miss you tickling me between my thighs tonight."

"Nolan's got a beard."

"Not as rough as yours. Maybe I can convince him to grow his out a little more."

Cam stared at the upward curl of her lips. "*Mmm.* I might not have time to tickle you between the thighs but we have enough time for this..."

He took her mouth and they shared a brief kiss. Anything more than that would get his blood rushing south.

But before he finished pulling away, Hope murmured, "Damn. I'm going to miss these lips," against them. "How long is she staying?"

"I'd assume only tonight since I don't think she has

classes tomorrow, but I know she does on Thursday. She's probably here to work me over for more money."

"Does she do that often?"

"No. And that's why I usually give in. If it's for necessities, that's one thing, but if it's for new shoes or a purse, she's shit out of luck."

"I don't blame you." Hope smacked him on the ass. "Okay, Handsome, let's go get some grub. My stomach is growling and I'm sure you're anxious to spend some time with your lovely daughter."

He was.

Speaking of...

"Hey." He grabbed her arm and stopped her from heading out of the bedroom. "Make sure Nolan doesn't stay over at your place all night. Laurel will wonder why he's not here, especially now that she knows we're sharing a bed." And that would spur further questions he wasn't ready to answer about Hope.

She raised an eyebrow. "You don't want her to know that we're *all* sharing a bed."

"Does that bother you?"

"Not at all."

"I just don't want her to think—"

Hope raised a palm. "I get it, Handsome."

Good. Now he could relax and enjoy dinner with his newly expanded family. Because that was what it was beginning to feel like. A patchwork family unit.

———

DINNER WENT SMOOTHLY, and after eating, they spent an hour hanging out in the lodge where all four of them shared some easy conversation.

Hope was great with Laurel. Thankfully, they seemed to get along just fine. Though, just as he figured, Laurel suspected that Hope was more than simply a friend or a Double D employee.

He'd expected his daughter to drill him about their relationship once Hope and Nolan left for the evening. He was surprised and a bit suspicious when she didn't.

Once they got back to the cabin, they hung out on the couch, ate some ice cream, and watched a movie together. Something they used to do a lot when she was younger.

His baby girl was growing up too quickly. She would soon be a college grad.

Jesus, that made him feel old.

As well as proud.

Also, just like he used to do when she was a little girl, once the movie was over, Cam tucked her in and pressed a kiss to her forehead before turning out the lights and heading to bed himself.

Unfortunately, sleep did not come.

His thoughts kept drifting to the unknown: what Nolan and Hope were doing without him. It quickly became clear that FOMO—fear of missing out—was a real thing he'd never experienced before.

While Laurel hinted that she guessed that Hope was more than a friend, she never came right out and asked. It could be she expected her father to admit it on his own. Or maybe she thought Nolan didn't know something was going on between Cam and Hope. Or between Hope and Nolan. When in reality, that could be farther from the truth.

He didn't want his daughter thinking badly of Hope at all, which could happen. Laurel would always side with her father or Nolan over someone new.

When he forced his eyes closed again, a more erotic movie began to play on the back of his eyelids.

One where a very naked Hope wore a strap-on and was pegging Nolan.

His cock stirred.

No, you horny bastard, you cannot masturbate with your daughter right in the next room.

Not only did the bedroom door not have a lock, when Laurel was younger, she used to sneak into bed with him and her mother in the middle of the night. Of course, it had been years, but no way would he risk getting caught jerking off.

He closed his eyes again, slowed his breathing, cleared his perverted thoughts, and willed himself to sleep. When that didn't work, he jackknifed straight up, shoved off the covers, rolled to his feet, and yanked on a pair of cotton shorts he kept within reach.

Cracking open the bedroom door, he peered out to see the glow of Laurel's cell phone lighting up her face.

Of course. Probably watching TikTok or texting her friends.

He opened the door wider and quietly padded out to the pull-out bed to sit on the edge.

The second his ass met the mattress, the phone went dark and so did the room. *Shit.*

"Hey, Dad, what's up? Is something wrong?"

"No, I need to talk to you about something, but we need a little bit of light first." Trying to read his daughter's emotions in the dark would be impossible. He reached over and switched on the small lamp on the side table, giving the room a soft glow.

"Is this something about Nolan?"

"Sort of. Yes." He squeezed her blanket-covered knee. "I want to be completely honest with you about our situation."

Her brow furrowed. "Situation?"

"With Hope."

"Okay?"

He thought she was catching on earlier at the lodge, but maybe he'd been wrong. Maybe he should've let this whole thing lie. "I figured you suspected something."

"Well, I mean, she walked right into your cabin without knocking. I guess friends do that, but honestly, the way she looked at you, Dad, made me wonder why Nolan went home with her."

"What do you mean?"

"Her camaraderie with you seems to be completely natural. She was faking nothing. Not the warm look in her eyes and certainly not the way she smiled at you. I also noticed how much she touched both you and Nolan. And all three of you were comfortable with it. The only thing I found odd was how, when she touched one of you, the other showed no signs of jealousy. That made me believe you were all just close friends."

"How are you so smart?"

"Your blood fills my veins. And Mom's, too, of course. She's pretty freaking smart."

"That it does. And yes she is."

"Dad, you were also a great cop and taught me to be observant."

"That I did." *Jesus*, he was proud of her earlier, now that pride was shining like a light beam shooting straight out of his chest.

"Are you about to tell me that you're more than friends?"

"That I am."

She blinked, then worried on her bottom lip. "Like friends with benefits or something more?"

"Right now, I'd say friends with benefits fits the bill, but she's not seeing anyone else."

"Except Nolan. Why else would he go over to her house and still be out at"—she unlocked her phone and glanced at the time—"midnight?"

"Movies and ice cream?" he teased.

She pressed her lips together and rolled her eyes. "Dad, please. You just called me smart. What you're saying is Hope is sharing those friendly benefits with both you and Nolan?"

"Well,"—he scraped a hand down his bearded cheek—"yes." He couldn't believe he was having this conversation with his daughter.

"And neither of you are jealous of the other? Neither of you mind this arrangement?"

Shit. Now came the sticky part. "Honey..."

Her mouth gaped. "Wait."

He waited.

He could see her working through the math problem. Only, this had nothing to do with math.

Or did it?

"Are all three of you...uh..."—she circled a finger in the air—"doing things together *together*? Like, at the same time?"

"Yes."

"Isn't that illegal?"

A chuckle burst from him before he could stop it. "You're thinking of polygamy, not polyamory. Polygamy, which has to do with being married to more than one person, is illegal. Polyamory, which has to do with relationships, isn't."

"That means you three will never be able to get married to each other." Her mouth took a downward turn. "That's sad. Consenting adults should be able to legally marry whoever they want, whoever they're in love with."

"I agree. But again, this is all new. For me and Nolan. For

me and Hope. And for Nolan and Hope. Right now, we're simply enjoying each other's company."

She air quoted, "Enjoying," as she repeated it and gave him a *"Sure, Jan"* look.

"You're smart enough to figure it out and I'm certainly not going into details."

"Thankfully. Because *eww*, I don't want to think of my father having sex with anyone. That's the stuff of nightmares."

"I'd rather you not think of it, either. Believe me. And I'm the same way about you. Good thing you'll remain a virgin until I'm dead and buried."

His daughter's tinkling laugh filled the room. When she was done, she gave him a pitiful look. "Oh, Dad."

He raised a palm. "All I need to know is you're being safe and smart. Anything else I don't want to know."

"Good. Because I wasn't going to share." She sobered. "If this is what you want, then I'm happy for you."

"After hiding my bisexuality for the majority of my life, I can honestly say I'm happy now that I can be myself."

"Well, since I love Nolan and Hope seems to be just as awesome, I hope everything works out between you three."

So did Cam.

Chapter Twenty-Two

"Give me a show."

Nolan's cock twitched at that husky command.

Cam cocked an eyebrow at Hope. "Are you sure you don't want to join us?"

"We don't want to leave you out," Nolan added. Of course, she would never be left out. Her not directly participating didn't mean she wouldn't be involved. She just wanted to be calling the shots.

"You won't be. I'll be right here watching." She pointed to the throne on a raised platform. With a smile, she sat, adjusted her short, tight skirt, leaned back, and crossed her sculpted legs. "And tonight, you two will address me as Queen instead of Mistress." She rolled her lips under as she rolled her hand in the air like she was royalty.

They were in Room Seven, and apparently, he and Cam would be her "subjects."

Really, her being the "queen" was just a different twist from when she stepped into her dominant role.

"Will you be participating in your own way, *Queen?*" Cam asked with a grin.

"It depends on you two. Your mission is to make me so horny that I can't resist touching myself."

"And if we don't, *Your Highness?*"

Cam was pushing his luck by calling her that, but Nolan was all for it. While their role playing was hot, it still needed to be fun.

"What do you think?"

Cam shot a look at Nolan. "You know what that means."

"Give her a ten out of ten performance?"

"Well, that, too, but I was going to say don't hold back. If you need to whimper, beg, cry out...do so. Let her see and hear your reactions."

"That would be a good start," Hope said, tongue-in-cheek. "But you'll need to do more than that."

"We'll do plenty," Cam assured her.

"Then I look forward to this show, Handsome. The curtain is just about to rise. The performers should take their places," she suggested with a slight upward curve to her lips. "And this is where my direction ends."

Oh shit. Normally, she made the demands; what to do, how to do it, and how often. Now it was up to them to figure out what she wanted?

He and Cam shared a glance. The confidence in Cam's eyes silently told him that they had this.

True. However they played didn't have to be perfect. All they had to do was entertain their temporary queen. Similar to how court jesters used to entertain the royals. Only, Nolan doubted they did it naked and by fucking and sucking another man.

But then, he wasn't up on his history.

The Royalty Room had a lot of the same equipment and

toys found in most of the other playrooms up in Heaven, but what made this one unique was the color scheme—all shades of purple—and the fact that a raised platform with a throne was the main focus. At the foot of that throne was a very narrow kneeling bench without padding. Also unlike in some of the other themed rooms, the St. Andrew's Cross wasn't padded, either.

Similar to the Puppy Play room, it had a cage in the corner, but the one in Room Seven was wood and made for a human. It wasn't a dog crate, but tall and super narrow. The person standing in it would be forced to remain on their feet the whole time.

A fully adjustable obedience chair was bolted down to a platform similar to a Lazy Susan. It could be turned so the person sitting on the throne could see whatever action was happening.

Of course, Nolan fully expected to be the one in that chair with his legs strapped down and spread wide. The seat height could be raised or lowered depending on whether one was getting head or getting fucked.

"Handsome, there's a suggestion wheel here if you'd like. You can use it if you need ideas on how to entertain your queen. Come get it."

The Wheel of Misfortune included various ways to "torture" the occupants. Its location indicated that whomever was sitting on the throne normally spun it and directed the entertainers to do whatever it landed on.

Here, Hope wanted Cam to use it instead so she could simply sit back and enjoy the show.

After Nolan skimmed what was listed on the wheel, he internally cringed. Normally, he'd be fine with ass spanking—as long as it wasn't too brutal—but it said: slap balls/pussy. He usually didn't have a problem with a Wartenburg wheel, either, but if the arrow landed on that particular act, the spiked metal roller had to be used on genitals. And those were just two of the twelve pie wedges.

When Cam grabbed his face and pressed his mouth against Nolan's, it made him forget the wheel for a moment. He parted his lips and Cam took that advantage to fully explore his mouth. Closing his eyes, Nolan melted into the kiss while heat swept through him and stirred his cock in his cargo shorts. He wrapped one hand around the back of Cam's head, pulling them even closer together.

With Cam already hard and Nolan halfway there, Cam scrambled to tug Nolan's shirt off, temporarily separating them. He then quickly peeled off his own and tossed it to the side. When their lips crashed together again, Cam quickly dropped his shorts and seconds later, Nolan's were also pooled around his feet.

Cam ended the kiss and their eyes met as he stroked Nolan's erection, thumbing the bead of precum that clung to the very tip. Cam held it up in front of Nolan's face. "Lick my thumb clean."

"Are you giving the orders now?" Nolan asked under his breath.

"Since Hope is handing the reins over to us, do you mind if I lead?"

Wow. Nolan hadn't expected Cam to ask. He naturally stepped in as Hope's number two. Or vice versa. Nolan was the only one out of the three who never took a dominant role. It simply wasn't for him. He'd done enough of that during his time with the state police. At this point in his life, he was perfectly happy to let others take charge. "Now that you asked, I don't mind."

"Sorry to assume."

"Too much chatter, boys," came the scolding.

Their eyes met and their grins were there and gone in a flash.

Nolan leaned in and pulled Cam's thumb into his mouth, giving him an amused wink while he did it. The salty tang of his own precum hit his tastebuds and his cock twitched when Cam hooked his thumb and pressed down on his tongue.

"Damn, that was hot," Cam whispered, his brown eyes heated. "Are you ready?"

"I'm always ready for you." Nolan's eyes flicked to the wheel Cam had placed nearby. "I'm not sure if I'm ready for the Wheel of Misfortune, though."

Unfortunately, Cam didn't give him any reassurance. Instead, he led Nolan to the obedience chair and strapped him in. The quick-release nylon straps went over his shins, waist, and chest.

Cam had set the incline of the chair's back so Nolan was at an angle, neither completely sitting up straight or flat on his back. Next, the two sections where his legs were restrained were pushed wide and locked into place. That position would give Cam easy access.

Nolan lifted his unsecured hands. "What about these?"

With his brow furrowed, Cam walked his sexy, naked ass behind the obedience chair to check. "I can secure them back here to the D-rings."

Great. Maybe Nolan should've kept his big mouth shut.

"Hands behind your head," Cam ordered.

"That sounds familiar," Nolan muttered as he raised his arms and offered Cam his wrists. Luckily, the nylon straps were much softer than the metal handcuffs that usually accompanied those words.

If he had to be restrained, doing it for sexual reasons was much more preferred. Especially if done by Cam.

As he circled the chair again, Cam dragged his short

fingernails lightly over Nolan's chest, flicking both nipples before following the path of dark blond hair that led from his navel to his cock.

Cam pumped it a couple times with his fist, then dragged his hot, slick tongue from his ball sack to the crown.

"Head would be perfectly acceptable about now," Nolan told him under his breath since he wasn't sure if Hope would mind them conversing.

So far, she hadn't told them to shut up. And until she did...

"I don't think head is listed on the Wheel of Misfortune."

Of course not.

Nolan jerked his chin toward the small, custom wooden wheel attached to a metal stand. "Are you going to show me where it lands first so I can mentally prepare, or am I supposed to go into this blindly?"

"What do you prefer?"

Shit. Nolan wasn't sure. What would be better? Anticipation or surprise?

He took the easy route. "You decide."

Cam tipped his dark head in acceptance, then spun the wheel. Nolan's cock flexed at the ticking sound created by the metal arrow hitting the pins that separated each wedge.

Round and round it goes, where it stops, nobody knows.

He held his breath as the room fell silent, wondering what the outcome was. Would it land on a sex act he considered torture or pleasure? What was torture for some was pleasure for others and vice versa.

Cam turned the wheel so Nolan could see it.

Shit. Fuck. Shit.

Okay, maybe it was better not to know.

It might not have landed on the Wartenburg wheel,

where it would feel like tiny needles were pricking his own prick and sensitive sack, but it was almost as bad.

Slapping his family jewels.

He'd been kneed in the nuts once by a woman resisting arrest, and that had been more than enough, thank you very much. Hopefully, this wouldn't be half as debilitating.

When he met Cam's eyes, Nolan could see his struggle to keep from either panicking or throwing up. Proof he had also experienced being kicked between the legs.

Nolan wasn't gagged. He hadn't even been given a gag order. So he could easily use his safe word. However, he signed up for this.

No matter what, he wanted to please Cam. He also wanted to please Hope. Even so, he couldn't forget this was supposed to be for his pleasure, too.

"Ready?"

Would he ever be ready for what was about to happen next?

Nolan squeezed his eyes shut and gave a short nod.

Three, two, one...

Nolan struggled to pull oxygen back into his empty lungs after Cam slapped his balls so lightly it could be considered no more than a "love tap." It was an uncomfortable reminder of just how vulnerable a man was in that area and why protective cups were highly recommended, if not required, while playing sports.

Nolan flinched, then tensed when Cam held up his erection. The next slap had more power behind it and, while it stung a bit, it wasn't nearly as bad as his balls, thankfully.

He'd vote for a hard dick spanking over a light ball tap any time.

Nolan opened his eyes once more when he heard the wheel spinning again, just in time to see it land on edging. It was an activity that was part of their regular routine, but not to any extreme. Nolan wondered how far Cam would take it since they were putting on a show for their "queen." He might take it farther than usual.

"Remember, the tables might be turned one day soon," he whispered, loud enough for only Cam to hear.

While he didn't get an answer, the look in his lover's eyes was reassuring. Cam wasn't one to lose his head. However, after he tracked Cam going over to the bag of toys he'd brought along and pulling out one he hadn't seen before, Nolan's relief was short-lived.

He owned a Fleshlight and, in the past, had used it quite often, but this masturbation tool seemed to be a Fleshlight on steroids. You simply fucked a Fleshlight like a pussy. While Cam held the toy, he rotated through every setting as a demo.

From what Nolan could tell, the inside chamber not only spun, but sucked at seven different speeds. He imagined trying not to come was about to be a *wild* ride.

Nolan usually didn't last much more than a minute when he broke out his Fleshlight. It was definitely both fun and efficient.

However, this might not be the right toy for edging. Or it could be perfect for it. Time would tell. And that time was now.

Cam laid the masturbation aid on his stomach, using Nolan like a coffee table before grabbing a nearby bottle of lube that had been sitting on a warmer. When he returned, he squirted some into his palm and stroked Nolan's cock until it was completely covered.

Cam working Nolan's cock like that didn't help in prolonging his orgasm. He could easily come from his lover simply touching him. They had jerked each other off more times than he could count in the past couple of months.

Including times they were on the trails taking a "break" from mountain biking.

Nothing wrong with a little rub and tug while hydrating.

"Handsome, turn him so I can see both of you better."

Once Cam unlocked the rotating platform and turned it until Hope had an unobstructed view, he slid the masturbator down onto Nolan's cock and pressed the power button.

Nolan instantly lost his mind.

If the current setting was only the first of seven levels of suction, rotation speed, and licking, he was in some deep shit.

Cam moved to his side, put his mouth to Nolan's ear and whispered, "Don't come, whatever you do. If it gets to be too much, give me a sign and I'll back off. If you come before she gives the word, then she might come up with some crazy punishment for both of us."

"Just don't go up any more levels."

"What if she orders me to?"

"Then prepare yourself for punishment. Have you used this on yourself yet?" Nolan gritted his teeth, fighting the urge to come. He forced his hips to remain still because if he started humping it, he was doomed.

"No, I haven't had a chance. She just bought it and wanted me to use it on you."

Nolan unclenched his jaws. "Just wait until it's on you."

One dark eyebrow rose. "That good, huh?"

"Yes, but bad for edging."

Cam muttered, "Shit," under his breath.

Chapter Twenty-Three

Despite fighting his response, Nolan's back arched and a groan forced its way through his clenched teeth.

Don't come. Don't come. Don't come.

This is just temporary. You'll get your release soon.

But not soon enough.

He groaned, then hissed when Cam began to massage his still-stinging balls.

"I'm struggling to stay in my seat and not join you two."

Cam held out his hand to Hope. "We would love for our queen to join us."

She shook her head. "Not yet. First, the show must go on." She once again rolled her hand in the air like she was a true queen.

Normally, Nolan would get a chuckle out of that, but in that moment he was too busy trying not to come. To him, this whole royalty role-playing was a bit over the top, but her sense of humor—tongue-in-cheek in this particular scenario—was one of many traits both he and Cam liked about her.

Sex didn't always have to be so damn serious. It could be fun and messy and awkward.

Luckily, Cam must have noticed his desperation. It was probably hard to miss. Just like his damn cock.

"My queen, he wants to come."

Not wants, *needs*.

"Of course he does. But not until I say so."

Nolan tipped his head back and silently mouthed a curse.

Cam shooting him a look of sympathy meant he knew very well that Hope could demand that Nolan do the same to him next. "How about if we get your mind off it?"

"How?" His question was a strained whisper.

When Cam leaned over him, Nolan lifted his head and met him halfway. Their mouths connected like two magnets and their tongues found one another, twisting and tangling.

His lover always tasted so good, as if sunshine had a flavor, and his kisses were perfection, even when messy and desperate.

While making out might be a good distraction, it wasn't—

He heard it then. The buzz of a small vibrator.

Knowing she was masturbating while watching them...

Was she *trying* to sabotage him?

Cam continued to work on distracting him by gripping the back of Nolan's neck and running his other hand across his chest before twisting one of his nipples, the light pain pulling some of his attention from the toy still working at his cock.

When Cam swiped Nolan's other nipple with his tongue before sucking it hard, it sent a shock of pleasure through his body that settled heavy in his balls and almost made him come. He moved to the other one and nipped the small, hard tip. Like his kisses, Nolan couldn't get enough of Cam playing with his nipples.

Or his balls.

Or his cock.

In truth, he couldn't get enough of Cam. Period.

It was the same with Hope.

In such a short amount of time, the relationship between the three of them had fallen naturally into place. Nothing between them was forced. The sex was awesome. The conversation easy.

In that moment, he couldn't ask for anything more.

Except to come, of course.

Soon. But, *man*, edging could be rough until that happened. Then the satisfying explosion at the end made it all so worthwhile.

Cam was now sliding the toy up and down Nolan's cock. That motion, along with the internal chamber spinning and the licking sensations at the tip, would quickly be his undoing.

He was about to beg Hope to put him out of his misery when he heard, "Hot Stuff, you can come now."

"Thank you, Queen," he gritted out, ready to kneel at her feet and kiss them.

Despite it being *so* unnecessary, Cam increased the intensity on the masturbation toy. Only, the man didn't jump one level, but two.

"I'm about to come," Nolan warned him, hoping Cam would take the opportunity to capture the cum in his mouth.

He thought that might happen when Cam jerked the toy off Nolan's throbbing erection. However, a warm, wet mouth did not replace it when Nolan's hips popped up off the seat as far as the restraints would allow. Instead, he emptied his balls all over his own stomach.

At least that would make for an easier clean up than him filling up that toy with his load.

Nolan's chest pumped and his pulse pounded as he slowly came down off his high.

"May I clean him up, my queen?" Cam asked.

Her approval sounded breathy. "You may, Handsome."

"Can I fuck him once I do?" Cam asked next while stroking his own hard-on.

He was probably anxious to come, too.

"Absolutely. After all, the show must go on."

When Cam disappeared, Nolan turned his attention to Hope. She continued to plunge the vibrator in and out of herself, sometimes pulling it all the way out and pressing it against her clit.

As soon as her hips would begin to dance, she'd pull it away and sink back onto the throne.

Was she edging herself? He wouldn't be surprised if she was.

Cam returned with a washcloth and quickly wiped off Nolan's stomach. But it wasn't the only thing he had brought back with him. As soon as he put the damp cloth aside, he rolled on a condom and generously lubed himself up before prepping Nolan's hole with the same slick fingers.

He had no doubt that Cam fucking him would make him hard again. It always did. Cam knew what he was doing and Nolan was thankful for that.

Cam growled, "That hole? That belongs to me."

If Nolan hadn't just come, Cam's possessiveness would've made him do so.

A sharp sound came from the throne before they heard, "It belongs to *me*. I'm only giving you permission to use it."

"Thank you, my queen," came out of Cam's mouth, but his eyes clearly showed he disagreed with Hope.

Nolan never thought he'd want to be claimed by anyone.

Until now. Knowing he now "belonged" to the man he lusted after for years was completely intoxicating.

And so was the fact that the smooth, bulbous crown of Cam's cock bumped against his entrance. Nolan sucked in a breath as Cam pushed forward slightly.

With a tilt of his hips, Cam nudged past Nolan's tight ring. "Do you need a second?"

Sometimes he did, sometimes he didn't, but he was more than ready in that moment. "No."

Cam paused and blew out a sharp breath. "Well, I do. With as tight as you feel right now, all I want to do is ram you hard and fast before filling you with my cum."

Nolan shuddered at his words, despite knowing that wouldn't actually happen because they were still using condoms. While he'd like that to change, that was a discussion for another time. "That might not make our queen happy."

"No, it won't, and I want her to be soaking wet from simply observing us."

"Then let's do it."

With one hard thrust, he took Nolan completely.

Despite Cam starting out thrusting slowly and cautiously, he quickly turned into a battering ram. With parted lips, his eyes unfocused and his breathing ragged, he slammed into Nolan over and over.

He wasn't gentle and he certainly wasn't taking his time, despite what they had just discussed, but Nolan was all for it. He'd waited long enough.

He stared up into his lover's eyes.

His lover.

Damn, had his life changed! He'd gone from thinking he'd never have this opportunity with his long-time friend to it becoming reality. He was now sharing his life with the man he'd wanted for so long.

And, as an unexpected bonus, Hope was coming along for that ride.

A loud mewl from the direction of the throne drew his gaze, only to see Hope's head thrown back and short puffs of breath escaping between her parted lips.

"Should we help?" Nolan whispered.

Cam stilled, glanced over at Hope, and shook his head. "No. Not without her permission. If she wants us to touch her, she'll tell us."

Good point.

Cam remained motionless, still deep inside Nolan as they both watched Hope sink her teeth into her bottom lip. A second later, her ass shot off the chair as an orgasm overtook her. When she slowly sank back to the throne, her eyes opened and she looked directly at them.

Busted. They were supposed to be the show, not her.

After turning off the vibrator, she gave them a lazy smile. "Did you like what you saw, boys?"

"Yes, Queen," Cam answered in a sexy grumble.

"Carry on, then. It's your turn, Handsome. But before you do, make sure he's hard again. Just don't make him come."

That last demand was a tall order.

"Yes, Queen," Cam repeated before once again focusing on Nolan.

Cam reached for the tube of lube and squirted more on his palm. He fisted Nolan's cock with one hand while the other traced along his jaw, down his neck, over his chest.

This was the man Nolan was making a life with. Who he went to bed with every night. Who he worked side-by-side with every day.

The man Nolan loved.

He suspected that Cam loved him back, but neither had admitted it to each other yet. Was it possible they were avoiding it so they didn't make things awkward with Hope and make her feel like a third wheel?

The real question was: would he be content only being with Cam? Of course. Is that what he preferred? Definitely not.

He and Cam weren't a couple. No, the three of them were now in a true polyamorous relationship. What was developing between them went much deeper than sex. What started off as just naughty fun had turned into so much more.

For all of them.

So after all this time, it would be weird not to include Hope. Without her, the dynamics of their relationship would be off.

Nolan wanted her to know just how important she was to them. Along with the topic of condoms, he needed to have a discussion with Cam about Hope, since communication was key in any relationship.

The sounds of their flesh slapping together dragged him from his thoughts and Cam's hand pumped Nolan's cock at the same pace he was fucking him.

A groan bubbled up from the back of his throat since, as Hope wanted, Nolan's hard-on was once again raging. But, *of course*, she didn't want him to come.

While his first initial thought jams she was being diabolical, he suspected there might be a good reason for her order. However, his balls were tight, his cock pulsing, and if Cam continued to jerk him off like that...

She would not get what she wanted.

His only saving grace would be if Cam came soon.

"Cam...if she wants me to remain hard, you need to come soon. Otherwise, I'm about to disappoint her."

With a slight nod and a determined set to his jaw, Cam dug his fingers deeper into Nolan's hips as he soldiered on. Unfortunately, the more his cock dragged over Nolan's prostate, the more difficult it became to hold himself together.

"Cam," he whimpered in desperation.

With a shudder, Cam's head dropped forward and his eyes closed, but he said nothing. A clear sign he was about to come undone himself.

Luckily, not a minute too soon.

As he suspected, Cam's next thrust was his last, deep and stuttering. But knowing he was coming made Nolan's cock swell even more and brought him closer to sliding down that slippery slope.

"Cam," Nolan whispered, drawing his fingertips along the man's bristly jawline. "I don't want to rush you, but I have no choice but to rush you."

As soon as Cam's brown eyes popped open, he quickly scrambled to collar the condom and pull free.

While relieved, Nolan also felt a loss with Cam no longer being inside him. Normally, Cam tended to linger after coming, whether while planted deep inside Nolan or Hope, until he could no longer physically do so. Nolan wasn't sure how Hope felt about it, but Nolan loved the extended intimacy. It was second to none next to cuddling afterward.

"Release him."

Cam unsnapped the nylon straps, freeing Nolan in record time and leaving him little time to wonder what Hope had planned next for him.

He didn't have to wonder for long before Hope patted the seat of the throne. "Hot Stuff, come sit."

Did the seat have some sort of electricity hooked to it?

Was she about to shock his ass? He visually searched for any attached wires or torture devices and saw nothing.

"Grab a condom, Handsome," Hope instructed Cam as Nolan sat. "And roll it on him." While Cam did so, she removed the narrow bench from the platform and placed it onto the floor nearby. She then pointed to it. "Kneel there."

A naked Cam immediately got into position. The perfect place to watch the next part of the show.

Hope gave him a brief kiss before approaching Nolan again, cupping her own breasts. "I'm so wet and ready for you, Hot Stuff. Are you ready for me?"

He sure as hell was. He was also ready to empty his aching balls. "Yes, my queen."

Her warm, slick thighs straddled his and her pussy hovered over his hard-on.

"Hold your cock in place."

He was liking this turn of events. He loved when Cam or Hope used him sexually, because he always benefitted in the end, and he considered Hope riding his cock after Cam finished riding his ass as a huge benefit.

Holding on to his shoulders, Hope shifted until the swollen head of his cock was tucked between her plump, slick folds, and after locking eyes with him, she slowly sank down.

The warm, velvety cocoon of her pussy surrounded him. Squeezed him.

Hell yes! It was so worth the wait.

He closed his eyes and pulled air in through his nostrils as she circled her flexible hips and ground against him, driving him even deeper.

The name Heaven was perfect for this area of the resort because that was the only way to describe it...

Heaven.

But then, it helped to be intimate with the right people,

too. He could say with one-hundred percent certainty that Cam and Hope were the right people.

Years of worrying that he'd never find anyone he was attracted to as much as Cam was now officially over. His future was looking bright between this unexpected relationship and his new job, which he also loved.

Her husky, "Pinch my nipples," had his eyes flashing open, only to see she was now looking over her shoulder to address Cam. "Don't touch yourself. You can only watch."

Whether Cam responded or not, Nolan didn't know because Hope was busy sliding down his cock and it was now difficult to think about anything else.

He rolled both dusky nipples between his thumbs and forefingers at the same time she reached back and cupped his balls, massaging them like Cam had.

"Twist them harder. And don't you come," Hope warned in Nolan's ear. "If you can hold off, I have a surprise for you."

While he wasn't sure how much longer he could hold off, he did his best as he continued to tug and tweak her nipples. She captured his lips and swept her tongue through his mouth. He enthusiastically returned the kiss, but soon separated as she began to bounce frantically on his lap like a wild woman. The sounds of her moaning, groaning, and whimpering on his cock made him feel as wild as she looked.

He gritted his teeth and willed himself to keep his cum contained, but his brain was spinning and his balls were crying. He felt his balls draw up against him and knew he was going to have to admit defeat.

Simply accept whatever punishment she deemed fit for his failure.

He wasn't a quitter, however, and wouldn't go down without a fight. He planned to do everything in his power to watch her come apart again.

With a tight grip on one breast, he dropped his other hand to where they were connected, where her pussy swallowed his cock every time she dropped all her weight onto his lap before freeing it as she pushed up on her toes.

He pinched and tugged on her swollen clit the same way he did her nipple.

"*Yessss*," hissed out of her. Her hooded eyes were now unfocused, her mouth gaping, and her chest pumping as she rode him frantically. "Yes, just like that...like *that*."

He blocked her words from his brain, which was spinning like a top.

Her arms wrapped around his head, pulling his face between her breasts, making it hard for him to breathe.

Hell, who needed oxygen, anyway?

He was okay with her "little death" causing his actual death.

Pleasurable torture. That was what it was. Fucking her was the pleasure, trying his damnedest not to come being the opposite.

She rocked back and forth, grinding her pussy against his thumb and cock until she froze and stiffened. Then her forehead slammed into his shoulder as she released a high-pitched cry as her cunt rippled around him.

Oh, thank fuck. His own relief was right around the corner.

Or he sure hoped it was since he couldn't take much more. "Can I come, my queen?" he forced out.

He waited desperately for her to give permission. Instead, she continued to rock against him as she rode out wave after wave of her orgasm. But as soon as her intense orgasm waned, she slipped off of him. "Soon."

After removing his condom, she then told Cam to stand

up. As soon as he did, she moved the narrow bench back to the foot of the throne at Nolan's spread feet.

She turned to where Cam stood, waiting for her next instructions.

She once again pointed to the bench. "Back on your knees."

Cam didn't hesitate. Most likely because he already figured out what would be asked of him. He also knew it wouldn't take much for Nolan to come once the man wrapped his mouth around his cock.

Nolan couldn't argue that.

As expected, Hope pointed at Nolan next and ordered Cam, "Finish him off."

Cam happily obliged.

Chapter Twenty-Four

"Knock! Knock!" A dark head peeked around Cam's office door. It was quickly followed by the rest of the woman. "Hey, Handsome."

Cam gritted his teeth at someone other than Hope using the nickname she used while dominating him. Having Danica, the youngest Lyons sibling, call him the same felt... wrong. Brain bleach needed to be added to his shopping list.

"Hey, Dani."

She leaned a slender hip against the door frame. "Have you heard the news?"

Apparently not. "What news?"

"Well, there's my answer. Dyl Weed, Ford, and Erin have picked a date."

A date? Wait... "They're getting married?"

Dani's face twisted. "Well, not legally, of course. Officially, they're having a commitment ceremony. You know, so they don't get arrested for polygamy." She scrunched up her face.

Smart. But he figured two of the three could legally marry, so...

Yeah. Maybe they were doing it the right and fair way so no one in the trio felt left out. That was something to consider if...

No, his own relationship wasn't even close to that point yet.

Was it?

No.

"When?"

"Christmas Eve."

"They want a winter wedding?" Since their relationship was unconventional, it made sense that the ceremony would be as well.

"Commitment ceremony," she corrected. "They're going to have a horse-drawn sleigh and everything!"

Sounded magical. As long as snow was covering the ground. But if that was something Erin wanted, he could see Dylan and Ford going the extra mile—and expense—of bringing in snow-making machines. "Good for them."

"That's not the only good news I come bearing. Dyl Pickle wanted me to tell you to tell Nolan that a spot in the bunkhouse will be opening up next month. He won't have to sleep on your couch anymore."

Cam's brow dropped low. That wasn't good news. At least not for him. "Who's leaving?"

Since being hired earlier this year, not one person had quit. He didn't know anyone who didn't like working for the Lyons siblings, which was not typical for most workplaces.

"The head groundskeeper is getting married and they bought a little place in town because his fiancé is four months pregnant."

"Oh nice. I guess."

Dani chuckled. "Nolan can move in right after Mike moves out."

"I'll let him know."

Dani tipped her head and stared at Cam. "Will you?"

"Of course."

"Then, I'll tell Dylan that Nolan will take it when I see him later."

What? "No! Don't tell him yet. Let me talk to Nolan first."

Dani pressed her lips together and the corners of her eyes crinkled. "Okay." She tapped the door frame. "I'm out of here. I have a week's worth of menus to plan."

As she turned to leave, Cam called out, "Hey, are you catering the wedding?"

She glanced over her shoulder. "Commitment ceremony. And yes."

"Good. Nobody could do a better job than you."

Dani snorted. "Well, aren't you sweet, Handsome?"

She disappeared.

He should really tell her to stop calling him that. While she meant it as a compliment, it was creeping him out. "Hey, Dani?"

A few seconds later, her head popped around the door again. "Yeah?"

Knowing Dani, she was going to want to know the reason for his request, and he really didn't feel like explaining the dynamics of his relationship with Hope. Or Nolan. "Never mind."

He would just have to grin and bear that nickname for now. At least until he could figure out a way to bring it up to her without her peppering him with a thousand questions.

Because that woman was a pro at getting the information she wanted, and was slick about it, too.

———

A TAP on his partially closed door had Cam calling out, "Come in!"

Nolan pushed the door open the rest of the way and stepped over the threshold.

"Close the door behind you."

Nolan's eyebrows rose in question, but he secured the door then dropped at an angle into one of the two chairs facing Cam's desk. He hooked one knee over the armrest and shot Cam a hell of a sexy smile that made his heart skip a beat.

He couldn't believe how far they'd come in only a matter of months. He'd always loved Nolan as a friend—as well as lusted after him for years—but the feeling that had since taken root deep inside him was more than friendship or lust.

It was solid.

It was real love. He not only loved Nolan, but Cam was *in* love with him.

He suspected Nolan felt the same way, but so far, they'd managed to avoid that particular discussion.

That needed to change. A fishing expedition might be in order.

"Are you busy?" Nolan asked him.

"Just finished up the weekly report." They switched over to weekly reports because, while the resort had plenty of activity throughout the week, none of it was of the criminal variety, making a daily report a waste of time.

Of course, even the weekly had only minor incidents listed. Like a guest imbibing too much and having to be escorted back to their room. Or a slip and fall accident.

"I just got done with rounds."

"Anything to report?"

"One of the goats grabbed hold of a guest and ripped his shorts down to his ankles." Nolan rolled his lips under.

Cam blinked. "Are you joking?"

Nolan shook his head. "Unfortunately, I'm not. I wrote Freckles a citation for harassment and put him in solitary confinement."

"He clearly committed a felony offense. Do you think he learned his lesson?"

"No, because he head butted me before I could get the stall door closed."

"Is the guest all right?"

"The guest is fine. He had a good laugh. I, on the other hand, might develop a bruise."

Concern creased Cam's forehead. "Do you need ice?"

Nolan chuckled. "No. Hope has paddled my ass a lot harder than Freckles' head butt. But if you want, you can kiss it better for me later."

He'd be glad to do that.

Cam sat back and studied Nolan.

Bringing up what Dani told him might be a way to open up dialogue on how they felt about each other. There was no point in denying it anymore. They had been sharing a bed for months now.

"Nolan," he started, hoping this talk didn't go sideways.

"*Hmm?*"

"Dani was in here earlier and she had some news."

"Is it about Dylan, Ford, and Erin's commitment ceremony?"

Was he the last to know? "That was one thing she brought up."

"Okay...what else?"

"A spot in the bunkhouse is opening up."

The smile Nolan had been wearing quickly flattened out. "Oh."

"Dylan said it's yours if you want it."

"Oh."

"But that's up to you." Cam wasn't going to pressure him or influence his decision in any way. "You look disappointed. Would you rather wait for a cabin instead? One might not be available for a long time."

"Do you want me to move out?" Nolan asked carefully.

"Well, I know my cabin is pretty small for the both of us..."

"But the spot in the bunkhouse would be even smaller and would lack privacy."

"That it would," Cam mumbled.

"I'll ask again, do you *want* me to move out? I know it was only supposed to be temporary. I don't want you to feel obligated to let me stay."

"It has nothing to do with obligations. If you stay, I want it to be because that's what *you* want."

"But what about you?"

"If you can continue to deal with sharing the cabin with me, I want you to stay."

Nolan set his boots on the floor and sat up. "Because of the convenient sex?"

Jesus. Was that what he thought? That Cam only wanted sex from him? "It has nothing to do with sex. Look how much sex we have with Hope and she doesn't live with us."

"Then, for what reason?"

"Nolan..."

Nolan's huge smile reappeared. "Yes?"

Cam rolled his eyes. "You seem to have figured it out already."

Nolan tipped his head to the side. "Have I?"

Cam closed his eyes and shook his head. When he opened them again, he surged to his feet, circled his desk and grabbed Nolan's arm, hauling him from the chair. He leaned his ass against the edge of the desk and sandwiched Nolan between his thighs. He curled one hand around the back of Nolan's corded neck and settled the other on his hip.

"Do I need to spell it out?"

Nolan's lips twitched slightly. "Yes."

"Then I will. We hid our true desires for each other for *years*. I don't want to do that any longer. It's a waste of time."

"I agree that we wasted time, but we're no longer hiding our desires. They're now out in the open."

"I'm not only talking about desires."

"Then what are you talking about?"

"Feelings," Cam answered.

"Which ones?"

He sighed. "You're purposely being obtuse."

Nolan chuckled and hooked his arms around Cam's neck. "I've suspected how you feel about me for a while now."

"What is it that you suspect?"

"That you love me."

"I've always loved you."

"I mean as more than a friend," Nolan added.

Cam nodded. "The truth is—"

Nolan took his mouth and cut off his next words.

While Cam was always happy to share a kiss with his lover, he wondered...

Did Nolan not want to hear the truth? If not, that was concerning. Maybe he didn't feel the same way.

But the kiss was brief, and when Nolan pulled his head back, he whispered, "The truth is, I'm in love with you. Not as a friend or co-worker, but as a lifelong partner."

Holy shit. Cam wasn't expecting for that confession to hit so hard. Suddenly his heart swelled too big for his chest. "I'm in love with you, too."

Nolan grinned. "So, no, I don't want to move into the bunkhouse. I want to wake up next to you every morning and lay my head down next to yours every night."

"And take my cock."

"That's one of the perks." Nolan's grin disappeared again. "What about Hope?"

"What about her?" Did Nolan want to cut her out and keep their relationship between the two of them? If so, that might be a problem.

"Do you agree what's going on between the three of us has gone beyond sex?"

Cam stared at the man he loved. "Are you asking if Hope feels the same about us as we feel about each other?"

Nolan shrugged. "Do you think it's possible?"

"I don't know. Maybe we simply need to ask her."

"I think we should, but I also don't want to force her hand," Nolan murmured.

"But do we feel the same way about her as we do each other? We need to address that first before asking her how she feels."

"She's an integral part of our relationship and it would suck if, in a few days, weeks, or even months, she decided she no longer wants to be involved with us. I don't want to lose her, Cam."

"I don't want to, either. I agree. Without her, we wouldn't be the same. Yes, you and I would still love each other, but the dynamics of what we have..." It was difficult to think about Hope not being in their lives. She really was an integral part.

"Right. It would change. I'll admit it right now, Cam, that I do love her. I hope you don't have a problem with that."

Cam looked deep inside himself. He had feelings for Hope, sure. But was it love? And was that love as strong as what he felt for Nolan?

It was.

Damn.

Yes, they needed to let her know. Then she could decide what to do with that information. "How about this? We can tell her how we feel with the caveat that she doesn't need to feel the same. We'll continue to welcome her into our bed however long she wants to join us."

"You love her, too?"

"What's not to love? You asked earlier if what we have—all three of us—has gone beyond sex. In my eyes, it definitely has. But if she doesn't love us the same way, then we need to respect that."

"I don't disagree." Nolan blew out a breath. "I hope she does. But if not, what would that mean for us?"

"We'd have to have that discussion with her first. We need to keep the communication open."

"We haven't done a great job of that if we both waited until now to declare our love to each other."

He was so right. "I'll admit we failed on that front. We need to do better in the future."

"I figured the reason we didn't bring it up with each other was so that Hope wouldn't feel alienated. We didn't want her feeling like a third wheel."

"She's definitely not a third wheel. If anything, we're a three-spoked wheel and her voice is as important as ours so our wheel remains balanced."

Nolan's eyebrows rose but his lips twitched at the corners. "That's actually really fitting, Cam. I'm impressed."

Cam chuckled. "I sometimes have intelligent thoughts."

"But if she doesn't love us the same way, my concern is

she might start feeling like one if she knows how much we love each other. I want to avoid that."

"I never said how much I loved you, only that I did."

Nolan poked him in the gut. "Ha ha. Funny."

"But if you have to know...I'd move the sun, the moon, and the Earth for you."

Nolan's hazel eyes went wide. "Wow, that sounded cheesy."

Cam shrugged. "It might sound cheesy, but it's true."

"Well, then good thing I love cheese."

"Good thing."

Nolan scraped his fingers down Cam's freshly trimmed beard. "When do we want to approach her about this?"

"Tonight after dinner?"

Nolan nodded. "The sooner the better. Especially now that I'll be living with you permanently."

Chapter Twenty-Five

WHOEVER WOULD'VE THOUGHT that Darren's moral outrage would lead to her becoming lovers with two men at the same time?

Scratch that.

Not just lovers.

Loves.

Two nights ago, with Nolan's arm wrapped around her waist and Cam's draped over her shoulders, they meandered back to Cam's cabin after dinner.

Scratch that.

Cam and *Nolan's* cabin.

Weeks ago, it had been clear—at least to Hope—Nolan would never move out and into his own place. She saw it before the men themselves did.

That night, once they returned to the cabin with both their stomachs and hearts full, the men revealed that they loved each other and hadn't told each other until earlier that day.

While that particular news was unexpected, to her, their

love was clear as day whenever they looked at each other or even talked about the other man. She had figured they expressed their love when she wasn't around since they had plenty of hours—even days—where they shared time together without her.

However, none of that was the surprising part. No, it was when they both expressed their love for her, too.

Hope hadn't anticipated those declarations.

Sure, the three of them were close and, of course, intimate. They all loved spending time together. The sex was the best she'd ever had and whenever she was in their company she always felt wanted. Appreciated. Respected. But she hadn't expected them to fall in love with her in only a few months' time.

Or ever.

Nor did she think she would feel the same about them.

She hadn't been looking for love, but it found her anyway.

They both assured her that it wasn't necessary for her to feel the same. That no matter how she felt about them, she was an important part of their life and they wanted her to remain in it.

So Darren leaving not only opened the door to taking two male lovers *at the same time*, but led her to fall in love with those same two men.

Thank you, Darren. Best thing you ever did for me.

Tonight, though, was a little different. It wasn't about her taking charge and ordering around her men. They promised tonight would be all about her.

She wasn't a fool. She wasn't going to say no to that type of spoiling.

She loved that their dynamic was flexible and that they stuck to no hard and fast rules.

But before they got to spoiling her, she wanted to do something for them first. Something she enjoyed, too.

With all three of them naked, she knelt between the two standing men. With their long, hard cocks gripped firmly by the root, it only took a turn of her head to alternate sucking each crown, licking their shafts and swallowing their lengths as far as she could.

She absolutely enjoyed giving them head as much as they enjoyed receiving it. Their physical reactions to what she was doing, accompanied by the groans and moans, caused a warm rush of wetness between her thighs. Add in the fact they were leaning over her and making out with each other, all while playing with each other's nipples, and her libido had flown into overdrive.

No man, not one, had ever gotten her as heated as Cam or Nolan. And together? How had she not self-combusted yet?

Tugging on both cocks, she drew the men closer so she could lick the tips at the same time. The salty tang of their precum coated her taste buds.

She loved being the center of their man sandwich.

She loved watching the men interact with each other. Turn each other on. Get each other off. The reality was even better than any fantasy.

She never thought being with two men would be the perfect scenario for her, but these two made it easy.

She tipped her eyes upward when Cam said, "Think it's time."

Nolan giving him an answering grin, along with a single nod, made her pussy clench and another trickle of arousal tickle her bare inner thighs.

The time had come for her to stop concentrating on them and for them to concentrate on her.

Once again, thank you, Darren!

Nolan grabbed under her arms and hauled her to her feet. Once there, Cam quickly swept her into his arms, carried her the four feet to the bed, and launched her into the center of it.

A giggle exploded from her as she landed with a bounce.

On the nightstand, condoms and lube were at the ready, along with bottles of water, hand towels, and wet wipes for quick and easy cleanup. The three of them had so much sex, they now had a routine.

In fact, she was now staying overnight at the cabin more than she was going home. Despite her house being a lot larger and more comfortable for three adults, they rarely spent a night there. Mostly because one of them seemed to always be on call.

However, she'd like that to change. While it made sense that they wanted to stick close to the property, her home was only twenty minutes away and it wasn't like the resort normally dealt with any kind of crime. Their security team was mostly made up of all former or retired trained law enforcement as it was.

Digging her elbows into the mattress, she used them to pull herself higher up the bed to give the men space to join her. As they did, her eyes roamed over both.

Both of her men were absolutely drool-worthy. How did she get to be so lucky?

Note to self: Send my ex a thank you card.

It was easy for her to see the slight changes to their physiques now that they were doing yoga more regularly, despite their initial resistance. She was pleased they now recognized the benefits.

Cam slid in on her left and Nolan on her right, once again keeping her sandwiched between them.

"We're here for you tonight," Cam reminded her. "Don't

hesitate to tell us if there's something you want us to do that we missed."

"I'm taking the night off from bossing you two around. Whatever you decide will be perfectly fine with me." And that couldn't be any truer. They've never let her down yet.

"I get that but—"

Hope reached out and cupped Cam's face. "Handsome, what I've discovered in the last few months is: you two don't need instruction, unlike some others I've been with in the past. You know how to satisfy me without me ordering either of you around. You two are quite well-versed in knowing how to make me orgasm."

"Well—"

Hope pressed a finger to Cam's lips to shush him. "You will not disappoint me, I promise."

"Aren't *we* supposed to promise that?" Nolan asked with a grin before sucking her nipple into his mouth and flicking the tip with his tongue.

With a smile, Hope dropped her head back to the pillow and simply said, "Do your thing."

Cam took her other breast into his mouth, gently scissoring the nipple between his teeth.

See? He knew exactly what she liked. In the past few months, the three of them had learned each other's likes and dislikes, as well as what got them off quickly and what built up the tension.

Like edging.

Her favorite night so far was the one they spent in the Restraint Room up in Heaven. She had cuffed Cam's wrists and ankles to a chair in the corner so he couldn't move, then gagged him. While their lover watched, she bent Nolan over a spanking bench, paddled his ass until it was almost purple, spread his ass cheeks wide, and pegged him until Nolan came all over the floor.

Cam was so sexually frustrated over not being able to touch them, or even himself, that, by the end, the veins in his neck and arms looked like a 3D road map. When she finally freed him, it was like releasing a Tasmanian Devil. However, she forbade him from touching her or Nolan and forced him to only touch himself.

Which he did. Like a maniac. His hand became nothing but a blur until he came all over himself.

But, *damn*, watching him jerk off was so freaking hot!

It was a memory neither she or Nolan would soon forget.

Of course, neither would Cam for a different reason. Once he recovered, he said he never wanted to be in that position again. So naturally, she put it back on their sexual to-do list.

Both of them pinching her nipples at the same time pulled her back to their present situation. At least Cam wasn't tying her up and making her watch the two of them go at it without giving her any way to relieve her sexual frustration.

Though, she wouldn't be surprised if it happened in the future. He'd probably enjoy watching her squirm in her chair, unable to take matters into her own hands.

Hope cocked her knees when Nolan rubbed her clit and stroked the soft flesh of her labia, occasionally dipping a finger or two into her very slick pussy.

Then, with both of their mouths latched *hard* onto her breasts, as well as Nolan finger fucking her, Cam joined in by thumbing her sensitive clit. Her hips jumped off the mattress slightly.

They were working toward her first orgasm. And she'd be glad to give them that. So, a few seconds later, she did.

They never said what their end goal was, how many orgasms they planned to give her tonight, but she had a feeling she would need a nap afterward.

"Take over up here while I go diving for pearls below," Nolan told Cam.

Cam's answer was sucking one nipple deep while twisting the other.

The bed shifted as Nolan moved until he was settled between her spread legs, his broad shoulders nudging her thighs even wider so he had room to work.

And such amazing work he did.

For her, the biggest issue with being with two men was figuring out where to concentrate. On Cam and what he was doing to her breasts? How he was nibbling her neck or playing with her hair? Or on Nolan tracing her cleft with his tongue and lapping expertly at her clit?

She tried to divide her attention, but when Nolan drew a path all the way down, it was hard to ignore. He tongued her ass for a second before working his way back up, giving her swollen, pulsing lips a quick nibble before dipping that skilled tongue inside her. She was now so worked up that when he added a finger to her throbbing clit, she jerked in reaction.

A recent discovery proved she could orgasm simply by them playing with, sucking, and biting her breasts, so Cam continued to do his part to help Nolan send Hope over the edge into bliss.

"*Yesss*," she breathed, tipping her head back to give Cam full access while digging her fingers into Nolan's dark blond hair.

Perfection.

Not thirty seconds later, her second orgasm started at her core and expanded out like a rock thrown into a lake. Her eyes closed, her toes curled, and with the way she tugged on Nolan's hair, she wouldn't be surprised if he worried about getting a bald spot by her ripping it out by the roots.

Luckily, she held on to enough control to keep all the beautiful hair on his beautiful head intact. Barely.

Were they going to make her orgasm a third time before they got to the main event? Or were they both at their limit, too?

Wearing a grin, Nolan poked his head up. "Good?"

"Perfect," she purred. "You're always so good at that."

"Hey now," Cam grumbled. "Are you saying he's better at eating you out than I am?"

"It's not a competition. But if you do want to compete, I'm volunteering to be your victim."

"Victim," Nolan huffed as he sat up.

She giggled and brushed her fingers over Cam's dark head of hair. "Now what?"

Cam put his finger against her lips to shush her the same way she had done to him earlier. "Just sit back and enjoy. Don't worry about what comes next."

She let out a fake, aggravated sigh. "Fine. Then, who's taking the lead?"

When Cam also sat up and cocked a brow at her in warning, she dramatically rolled her eyes. She pinned her lips together to contain a giggle when Nolan asked, "Now what?"

"She's going to ride your cock as I fuck her ass."

Cam's answer caused a little orgasm aftershock.

Before meeting Cam and Nolan, she hadn't had anal in at least ten years. Not since the man she'd been seeing at the time had wanted to try it. She was shocked to find how much she loved it. Unfortunately, he decided he didn't.

But it was also then when she realized she had a more kinky side. Not that anal was considered kinky, but it opened her eyes to the rest of the possibilities. Only after that, the partners who liked to experiment were few and far between. And then she met Darren, who slammed his foot on the brake when it came to any and all experimentation. And anal? She hadn't even bothered to ask.

It had become clear just how much she'd missed out on what she liked due to Darren's unwillingness to be open-minded. She quickly pushed that regret aside.

She reminded herself that chapter of her life was over and she had moved on to bigger and better things.

Two of them.

It took a few weeks of preparation before the men thought she was ready for double penetration. And as soon as they—including her—did, Nolan got first shot at her.

That night cemented two things: she still loved anal—with the right person, of course—and it wasn't Nolan's favorite. One reason he preferred to be a bottom.

They didn't have to ask Cam what he preferred because he'd never hid his feelings about it. He loved everything about ass. Whether spanking it, eating it, or fucking it.

Cam swiped the condoms off the nightstand, gave one to Nolan, and rolled the other down his own hard length. He then squirted lube all over his cock before handing the bottle to Nolan. "Prep her for me, baby."

That endearment was a recent addition and she was loving the fact that Cam had started using it for both Nolan and her. She'd caught Nolan using it a few times himself.

As soon as Nolan had his own condom secured, he lubed up two fingers and slipped them inside her, working them in and out.

Once he was done, Cam hooked an arm around her middle and pulled her to him. She shuddered in anticipation when he announced, "You're going to face him as you ride my cock."

With his hands on her hips, Cam helped her into place. Luckily, his were narrow enough that she had no problem straddling them, but she wouldn't be doing that for long. They had tried this position once before and it had worked out fabulously.

Cam gripped the root of his cock and held it steady as Hope slowly lowered herself onto him, pausing every few seconds to allow her body to adjust to his girth.

The sensation of fullness was absolutely delicious. She might have to put anal into their regular rotation. For her, anyway. Nolan already got plenty of it, even when Hope wasn't around.

They were both open with her about how much sex they had when she wasn't on the ranch. While she loved that they were connecting, sometimes she couldn't help but feel left out, despite how hard the men worked to ensure she didn't.

Naturally, she'd be more involved if they all lived together, but they were nowhere near that point.

Maybe someday, if they kept on their current path.

She had no idea how that would come about with Cam's cabin being barely big enough for two, forget three people. Obviously, it wasn't like they could build a house on the Double D like Dylan and Dayne had for their triads.

And as for her place...Cam would have to get over the concern that twenty minutes was too far away.

Realistically, it was not. And knowing the Lyonses, she doubted they'd care if both their head and assistant head of security didn't live on the premises. Not with the experienced team they had in place.

With Cam's hands on her ass, he kept her spread open until she was fully seated. Once she was, she knew what to expect next. Leaning back into his chest, he held her thighs up and open to give Nolan easier access.

Nolan slipped a finger through her folds and whispered, "Look at that pretty pink pussy."

"All yours," Cam told him.

In this position, Hope had no way to move, so of course, it was up to the men to take care of business.

With his hard-on in hand, Nolan shifted forward, the head of his latex-covered cock following the previous path as his finger before he surged forward.

It took a little work—and a lot of patience—to wedge himself inside her at the same time Cam filled her ass, and once he was, he paused and waited for her to give him the go ahead.

Last time it took a little planning to make this position work, but now they knew...

Nolan pressed his lips to hers and murmured, "Ready?"

"Yes," she breathed. At first, having both of them inside her was uncomfortable, but it didn't take long for her body to adjust.

And the fact she could take them both at the same time was such a turn on. Not only for her, but for both Cam and Nolan, who nibbled on her lips for a second before straightening and beginning to move.

Despite not being one to take control, he had no choice in this. She couldn't do much to contribute and neither could Cam when it came to rhythm and timing. But that didn't mean Cam didn't help by keeping her bent knees up and open. He also made a great chair, his lap being the seat and his chest being the chair back.

An idea popped into her head. She had seen adjustable nylon straps that would work perfectly for this particular scenario. They would go around her thighs and hook around his neck so she could be held in that position hands-free.

She'd have to suggest it. Because, *holy crap*, this had to be her favorite position right now. Especially with Cam sucking on her neck and Nolan kissing her as he slowly and carefully plunged in and out of her.

Despite her facing away from Cam, if she leaned her head back far enough, she could share kisses with him, too.

Cam nipped her shoulder playfully. "Can you plant your feet on my thighs?"

Well, great minds and all that...

Only, he had come up with a much easier solution. At least for their current situation. They could try the straps next time.

Once she had her feet securely on Cam's thighs, his breathing beat a pattern against her ear. His hands began to move faster. Twisting her nipples, squeezing her breasts, snaking down her belly to where his fingers brushed the point she and Nolan were connected. He then thumbed her clit, making her clench tighter around Nolan. She felt him shudder and pause while the breath hissed out of him.

Oh yes, it was a great idea to keep his hands free to explore. They all benefitted.

Hope and Nolan shared another kiss before he leaned over Hope's shoulder and shared one with Cam.

That was such a turn on. Knowing they loved each other. Knowing their deep connection. And, lucky her, she got to share in both.

Of course, their relationship was unorthodox, but it was also perfect for them.

She thanked her lucky stars that Cam approached her on the dock that day. She had no idea at the time where that interaction would lead them and how much her life would change.

She had zero complaints.

How could she? She was currently sandwiched between the two men she loved as they pleasured her.

Life was good.

No, life was great!

She could only think of one thing that would make it even better.

Cam wrapped his fingers around her throat and pulled her head back until it rested against his collarbone. Once she relaxed, he began to gently squeeze and release.

Besides loving to edge the men, breath play was another favorite.

Cam was great at it. He knew the perfect amount of pressure. It was a huge turn on to allow herself to be so vulnerable with someone she trusted one-hundred percent. He had previously admitted her trust in him turned him on, too. A win-win situation for them both.

"Fuck," came out on a grunt as Nolan continued to thrust deep, her body automatically making room for him, even though it was already full.

Cam was most likely fighting the urge to thrust so he didn't hurt her. He was patiently waiting for Nolan to come first before he let himself follow those instincts.

But first, she needed to come. Because once Nolan did, Cam was sure to quickly follow.

Cam was aware of that, too. Using the hand not wrapped around her throat, he pinched her clit hard before circling and pressing.

"*Yesss*," came from her on a hiss. "Yes, fuck me. Make me come."

Her head rolled back and forth on Cam's collarbone and

her eyes drifted shut as Nolan continued to plunge in and out of her.

"Soak his cock, baby." Cam's whisper was husky and sounded a little bit desperate. "Show him how much you love his cock wrecking your pussy."

Cam wasn't a huge dirty talker but, *damn*, when he did it, it flipped a switch inside her. It caused a fire to roar at her core and her pussy to clench around Nolan's cock, which was even harder now.

That meant he was close. *Very* close.

So she let herself go. The intense climax, starting at her clit and encompassing Nolan, made every muscle twitch.

No surprise when Nolan warned a few seconds later, "I'm coming," before thrusting deep and staying there. He closed his eyes and dropped his head.

Cam continued to squeeze her neck gently until her own waves of orgasm subsided. Not unexpectedly, Cam, with a deep grunt, sank his teeth into her shoulder as he thrust up slightly and also came.

The room went silent except for their heavy breathing and no one moved for a few pounding heartbeats.

Once Nolan finally disengaged, he helped Hope climb off Cam. When she was free from him and on her back recovering, they insisted she remain in bed so they could clean her up.

They were definitely taking care of her tonight. It made her feel wanted and loved. As well as appreciated.

After taking their time and care using warm, damp wash clothes, they joined her again in bed, tucking her tightly between the two of them. They pressed soft kisses everywhere they could reach while softly brushing their fingers along her heated skin.

Her heart was so full she thought it might burst.

Chapter Twenty-Six

The squawk from his portable radio had Nolan pulling it off his waistband and pausing on his way to the stables. Since the weather was perfect this afternoon, he had decided to forego using the ATV for his rounds and hoof it on foot instead.

He could use the exercise, despite the fact that he'd had plenty already this morning. While Cam still slept, he had sex with Hope in the shower before she left to go teach yoga. As soon as Cam woke and found out they had let him sleep in, he bent Nolan over the end of the couch and ate his ass for a good ten minutes before grabbing the coconut oil off the kitchen counter. Then, after lubing up his bare cock, Cam fucked him hard and deep until they both came.

He and Cam had stopped using condoms right after they both got their negative test results a couple of weeks ago, but they were still using them with Hope until she had a chance to get to her gynecologist to get on some form of birth control.

If Cam thought fucking him over the couch would be punishment for not waking him earlier, then Nolan would accept every minute of it. He would, in fact, encourage more of it.

"Gate to Supervisor."

Instead of letting his thoughts wander to his two quickies this morning, he should answer the radio.

He pushed the button. "Supervisor to Gate, go."

"Have an issue here, if you can come advise."

That didn't sound good. Normally, the guards didn't need assistance. Cam had previously joked about Nolan taking a security job at an old folks' home. Truthfully, there were probably a lot less issues at the Double D.

"On my way," Nolan answered before slipping the radio back onto his belt.

Since walking to the resort's entrance would take too long, he stopped at the equipment shed to grab the ATV Cam and he now shared.

As Nolan approached the guard shack, he saw a vehicle parked in front of the metal barrier gate and a dark-haired man he didn't recognize standing almost toe-to-toe in a threatening manner with their gate guard.

Whoever he was, he was clearly irritated. His tense shoulders were pulled back and his chest puffed out in an attempt to intimidate Kirk, a Navy veteran.

Nolan's guess? Kirk wasn't going to back down and would do whatever was necessary.

He parked the ATV up close to the barrier, blocking the lane, just in case, and as soon as he shut off the engine he heard, "I know she's here!"

She?

"Let me in. I have every right to see my girlfriend."

Girlfriend?

Did a guest book a stay without her significant other and this guy was bent out of shape over it?

"You!"

A finger was jabbed in Nolan's direction.

"Make this asshole open the gate."

Nolan calmly asked Kirk, "Does he have a reservation?"

"No."

"Is he on the visitors' list?"

Kirk shook his head. "Nope."

Even Nolan could tell Kirk was clinging hard to his patience.

Great. Good thing the gate was far from any guests so no one would be witnessing this shit show.

"I know she's here. At this"—he flung a hand around, barely missing Kirk—"this place."

Nolan pulled in a breath to cool his annoyance. "Who's the guest you're seeking?"

One side of the man's lip pulled up in a sneer. "She's not a guest! She works here."

Great. "And her name?"

"Hope Reed."

All the blood drained from Nolan's face. This jack wagon had to be Darren, her ex. Because Nolan and Cam were her current boyfriends—and lovers—but he kept that important tidbit to himself.

Nolan wasn't sure that Hope was even on the property since he didn't check to see if her vehicle was still parked in front of the cabin. Sometimes she hung around the resort if she didn't have to run home to teach another class from her home studio or get housework done.

"She's probably at home," Nolan forced through clenched teeth.

"She's not. That was the first place I checked."

The hairs on the back of his neck stood up.

First of all, why was Darren back in town? Second, why was he looking for Hope?

Whatever the reason was, it couldn't be good.

It took everything in him to ask, "Did you try to contact her?" since he'd rather Darren not contact her at all.

"She's not answering. What have you perverts done with her?"

Nolan ground his teeth to avoid knocking Darren's out of his mouth. His law enforcement training taught him to deescalate, not throw punches.

No matter how much he wanted to knock out Hope's ex.

You like your job here. Don't do anything stupid.

A screaming engine could be heard coming up the lane.

Nolan spared a glance in that direction to see Cam speeding toward the gate in one of the trucks belonging to the maintenance crew.

The pickup came to an abrupt halt at an angle directly behind the ATV. As soon as the driver's door was flung open, Cam burst from the driver's seat. Before his feet even hit the ground, he asked, "What's going on here?"

When Nolan's eyes flicked to Kirk, the guard gave him a chin lift that said he could hold down the fort while Nolan pulled Cam off to the side.

Nolan kept his voice low. "Did you hijack that truck?"

"It's commandeering when the good guys do it, and of course I did. What's going on?"

"Where's Hope?"

Cam jerked his chin into his neck and frowned. "She texted me earlier and said she'd be spending a few hours at the spa."

Good. She needed to stay far away from this belligerent asshole.

"Sir, you need to calm down," Kirk warned with extreme restraint.

"I want to speak to my girlfriend! By barring me from entry, I'm beginning to think this is a hostage situation. Don't make me get the police involved."

Nolan rolled his eyes so hard, he swore he busted a blood vessel.

"For fuck's sake," Cam muttered. "Is that her ex?"

"Yep. The one and only Darren Von Dump Her."

Cam blinked at Nolan's snarky answer before walking away. Out of the corner of Nolan's eye, he saw his lover on his cell phone. Was he calling for backup?

Between the three of them, they could easily handle one pissed off man. As long as Darren wasn't packing. If so, they'd soon be wishing they were, too.

A few seconds later, Cam took determined strides toward the gate and Nolan followed closely behind him.

Cam's nostrils flared in irritation when he asked, "What do you want with Hope?"

"I need to talk to her. That's all."

"Does she want to talk to you?"

"Of course she does. I left her, not the other way around."

What an asshole.

"You left her and you truly believe she wants to listen to what you have to say now?"

"Stay out of our business."

"You're making it our business by showing up here,"—Cam jabbed a finger toward the ground—"and creating a scene."

"I wouldn't be making a scene if you'd give me access to her."

"She has a phone."

"She's not answering."

"That should be a sign she doesn't want to hear from you."

Nolan realized exactly who Cam had called when he glanced over his shoulder to see Hope's Subaru coming up over the rise.

As soon as she parked and climbed out of her car, Darren leaned into the metal barrier gate. "Hope! I need to speak with you."

"If you walk around that gate, you will be arrested and charged with trespassing," Nolan warned. "This is your one and only warning."

Darren ignored him. "Hope! You owe me that much!"

"You don't owe him anything," Cam said with his expression hard and his hands balled into fists as she joined them.

With her features grim, her eyes slid between Cam and Nolan before fully focusing her attention on her ex. She shrugged. "So talk."

"Not here. Not in front of these people."

These people.

What did Hope ever see in this cretin?

"I don't think we have anything to talk about. You made it clear with what you believed about me, my career, and about working here before deciding to give up on us."

"I've had time to reflect—" When Nolan snorted, Darren scowled at him. "See? This is why we need to speak in private."

"We don't need to do anything, Darren."

Nolan silently cheered at her response.

"Are you willing to throw away everything we had?"

Her mouth dropped open. A second later it snapped shut. "Me? *I'm* to blame?"

A muscle jumped in Darren's clean-shaven cheek. "Please, just give me a chance and hear me out."

Before Hope could respond, Cam pulled her away and stood between her and her ex. Nolan stepped up next to Cam, creating a wall to block Darren's view.

"If you go with him, one of us is going with you, Hope."

"He's not going to hurt me," she assured Cam. "Maybe if I let him have his say and I'm clear that I'm no longer interested, he'll leave me alone."

Oh, sure. Nolan wondered how many women thought that and ended up regretting it afterward. If they were still alive to regret it.

"I don't like this."

Nolan agreed with his lover. "I don't, either."

Hope sighed. "Well, then we all agree, but unless I squash this, he might not give up."

"I'll squash him for you," Cam growled.

"No, you won't. He's not worth losing your freedom or your job. Or your self-respect. I can handle this."

"Hope," Nolan started, not comfortable with her *handling* what appeared to him to be an unreasonable man.

She lifted a hand. "It'll be fine." She yelled over to Darren. "Because we have a past, I'll give you a few minutes of my time."

Shit. He didn't like that one bit.

"Not here," Darren insisted.

"Fine," came out on another sigh. "Let's go to the house."

Cam and Nolan reluctantly moved their vehicles and Kirk opened the gate so Hope could drive out.

Nolan and Cam shared a worried glance as she drove away and Darren followed in his own vehicle.

"I don't like this," Nolan grumbled under his breath.

"I don't, either. But she'll be fine," Cam assured him.

Nolan wasn't so sure. "What if he convinces her to take him back?"

"She won't."

He'd like to think the same, but he didn't know how persuasive Darren could be. "How do you know? They were together a lot longer than us. In fact, they lived together. That's serious. We don't even have that. With him, she was getting all of his attention. Unlike with us."

"Shit," Cam said. "Do we need to go fight for her?"

"If there's even a slim chance she would take him back. I don't want to lose her, Cam. And not only that, I don't like the way he's acting." Something about the guy was setting off his cop instincts, he just couldn't put his finger on it exactly..

Cam grimaced. "I don't, either."

Not only would losing Hope feel like lopping off a limb, he couldn't simply sit back and let Darren intimidate or possibly hurt her. "Then we have to make sure she knows that and we need to head to her place."

"We should give her a chance to handle this first."

"Cam..."

Cam closed his eyes and pulled in a sharp breath. "You're right. We can't just sit back and let him convince her that she should give him a second chance. And I don't like that he'll be alone with her. If something happens to her on our watch, I'll never forgive myself."

Nolan blew out a relieved breath. "Same. I'm going to grab my SUV and you return that truck. I'm sure they need it. Then we can head over to her place. I'm willing to fight for her and protect what's ours. Are you?"

Cam stared at him for a second and then gave him a single nod. "Let's go claim our woman. And if we need to, kick some ass."

Hell yeah.

———

"You made the wrong choices. But so did I. I see that now, Hope, and I want to correct my mistake."

Sure he did. Hope doubted Darren's narrow views magically changed, especially in only a few months' time. "And how will you do that?"

"If you allow me to move back into our home, I'll let you work at that place, if that's what you really want."

Hope refrained from rolling her eyes.

Our home.

It hadn't been their home for quite a few months. She had made sure to exorcise the house of everything that was Darren, except for two small boxes he'd left behind that she had shoved to the back of the closet.

If she'd had his forwarding address, she would've mailed them to him, but since he was there in the flesh, he could take his stuff with him when he left this time.

Hope did a double-take. "You'll *let* me?"

"A lot of people would love to make money from their hobby. You're one of the lucky ones."

"Lucky?" she spit out.

Darren was digging a hole so deep, it was about to cave in on him.

He clearly didn't know—or care—how dedicated she was to her students, whether they be her regulars or the resort's guests.

"Why are you here, Darren? Other than to insult me all over again."

"I...It's..."

Hope lifted a palm to stop his sputtering and pushed off the kitchen counter where she'd been leaning. "By the way, you left a couple of boxes behind. I'll get them for you."

"No need. I'll just be bringing them back when I move back in."

Hope's head jerked back from his audacity. "I said I'd give you a chance to speak. I let you speak. Now it's my turn. You won't be moving back in, Darren. You not only disrespected me by trying to dictate where I could work, but you disrespected everyone—guests and employees alike—at the Double D by calling them perverts and worse. I'm done. Truthfully, I'm much happier without you. I want to keep it that way."

"Ouch."

"Funny, I felt the same way when you insisted that teaching yoga wasn't a real job."

"I didn't mean it."

"It came out of your mouth," she reminded him.

"I was worried about you teaching there. Anyone who goes to a place like that has no morals."

"Then you're also saying that *I* have no morals."

"Hope, we were good together. We were happy together."

"I thought so, too, until you showed your true colors. But once you left, I realized I wasn't as happy as I thought." She wasn't going to unnecessarily get into the boring sex.

"You just need to give me a chance."

"No, I don't. You had your chance and you blew it."

"This is my house, too."

"It was your house until you left me with the mortgage payments."

"There's equity in this house that belongs to me."

She tipped her head to the side. "Is there? Have you seen the mortgage statement recently? Do you know how much was paid down on the principal? And I made the down payment, not you. So, it's my house, not ours. If you want to take over the monthly payments and all the expenses, you are free to buy me out. Take the house and I'll move out."

She really didn't want to do that, but she didn't doubt

that Darren wouldn't want to take over the payments on his own.

"Now, you had your say. I'm going to grab the boxes you forgot." Without waiting for a response, she headed over to the coat closet and pulled out the two small boxes.

She returned to the kitchen and shoved the stacked boxes at him. "Here you go and please don't come back. I'm loving my life right now with you not in it."

She ignored his muttered curse and as soon as he had a good grip on the boxes, she went to the junk drawer and pulled out the card she had written one night.

"And don't forget this." She placed the envelope on top of the boxes he was holding. "I would've mailed it but you never left your forwarding address."

His eyes dropped to it. "What is it?"

"A thank you card."

His brow furrowed. "For what?"

"For leaving and letting me find the two men who love and accept me as I am."

His mouth dropped open. "What do you mean, two men?"

"Just what I said. But I'm no longer your business so I don't have to explain."

"It sounds like you're being a slut."

"You're welcome to think what you'd like. Just do it elsewhere." She went to the door and opened it, swinging out a hand. "I hope you have a great life, Darren. I plan on doing the same."

After a slight hesitation and a mumble she couldn't understand—nor did she want to—he headed outside. She gave him a wave and shut the door to that particular chapter of her life.

A few minutes later, a pounding at her front door made her heart take a tumble.

Now what? She thought she'd made herself clear.

When she flung open the door, she swallowed the words she had geared up to say to her ex.

"He's gone."

"Of course he's gone," she told Cam. "Did you really think I was going to let him slide back into my life and my home?" Nevermind that he had called her a slut. Cam and Nolan didn't need to know that.

Hope stepped back to allow them inside.

But before she even finished closing the door, Cam said, "We need to have a serious discussion."

"Right now?" she asked his back as he moved farther into the kitchen.

He turned, leaned back against the counter and crossed his arms over his chest. "Is there a better time?"

"Is this because of Darren trying to get me back?"

"Having him show up was a reality check. It reminded us how we don't want to lose you. Ever."

"You're not going to lose me."

MAYBE, maybe not, but they needed to stake their claim to be completely sure it never happened. "Nolan and I discussed it on the way over."

Her brow furrowed. "Discussed what?"

"I'm getting to that."

Hope rolled her eyes. "Well, hurry up!"

When he chuckled at her fake outrage and she whacked him in the gut with the back of her hand. He released an overly dramatic *oof*, then pulled her into his arms.

While they had never discussed being exclusive, it had been over six months that none of them had been with anyone else. They had no reason to make it official with Hope at this point.

Yes, it had only been six months. And in reality, six months wasn't very long in any relationship, but—

Bottom line was, they didn't want to share her with anyone else. And they also didn't want to risk losing her to anyone else. Not just Darren.

They were happy and he could envision a future that included all three of them.

He was someone who knew what he wanted.

Nolan was quite clear with what he wanted.

They just needed to make sure Hope wanted the same as them.

He glanced over at Nolan first—who gave him a subtle chin lift to proceed—before locking eyes with Hope. "I..." He shook his head before correcting himself. "*We* want us to take the next step and live together."

Her expression wasn't one of surprise but of relief. Had she been waiting for them to propose this?

"That would be ideal, but where would we live? I know how much you two love living on the ranch. Not to mention I know you feel obligated to stick close. Handsome, you always seem antsy to return the nights you guys come over here."

Unfortunately, that was true. He appreciated his job. He appreciated the Lyonses and how they ran the ranch resort. But it was actually during one of their recent meetings where they mentioned that, if the cabin was too small for them—Dayne's eyebrows had raised at that word—their positions didn't require Cam and Nolan to live on site. Especially since Fisher Falls was only about twenty minutes away.

"The resort will be fine," Dayne had assured him. "The

team you put together is top notch, Cam. We have no doubt they can handle anything crazy until you get here."

"Since opening, we've only had one problem guest. For the most part, this is a place where people leave their emotional baggage at the front gate and forget their problems," Dylan had added.

"Copious amounts of sex will do that," Dayne said with his typical shit-eating grin. "Take it from me."

Everything their bosses had said was true.

Nolan moved to stand next to Cam, so they both faced Hope. Her eyes flicked between the two of them.

Cam grabbed her chin and had her focus solely on him for a second. "We do love living on the ranch, but not as much as we love you. We want you in our lives full-time."

"Absolutely," Nolan agreed with a nod. "It's not the same when you're not with us. When you're gone, we miss you."

Despite her face softening at Nolan's words, she reminded them, "I'm with you two a lot."

While that was true... "Both Nolan and I want all three of us to build a home together. A life." He was damn sure Hope wanted that, too. Which was why he didn't think it was too early to bring up this topic.

"Like a couple. But better," Nolan added.

"And Dylan and Dayne are proof of how polycules can work."

"It's always nice to have an extra set of hands around," Nolan added with a wink.

"And not just during sex," Cam clarified.

Nolan's lips tipped upward. "Sure, sure. That's what I meant."

Her brow furrowed. "But what about your jobs?"

"Dayne and Dylan have told me that they're fine with us moving off the resort. They actually encouraged it. I guess it was obvious on what path we are headed." Already being in established polyamorous relationships probably made it easier for them to recognize said path.

"But you didn't think to ask me first before talking to them?"

"They brought it up before I could. Then I thought about all the times you've mentioned that you didn't want to go home. That you wanted to stay."

"Most times I do."

Could it be that he has misread the relief on her face? Or was she just making sure they really wanted this?

"But not every time. You should be sleeping beside us every night and waking up beside us every morning."

Nolan nodded. "As you know, you're a major part of this relationship. We don't want you feeling the slightest bit left out. I can't imagine me leaving you and Cam some nights to go home to be by myself. I'd feel like I'm missing out. The truth is, you shouldn't be missing out on anything."

If there was any chance she thought she missed out on intimacy or conversations, living together might solve that.

Her eyebrows knitted together. "But where would we live? You haven't answered that yet."

Cam's eyes met her blue ones. "Unless you have any objections, we thought this house would work. It's not huge, but it's plenty big enough for us at this point. Plus, it would open up one of the cabins for another employee."

"What do you mean 'at this point?'"

"Well, if we eventually decide to raise a family..." Cam let that drift off because this was something they hadn't discussed. But Nolan mentioned one night that he regretted never having children. Cam only had one. Laurel would probably love having younger siblings. To visit, not help raise them, of course.

He had no idea where Hope stood on having kids. Since she'd be the one bearing them, ultimately, that decision would be up to her.

Kids or not, he still wanted them all to share their lives together. Forever. "What do you say?"

She tucked her bottom lip between her teeth as she stared past him. Her gaze suddenly swung back. "I'll give you one guess because one will be all you'll need."

He placed his hands on either side of her face and pressed their foreheads together. "I'll take that as a yes." Before he let her go, he brushed his lips over hers. Once she was free, Nolan enveloped her into his arms and shared a kiss with her next.

"Should we go upstairs to celebrate?" Hope suggested.

While their work day wasn't quite over yet, they could probably get away with a quickie.

As they headed upstairs, their smiles were bright. But not as bright as their future.

Cam didn't think he could be any happier.

It turned out, he was wrong.

Epilogue

Hope stuck out her tongue to capture some of the cold flakes falling softly from the sky.

When it snowed, she normally wouldn't say the weather was perfect, but in this case, it was. It was exactly what Erin had wanted for their commitment ceremony. Since Mother Nature cooperated, no snowmakers were needed.

The day was turning into a real winter wonderland with the sun shining brightly, making undisturbed snow sparkle like glitter and diamonds. The ground was covered enough so the sleigh, pulled by two of the ranch's rescue horses, glided with ease as it delivered the stunning "bride" to her two waiting men, Dylan and Ford.

Their huge smiles and obvious love between the three of them made her heart swell. It also proved that, while polyamory was unorthodox, it could be successful. As with any relationship, it just took dedication and work.

Plus, a whole lot of love.

"You keep sticking out that tongue of yours like that and

we might have to cut out of here early," came the deep voice to her right.

She glanced over at Cam. "That would be rude."

"Then we can just dip out and return before anyone realizes we were missing."

Hope elbowed Cam's ribs and smothered a giggle. "It sounds like you're saying you have no staying power."

"You should know." He shot her a grin that warmed her all the way to her toes as he squeezed her blanket-covered knee.

She certainly *did* know. Very well. It all depended on who was doing what to whom. No matter if it was fast or slow, the men always made it great.

She had no complaints.

Nolan, sitting on her left, leaned in closer, whispering, "What do you think?"

She swept away a snowflake stuck to his beard. "About?"

"Having one of these of our very own."

"Pledging our love and commitment in front of friends and family?" she asked in a whisper.

"I'm all for it. Though, can we not do it at the end of December?" Cam muttered.

"You can't say today isn't completely magical. It's exactly what Erin wanted," she told him.

"I'm hoping you prefer somewhere warm, with turquoise water, where our toes would be in the sand."

"*Ooooh.* That does sound good," Hope breathed. "As long as you two can tear yourselves away from work."

"I'm sure we can make an exception," Cam teased.

They quieted down as Dylan's twin assisted Erin out of the sleigh at the end of the makeshift aisle. The guests stood as she made her way on Dayne's arm to her waiting lovers.

Their slow stroll was accompanied by string musicians playing *Beautiful In White.*

Hope swiped at the sting in her eyes. She really could picture herself in Erin's place, wearing a gorgeous dress and committing herself forever to the men she loved.

Once the ceremony was over, the happy trio headed hand-in-hand back down the aisle to the waiting sleigh while the guests began to head over to the event hall for the reception.

The biggest issue with sitting outside on Christmas Eve was the cold temperature. Luckily, the hall had heat so they could all shed their blankets, gloves, and winter coats to show off their fancy outfits while they celebrated.

She couldn't wait to get a glimpse of her men in their tuxes again. When she got a good look this morning before they had headed out, she'd lost her breath with how handsome and debonair they both looked.

It once again reminded her of how happy and lucky she was.

Nolan stood, put her blanket aside, and offered a hand to help her stand. Once she was on her feet, she realized Cam remained in his seat, not moving.

"What's wrong?" Her eyebrows knitted together. "Do we need to use a blow torch to unfreeze your ass from the chair?"

Wearing a serious expression, he shook his head. When he stood, he faced her and Nolan. "I know it's too early for us to consider having children, but..."

"But you really want some," Hope finished for him.

"At least one," he confirmed.

"Or two." Nolan dropped his arm over her shoulders and bumped his hip into hers. "If you don't want any, that's fine, too. We'll leave that decision up to you."

"Well, that's good," she said dryly.

Nolan barked out a laugh. "I'm glad you're onboard."

"Well, it's not like I have a choice at this point."

Cam frowned. "What does that mean?"

With his brow furrowed, Nolan moved to stand next to him and stare at her.

She smiled.

And waited.

And waited some more.

She swore their mouths dropped open at the same time when it hit them.

Before they could say a word, she said, "I'm glad you two moved into my place." While the Double D was beautiful, it wasn't a place to raise a child.

"Holy shit," Cam whispered.

"What? How?" Nolan shook his head and grimaced. "Not how, but *how?*"

"Apparently, we didn't wait long enough for the birth control pills to kick in once we stopped using condoms. I know this wasn't planned but—" The corner of her lips tipped up and she shrugged. "Merry Christmas?"

Nolan grabbed her by the waist, lifted her off the ground, and swung her in a circle with a loud whoop, almost taking out the nearby chairs. "Damn right this is a merry Christmas! I'm going to be a dad!" He gently set her back on her feet. "I mean, *we're* going to be a dad." He shook his head. "Dads! Whatever! Best Christmas ever!"

"Remember you said that when you're dealing with dirty diapers next Christmas," Hope warned him.

Nolan shot Cam a glance. "Good thing Cam's already an expert with them."

"Oh, hell no," Cam said with a fake scowl. "Don't think you're off the hook." His expression smoothed out and he pulled both Nolan and Hope into his arms, squeezing them tight. "I guess we have something else to celebrate tonight."

"We definitely do. Merry Christmas to us," Nolan said, picking up a handful of fluffy snow and tossing it in the air like confetti.

"Merry Christmas to us," Cam repeated, giving each of them a kiss. "I can't wait to tell Laurel."

"Not yet," Hope said. "Let me get through this first trimester, then we can tell the world."

"Can't wait."

Hope couldn't, either.

Spending that Christmas with the two men she loved would be special.

The following year would be even better.

———

Sign up for Jeanne's newsletter to learn about her upcoming releases, sales and more! https:// www.authorjeannestjames.com/

———

What could be better than waking up next to a hot guy? Waking up sandwiched between two of them.

Quinn Preston, a financial analyst, is not happy when her friends dare her to pick up a handsome stranger at a wedding reception. What better reason to give up men when her previous long-term relationship had not only been lackluster in the bedroom but he had cheated?

Logan Reed, a successful business owner, can't believe that he's attracted to the woman in the ugly, Pepto-Bismol pink bridesmaid dress. And to boot, she's more than tipsy. After turning down her invitation for a one-night stand, he finds her in the parking lot too impaired to drive. He rescues her and takes her home. His home.

The next morning Quinn's conservative life turns on its ear when Logan introduces her to pleasures she never even considered before. And to make things more complicated, Logan already has a lover.

Tyson White, ex-pro football player, is completely in love with Logan. He has mixed emotions when Logan brings home Quinn. But the dares keep coming...

Turn the page to read the first chapter of Double Dare (Dare Menage Series, Book 1)

Double Dare

Dare Menage Series, Book 1

LOGAN REED JAMMED a finger into the neck of his white oxford and pulled. He needed some fucking air.

What the hell was he doing here anyway?

As he surveyed the church, a bead of sweat popped out on his forehead. His breathing had become shallow and quick. He was going to hyperventilate right there and pass out, making a fool of himself in front of everyone.

With a start, he realized one of the ushers was speaking to him. "What?"

"Bride or groom?"

Bride or groom? Did he look like a bride?

All he wanted to do was strip off his stiff shirt, strangling tie, smothering jacket; throw on a soft, worn pair of jeans and one of his comfortable shirts; sink into his couch; toss his feet on his coffee table; and chug a nice frosty beer.

Now that was a fantasy!

But here he was, standing in a monkey suit in a church, about to be struck down by lightning at any second. He blew out a long breath to settle his thumping heart.

Logan stared at the confused usher. Unfortunately, he understood the feeling. "Neither."

"Are you okay?"

Logan had vowed to himself to never do this again. Never be in a church again.

He reminded himself he was only there to observe. He didn't have to participate. But it didn't help. Anyone with as many sins as Logan should've been barred from religious houses. That should've been a law. But it wasn't.

For fuck's sake, he had to get a grip. This was a wedding, not a crucifixion.

He had promised his sister he would be here. And even though Logan was a sinner, he never broke a promise. Never.

The usher cleared his throat.

"Dude—"

Logan pinned the suddenly flushed, sweating kid, whose suit looked two sizes too big, with a glare. "Dude?"

He watched the teen's Adam's apple bob up and down a couple of times before he felt a *whoosh* of air against him, and someone grabbed his elbow. Hard.

"Logan! How nice of you to get here on time." The female voice was singsong and syrupy sweet. And it held a lot more meaning in the tone than in the words.

Logan turned to face his sister. He had to look down because she was nearly a foot shorter than him. "Hey, Shorty. Good timing."

The petite brunette gave him a tight smile. "I see that." She turned to the usher. "We're with the bride," she said sweetly. "We'll just seat ourselves. Thank you."

The usher looked relieved, and Logan almost felt bad. Almost.

The grip on his elbow tightened, and without warning,

his sister dragged him down the aisle and over into one of the pews on the left.

"*Sit down*," Paige said through gritted teeth, even though her face held the biggest smile.

He sat.

She smoothed her dress and tucked it ladylike as she settled into the pew beside him.

"Jesus Christ, Shorty. What the hell is your problem?"

Logan watched her plastered smile falter.

"Logan, you're in a church, for God's sake. It's not the best place to take the Lord's name in vain. And if you keep doing that, I might have to move to another pew so when lightning strikes you dead, I'm in a safe spot." She smoothed her done-up do and gave a pacifying smile across the aisle to the older couple staring at them, mouths agape.

"Hey, I didn't want to be here in the first place."

"I ask you for one favor—"

"One? Hmm. You must have a short memory."

"Okay, okay. Knock it off. Believe me, I appreciate your coming."

"And the thanks I get is a bruised elbow?"

"Sorry, I thought you were going to make that guy piss his pants."

"Well, shit, he called me *dude*."

"Oh yeah, that's so much worse than you calling me *Shorty*."

"I thought you liked it—" Paige elbowed him in the gut before he could say anything besides "ooof."

The wedding march started, and the double doors opened to reveal the bride.

His sister owed him big-time.

———

Quinn Preston almost choked on her Alabama Slammer when her friend elbowed her in the ribs. "Ooof."

She saved her drink before it could spill all over her ugly bridesmaid dress. Yeah, that would have been a shame: to ruin such a nice, frumpy, pukey pink taffeta dress. One the bride had said she would be able to wear in the future. Like to a cocktail party. Or maybe her own funeral. *Yeah, right. No one in their right mind would want to get caught dead in this thing.*

Ruining the dress wouldn't have been a loss, but losing her drink would have. She was drinking Slammers for a reason—to get good and drunk.

Lana nudged her again. "You see that?" She nodded her head toward the back of the room.

"What?" Quinn really didn't care what Lana was excited about. She just wanted to get this day over with. She was tired of watching the happy couple. She was tired of pasting on a plastic smile for the photographer. And she was really tired of listening to the sappy congratulations. All things she might never have—the wedding, the husband, the bridal bliss. Something her parents never failed to remind her. Especially now that she was in her early thirties. And single. Again.

"Not what. Who."

"Huh?" She sucked on the dainty little straw the bartender had put in her drink. Hardly anything would come out of it. Maybe it was designed just for stirring. She pulled it out and threw it onto the bar. She really needed one of those giant straws that came in those fancy frozen drinks.

"Him. Over there." Lana grabbed Quinn by the shoulders and turned her around to face whatever had caught her friend's attention.

"Oh, him." She took a deep draw of the punch-like drink,

only there wasn't a bit of punch in it. Not the fruit kind anyway.

"Yeah, him." Lana dragged out *him* like she was sucking on a maraschino cherry and enjoying the sweetness on her tongue.

Quinn didn't even take a good look. Men were on her shit list at the moment. She didn't care how hot they were. The potent drink in her hands was all the company she needed. She smiled into her glass; it was the best date she'd had in a while.

Another pink taffeta blur whirled up to them, out of breath.

"Jeez Louise. Did you see that hunk of man meat?" Paula, another victim of the wedding fashion nightmare, was flushed and had a bead of sweat running down her chipmunk-like cheeks. "Do you think he's single?"

Quinn raised one shoulder in a half shrug and turned back to the bar. It was bad enough when the three of them had to stand next to each other at the altar, then throughout the grueling pictures, followed by having to sit beside each other at the head table. All in that awful pink froth. But now that it was all over, and they had done their duty for their friend Gina, there was no reason they all had to stand there looking like someone threw up Pepto-Bismol.

She leaned into the bar and asked the semi-cute bartender the time. When he answered that it was six, she gritted her teeth. They had only been at the reception for an hour. It was way too early to bail.

Damn.

With a sigh, she turned back to her friends. They were still ogling the male eye candy across the room.

Paula's sigh drifted over her. "I wonder if he likes women with a little meat on their bones."

A little meat? She opened her mouth to correct Paula, but shut it quickly. Her friend didn't need to be on the receiving end of her miserable mood.

"Quinn, I bet he'd make you forget Peanut."

Quinn winced and took another long draw from her drink. She loved the flavor and the tanginess on her tongue. And she was trying to forget Peanut. She hated the nickname her friends had called her ex-boyfriend, Peter. Once they had actually called him Peanut in front of his face—by accident, of course. *Right.* It had taken her a while to brush that one under the rug. He had never liked her friends after that.

On the other hand, her friends had never liked Peter from the beginning. Unlike her parents, who loved the bastard. Probably more than they loved her.

"Yeah, Quinn, he could probably fuck your brains out, and you'd never remember that douche again."

Quinn frowned at Paula. She noticed her friend's string of pearls hiding in the skin around her neck. Quinn's hands automatically went to her neck to finger a similar necklace—a part of the stupid wedding costume. *Ugh.* She hated pearls!

She hated taffeta. She hated pink. She hated frilly dresses.

She took a long swig from her glass.

And she hated Peter. The asshole.

His gift to her last Valentine's Day wasn't an engagement ring. Oh no, after five long, wasted years of dating the shit, he couldn't have gotten her a ring. Nope. Instead he sent her a text message.

That was it.

A stupid little text message. Two simple lines.

This isn't working anymore. I've found someone new.

She deserved more than that. Something better. After all those years of loyalty, standing by his side, being the "good, proper" girlfriend. As Peter had expected. As her parents had expected. The girlfriend any decent man would want on his arm. Right?

Not even a sorry. Not even an explanation. Nothing.

And the next day, FedEx had delivered a box with all the things she had left over at his apartment during the last half decade.

Quinn emptied her glass and turned back to the bar, blocking out her friends' chattering over that man.

She needed another man like she needed a hole in the head.

She slid her glass over the bar top, and before she could ask for another, a deep voice washed over her.

"Put her next drink on me."

Dumb ass. The drinks are on the house. She turned to ream out whoever it was, and stopped. Her mouth opened, but nothing escaped.

"You look like a fish out of water with your mouth hanging open like that." When he smiled, the lines around his eyes crinkled. He was tan, an outdoorsy tan, not a manmade one. And he had beautiful green eyes. Shit. She had never seen such beautiful eyes on a man. His nose was a little crooked, like it had been broken, and it made him even more beautiful. No. Not beautiful. He was... He was...

Quinn closed her mouth and swallowed hard. He was so *unperfect,* he was perfect. His hair was a dark brown with natural highlights, more proof he liked being outdoors. It was long and pulled back into a neat ponytail.

She hated long hair on men. But it was right on him.

He had a beard that wasn't a beard. It was like a longer five-o'clock shadow.

She hated facial hair.

He had a strong, corded neck that disappeared into a stiff

dress shirt. The collar had been already released and one more button undone below that. The knot of his tie was loose and hung crookedly from around his neck.

The sleeves of his crispy white shirt were rolled up to his elbows, and his forearms were tan covered in dark hair. His hands...

Oh. Damn.

His hands were large. Working hands. Not soft and pampered, but calloused, thick and strong.

Capable. Capable of doing all kinds of things.

Quinn's nipples hardened under the scratchy taffeta.

His hands could do all kinds of dirty, nasty things.

Things Peter had never wanted to do...

Quinn ripped her gaze from him and spun back around to the bar, bracing herself against it for a second to catch her breath. She grabbed her fresh drink and took a gulp.

"Whoa. Slow down there."

Pressing the cold drink against her forehead, she attempted to cool herself off.

She needed to go change her panties, she was so freaking wet.

She could feel his heat next to her; his body was like a furnace. She wanted to plant her hands on his chest and feel how hot he really was. Her fingers convulsed around her glass.

"Are you okay?" The deep timbre of his voice sent a shot of lightning through her body, landing right in her core.

Quinn could only nod her answer.

Palming her bare shoulder, he turned her to face him. He stared down into her eyes, his lips widening into a smile.

His lips. *Oh man.* Those lips probably could do all sorts of things to her, with her. Lips that were made for more than kissing...

"*Yes.*"

Holy shit. That was the kind of yes she blurted when she was in the midst of an orgasm. At least from what she could remember. It had been so long since she'd come... with a partner, anyway.

Heat crawled up her neck as she stepped back, breaking the contact.

"I... I'm fine." She cleared her throat. "Thank you for the drink." She took another sip before raising the glass to him in thanks.

"It was nothing." When he laughed, her knees almost buckled. "Enjoy it."

He stepped away and then paused. But it looked as though he thought better of whatever he was contemplating, and he continued on his way.

Quinn leaned back against the bar and let out a shaky breath.

She was suddenly flanked on either side by her friends. She had been so distracted, she hadn't even realized that they disappeared.

"Quinn—"

"Quinn!"

"Oh. My. God!"

"I told you he was hot!"

"Oh! I wish I weren't married already."

"I wish he liked chubby chicks."

Quinn couldn't take any more. She raised her palms in surrender. "Stop. Enough."

"But, Quinn—"

"But nothing," Quinn answered Paula.

"You're just going to let him walk away?"

"Paula, he isn't going anywhere. Unfortunately, I'm not

going anywhere. We have to be here for two more hours, at least."

Lana said, "Are you going to let Peter ruin the rest of your life? All men aren't assholes like him."

Quinn snorted and took another sip of her Slammer.

"Why don't you at least dance with him?"

"No."

"Why not?" Lana asked.

Why not? Because if she did, she might come right on the dance floor. Because she might end up in a puddle of her own juices. The picture in her head shocked her: it was of her lying in a heap in the middle of the dance floor in the throes of an orgasm. Surrounded by all the wedding guests...

This drink was stronger than she thought.

"Because no one is dancing yet."

"Sure they are. Look."

Quinn glanced over at the area cleared for dancing, and sure enough, a crowd of people were out there shaking their groove thing. Quinn had been too busy trying to get her drink on to notice.

From the looks of the participants on the dance floor, a few of them had been partaking in the open bar also. Even the bride and her new husband were bouncing and shimmying in the crowd.

At least *they* were a happy couple.

Quinn took another drink.

Lana frowned at her. "Are you just going to drink tonight, or are you going to do something about your situation?"

"Situation? What situation?"

"Getting laid."

Quinn checked over her shoulder to see if the bartender was listening. He was. He had a big grin plastered on his face. *Great.*

The father of the bride came up and asked for a gin and tonic. While he was waiting, he turned to them. "Hi, girls. Enjoying yourselves? You look great in those dresses. My wife picked them out."

Oh joy. Quinn would have to remember to smack—she meant thank—her. She couldn't wait to rip the scratchy, ugly piece of shit off.

All three women gave him a smile but bit their tongues. Eventually he wandered away, and Lana and Paula jumped right back to harassing her. Good thing they were her friends.

"C'mon. It's not going to hurt to have a one-night stand. Look at him."

"I already saw him." Holy crap, she knew they meant well, but they were getting on her last nerve.

"Yeah, and we saw how you were drooling, too."

She had not drooled. Her hand automatically went up to her mouth.

Paula said, "He probably isn't interested in you anyway."

"Yeah, you couldn't get someone like that. You attract losers like Peter," Lana said.

If they thought their reverse psychology was going to work, well, it wasn't.

"Looks like he's with Paige Reed, anyway."

Quinn's gaze shot over to the corner of the ballroom where the tall man stood next to the petite, dark-haired beauty. Paige Reed. *Figures.*

"I thought Paige was dating Connor Morgan," Quinn mumbled.

She must have mumbled loud enough, because Lana answered her. "She is. Connor had to fly back to Australia for something to do with his job."

"So why is she with him?" Quinn asked. Why was she so curious all of a sudden? Why did she care?

She didn't. She nursed her drink. After one and a half Alabama Slammers, she was starting to feel pretty tipsy. She wasn't used to drinking. And when she did drink, she usually had wine, not hard liquor, and especially not such a hard-hitting mix of liquors.

Paula leaned into the both of them and said in an exaggerated whisper, "Maybe he's an escort," like it was a scandal, and then laughed.

Maybe he *was* an escort.

He was probably worth every penny, too.

His back was to them now, but that just gave Quinn the opportunity to study how broad those shoulders were in his dress shirt. When he moved, the fabric bunched and pulled with his muscles.

Lana gasped, jerking Quinn out of her thoughts. "He's not an escort! That's Logan Reed, Paige's brother. I haven't seen him since we were kids. Holy shit, did he grow up."

"I'll say." Paula agreed. "Quinn, I dare you to go ask him to dance."

"Not interested."

Lana joined in. "Yeah, I dare you too. Don't be a wuss."

If she were a wuss, she wouldn't have come out in public in this pink atrocity. And the matching shoes were killing her feet. The last thing she needed was to be dancing. She'd be crippled.

"That's a double dare, you know, with the two of us daring you."

Oh, boy, a double dare. She would definitely do it now—not. "You're crazy."

"No, you are, if you pass up this opportunity."

"How do you know he's available?" Quinn asked them.

"You don't know until you ask him," Lana said. "But if I

remember correctly, his wife left him a while ago. There had been some rumors…"

There had been some rumors about her and Peter too, but rumors were just that: rumors. She didn't take any stock in them.

Paula suddenly shouted, "Truth or dare?" making Quinn jump. It was like they were teenagers all over again.

Lana quickly said, "Truth." And bounced on her toes like she was fifteen.

Jesus, would someone please put a bullet in my head? Quinn needed to be put out of her misery.

Paula asked Lana, "Do you shave or wax?"

"Shave. Okay, Quinn, your turn. Truth or dare?"

Quinn was not playing this juvenile game. It was stupid; she was not going to fall into what was clearly a trap.

"Truth."

"How bad was Peter in bed?" Lana asked.

Damn. She wasn't going to answer that one. Even as drunk as she was. She didn't want to relive their vanilla, boring sex life. And she definitely didn't want to admit it or talk about it.

There was only one thing left for her to do.

Get the rest of the story here: https://buy. bookfunnel.com/lposmjspfq

If You Enjoyed This Book

Thank you for reading Unrestrained. If you enjoyed this polyamory romance, please consider leaving a review at your favorite retailer and/or Goodreads to let other readers know. Reviews are always appreciated and just a few words can help an independent author like me tremendously!

Want to read a sample of my work? Download a sampler book here: BookHip.com/MTQQKK

Also by Jeanne St. James

Find my complete reading order here:

https://www.jeannestjames.com/reading-order

Buy direct from the author here: https:// jeannestjamesauthor.com

<u>Standalone Books:</u>

<u>Made Maleen: A Modern Twist on a Fairy Tale</u>

<u>Damaged</u>

<u>Rip Cord: The Complete Trilogy</u>

Everything About You (A Second Chance Gay Romance)

Reigniting Chase (An M/M Standalone)

<u>Brothers in Blue Series</u>

A four-book series based around three brothers who are small-town cops and former Marines

<u>The Dare Ménage Series</u>

A six-book MMF, interracial ménage series

<u>The Obsessed Novellas</u>

A collection of five standalone BDSM novellas

<u>Down & Dirty: Dirty Angels MC®</u>

A ten-book motorcycle club series

<u>Guts & Glory: In the Shadows Security</u>

A six-book former special forces series

(A spin-off of the Dirty Angels MC)

<u>Blood & Bones: Blood Fury MC®</u>

A twelve-book motorcycle club series

<u>Motorcycle Club Crossovers:</u>

<u>Crossing the Line: A DAMC/Blue Avengers MC Crossover</u>

<u>Magnum: A Dark Knights MC/Dirty Angels MC Crossover</u>

Crash: A Dirty Angels MC/Blood Fury MC Crossover

Romeo: A Dark Knights MC/Blood Fury MC Crossover

Beyond the Badge: Blue Avengers MC™

A six-book law enforcement/motorcycle club series

<u>Double D Ranch</u>

A six-book MMF ménage series

<u>COMING SOON!</u>

Property of Stone (Kings of Anarchy MC: Pennsylvania)

Dirty Angels MC®: The Next Generation

WRITING AS J.J. MASTERS:

The Royal Alpha Series

A five-book gay mpreg shifter series

About the Author

JEANNE ST. JAMES is a USA Today, Amazon and international bestselling romance author who loves writing about strong women and alpha males. She was only thirteen when she first started writing and her first published piece was an erotic short story in Playgirl magazine. She then went on to publish her first romance novel in 2009. She is now an author of almost 70 contemporary romances. She writes M/F, M/M, and M/M/F ménages, including interracial romance. She also writes M/M paranormal romance under the name: J.J. Masters.

Want to read a sample of her work? Download a sampler book here: BookHip.com/MTQQKK

Buy ebooks and audiobooks directly from the author here: https://jeannestjamesauthor.com

Newsletter: https://www.authorjeannestjames.com/
Jeanne's Down & Dirty Book Crew: https://www.facebook.com/groups/JeannesReviewCrew/

facebook.com/JeanneStJamesAuthor

instagram.com/JeanneStJames

bookbub.com/authors/jeanne-st-james

goodreads.com/JeanneStJames